MARVEL UNIVERSE ALL-NEW AVENGERS ASSEMBLE VOL. 4 DIGEST. Contains material originally published in magazine form as MARVEL UNIVERSE AVENGERS ASSEMBLE SEASON TWO #13-16. First printing 2016. ISBN# 978-0-7851-9441-5. Published by MARVEL WORLDWIDE, INC., a subsidiary of MARVEL ENTERTAINMENT, LLC. OFFICE OF PUBLICATION: 135 West 50th Street, New York, NY 10020. Copyright © 2016 MARVEL No similarity between any of the names, characters, persons, and/or institutions in this magazine with those of any living or dead person or institution is intended, and any such similarity which may exist is purely coincidental. **Printed in the U.S.A.** ALAN FINE, President, Marvel Entertainment; DAN BUCKLEY, President, TV, Publishing & Brand Management; JOE QUESADA, Chief Creative Officer; TOM BREVOORT, SVP of Publishing; DAVID BOGART, SVP of Business Affairs & Operations, Publishing & Partnership; C.B. CEBULSKI, VP of Brand Management & Development, Asia; DAVID GABRIEL, SVP of Sales & Marketing, Publishing; JEFF YOUNGQUIST, VP of Production & Special Projects; DAN CARR, Executive Director of Publishing Technology; ALEX MORALES, Director of Publishing Operations; SUSAN CRESPI, Production Manager; STAN LEE, Chairman Emeritus. For information regarding advertising in Marvel Comics or on Marvel.com, please contact Vit DeBellis, Integrated Sales Manager, at vdebellis@marvel.com. For Marvel subscription inquiries, please call 888-511-5480. **Manufactured between 3/25/2016 and 5/2/2016 by SHERIDAN, CHELSEA, MI, USA.**

10 9 8 7 6 5 4 3 2 1

MARVEL

AVENGERS ASSEMBLE

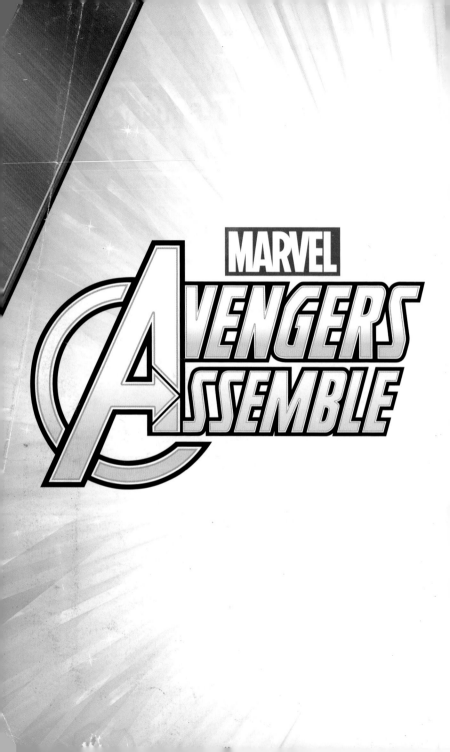

Based on the TV series written by
EUGENE SON, DANIELLE WOLFF and **KEVIN BURKE**
& **CHRIS "DOC" WYATT**

Directed by
TIM ELDRED & **PHIL PIGNOTTI**

Art by
MARVEL ANIMATION

Adapted by
JOE CARAMAGNA

Special Thanks to **Hannah MacDonald** & **Product Factory**

Editor
SEBASTIAN GIRNER

Consulting Editor
MARK BASSO

Senior Editor
MARK PANICCIA

Avengers created by **Stan Lee** & **Jack Kirby**

Collection Editor
ALEX STARBUCK

Associate Editor
SARAH BRUNSTAD

Editors, Special Projects
JENNIFER GRÜNWALD & **MARK D. BEAZLEY**

VP, Production & Special Projects
JEFF YOUNGQUIST

SVP Print, Sales & Marketing
DAVID GABRIEL

Head of Marvel Television
JEPH LOEB

Book Designer
ADAM DEL RE

Editor In Chief
AXEL ALONSO

Chief Creative Officer
JOE QUESADA

Publisher
DAN BUCKLEY

Executive Producer
ALAN FINE

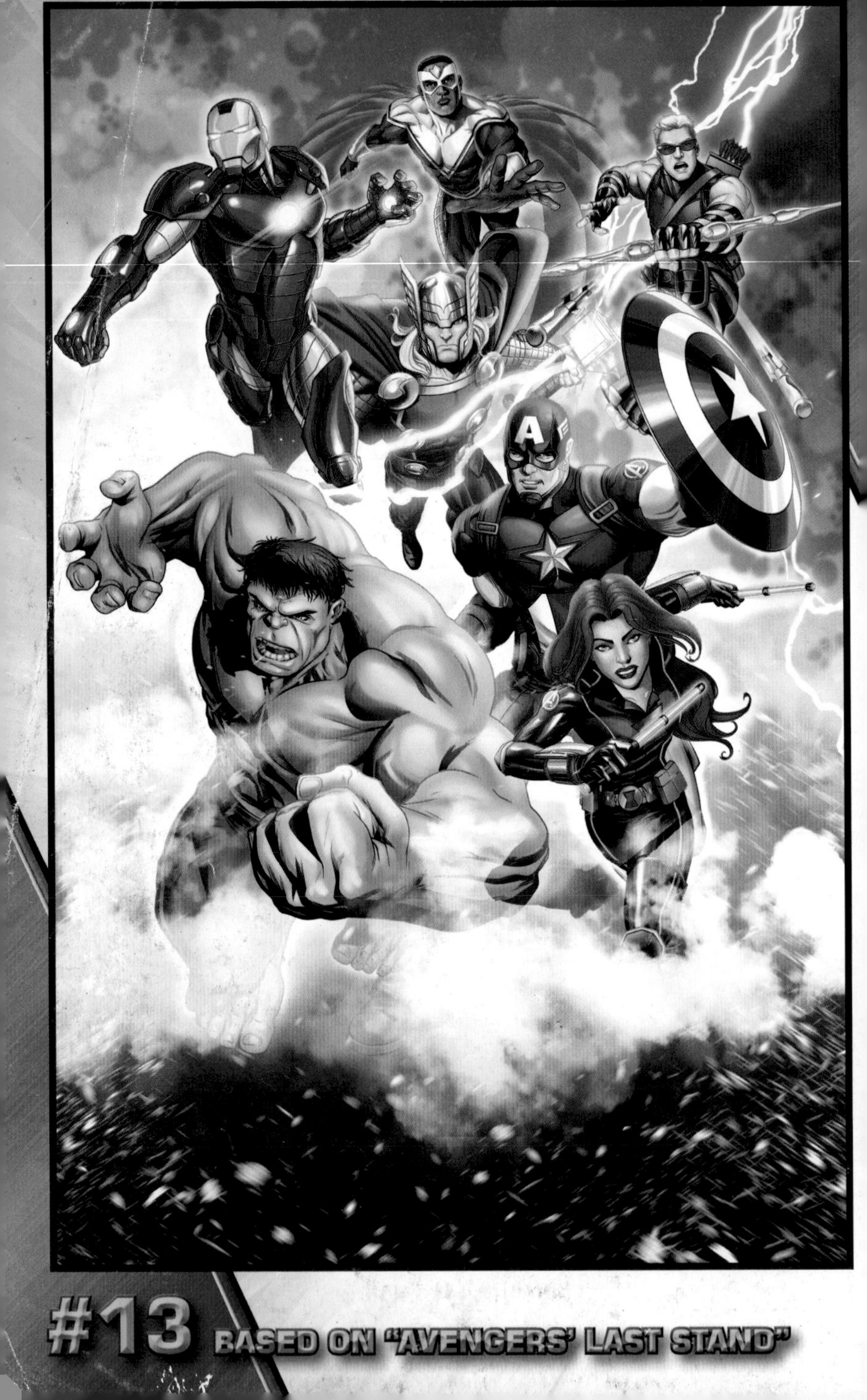

#13 BASED ON "AVENGERS' LAST STAND"

MARVEL AVENGERS ASSEMBLE SEASON 2

In an effort to learn more about the mysterious SQUADRON SUPREME, Falcon infiltrated the Citadel, the Squadron's warship. When he was discovered, a battle erupted that sunk the Citadel to the bottom of the East River.

Now the Squadron is planning another attack, and the Avengers must be ready...or Earth will meet its doom.

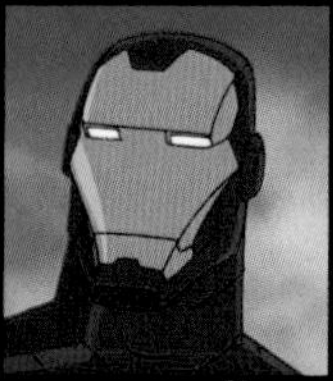

IRON MAN

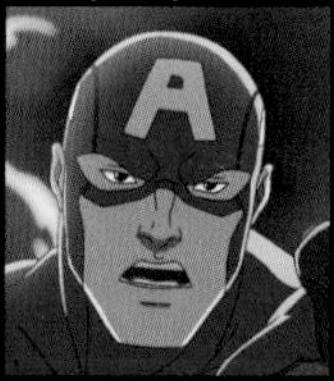

CAPTAIN AMERICA

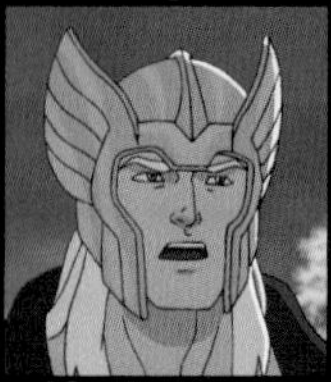

THOR

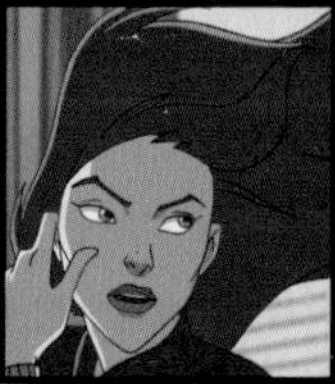

BLACK WIDOW

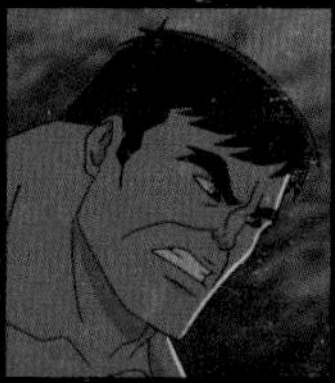

HULK

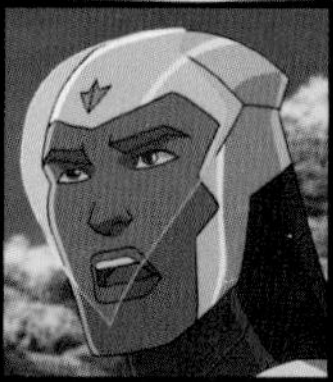

FALCON

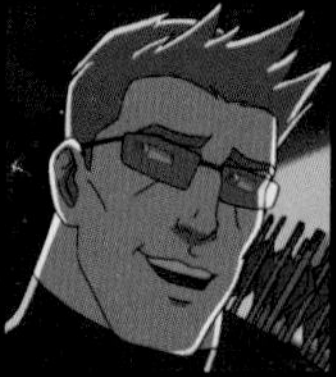

HAWKEYE

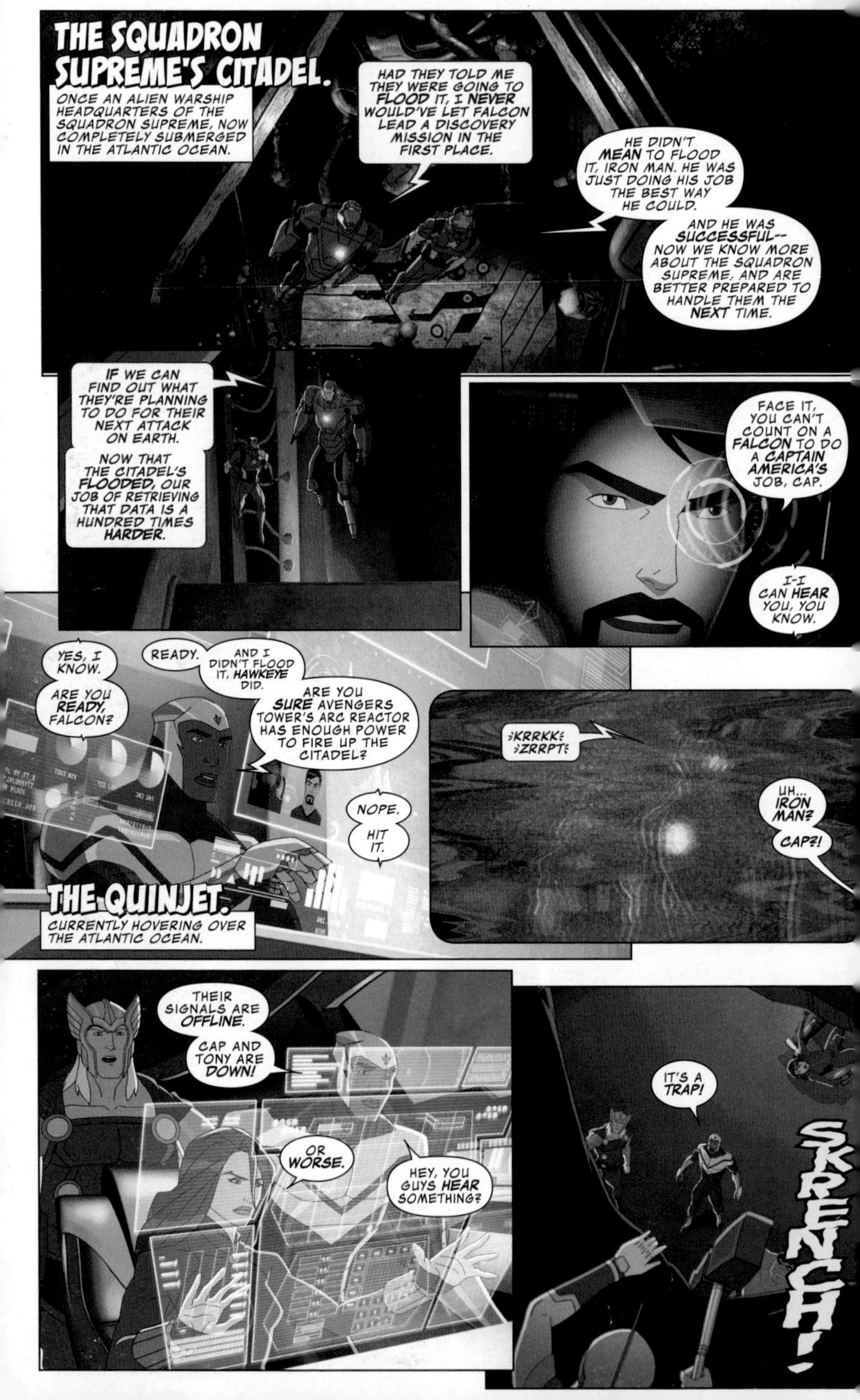
THE SQUADRON SUPREME'S CITADEL.
ONCE AN ALIEN WARSHIP HEADQUARTERS OF THE SQUADRON SUPREME, NOW COMPLETELY SUBMERGED IN THE ATLANTIC OCEAN.
HAD THEY TOLD ME THEY WERE GOING TO FLOOD IT, I NEVER WOULD'VE LET FALCON LEAD A DISCOVERY MISSION IN THE FIRST PLACE.
HE DIDN'T MEAN TO FLOOD IT, IRON MAN. HE WAS JUST DOING HIS JOB THE BEST WAY HE COULD.
AND HE WAS SUCCESSFUL-- NOW WE KNOW MORE ABOUT THE SQUADRON SUPREME, AND ARE BETTER PREPARED TO HANDLE THEM THE NEXT TIME.
IF WE CAN FIND OUT WHAT THEY'RE PLANNING TO DO FOR THEIR NEXT ATTACK ON EARTH.
NOW THAT THE CITADEL'S FLOODED, OUR JOB OF RETRIEVING THAT DATA IS A HUNDRED TIMES HARDER.
FACE IT, YOU CAN'T COUNT ON A FALCON TO DO A CAPTAIN AMERICA'S JOB, CAP.
I-I CAN HEAR YOU, YOU KNOW.
YES, I KNOW.
ARE YOU READY, FALCON?
READY.
AND I DIDN'T FLOOD IT, HAWKEYE DID.
ARE YOU SURE AVENGERS TOWER'S ARC REACTOR HAS ENOUGH POWER TO FIRE UP THE CITADEL?
NOPE.
HIT IT.
THE QUINJET.
CURRENTLY HOVERING OVER THE ATLANTIC OCEAN.
KRRKK *ZRRPT*
UH... IRON MAN?
CAP?!
THEIR SIGNALS ARE OFFLINE.
CAP AND TONY ARE DOWN!
OR WORSE.
HEY, YOU GUYS HEAR SOMETHING?
IT'S A TRAP!
SKRENCH!

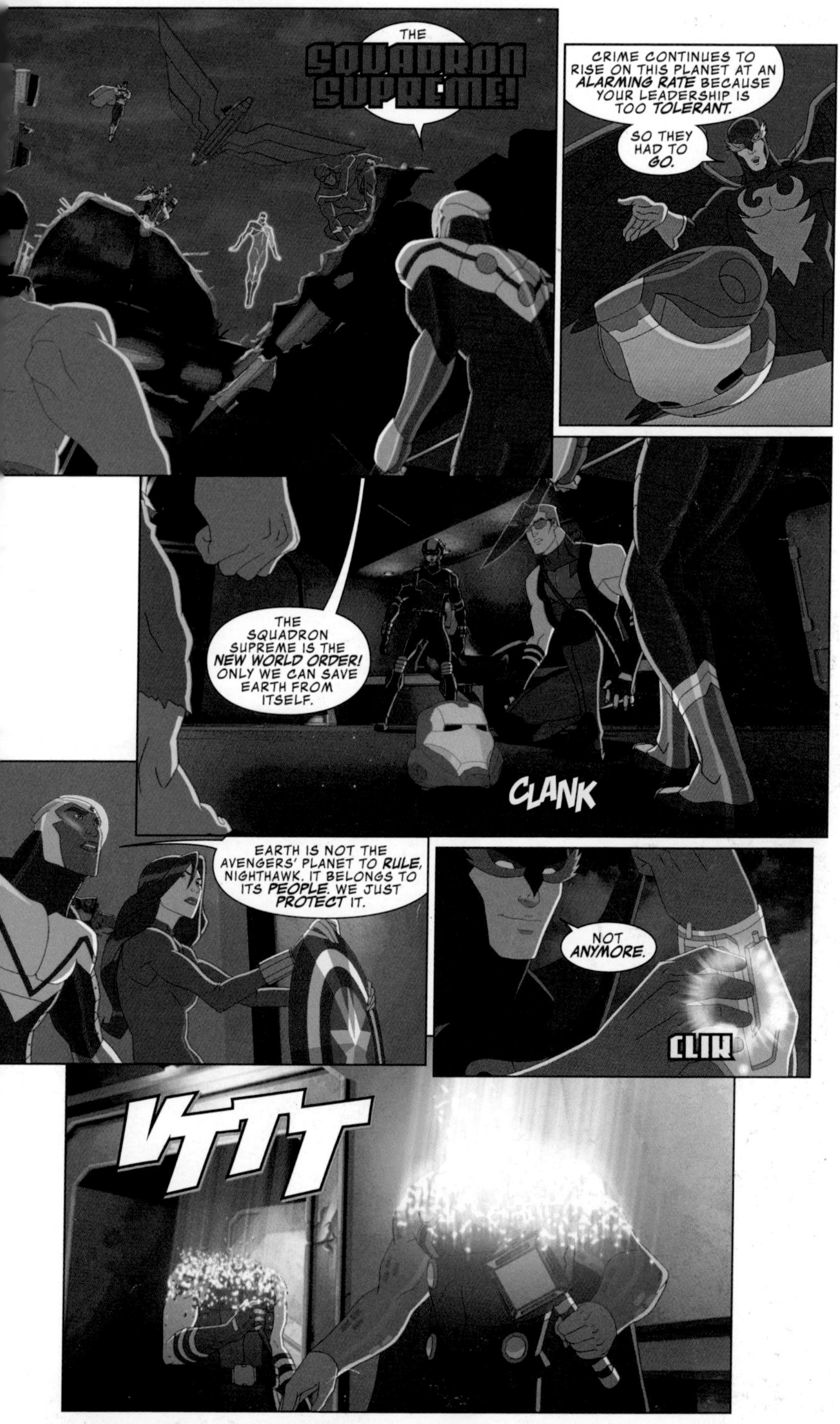
THE SQUADRON SUPREME!
CRIME CONTINUES TO RISE ON THIS PLANET AT AN ALARMING RATE BECAUSE YOUR LEADERSHIP IS TOO TOLERANT.
SO THEY HAD TO GO.
THE SQUADRON SUPREME IS THE NEW WORLD ORDER! ONLY WE CAN SAVE EARTH FROM ITSELF.
CLANK
EARTH IS NOT THE AVENGERS' PLANET TO RULE, NIGHTHAWK. IT BELONGS TO ITS PEOPLE. WE JUST PROTECT IT.
NOT ANYMORE.
CLIK
VTT

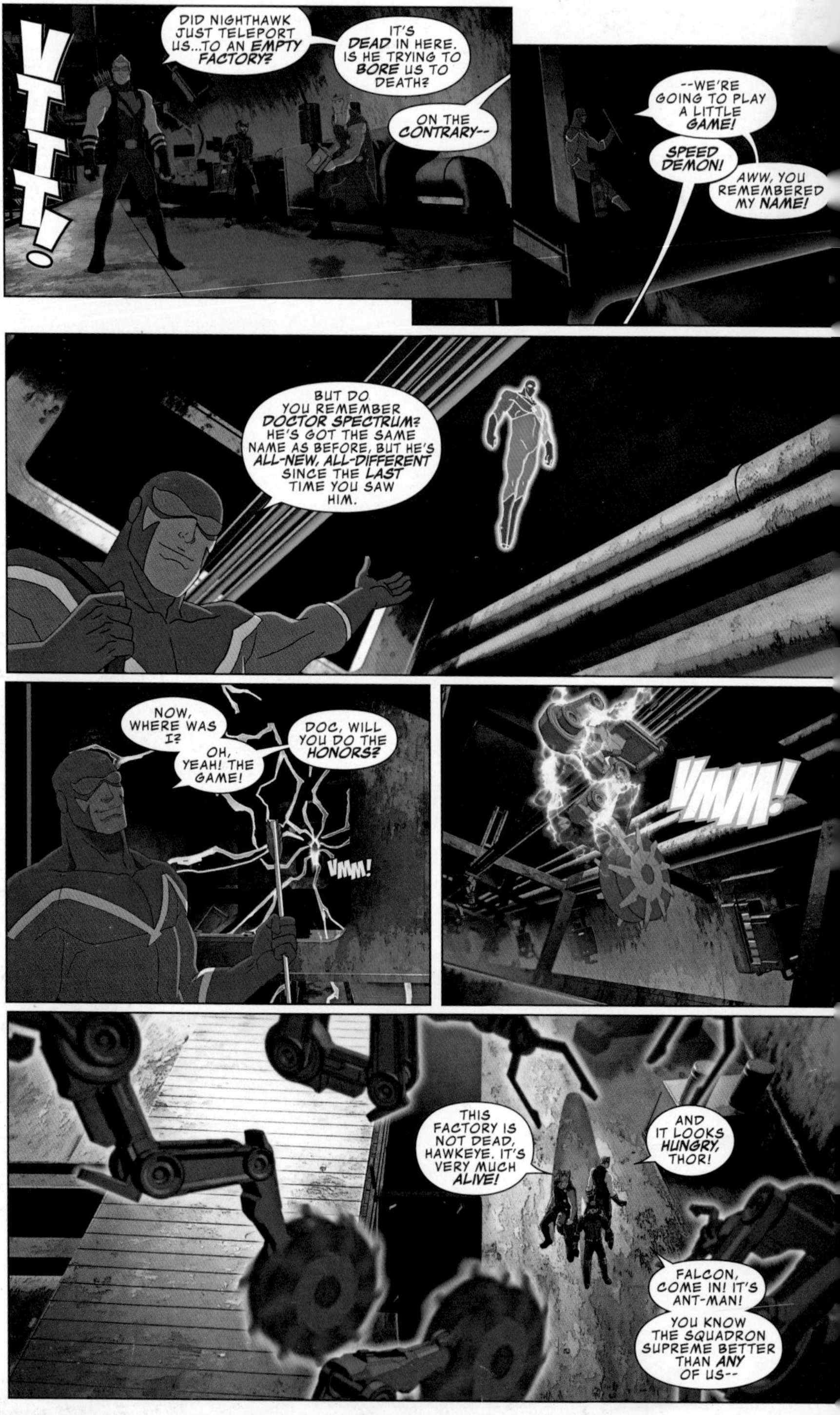
VTTT!
DID NIGHTHAWK JUST TELEPORT US...TO AN EMPTY FACTORY?
IT'S DEAD IN HERE. IS HE TRYING TO BORE US TO DEATH?
ON THE CONTRARY--
--WE'RE GOING TO PLAY A LITTLE GAME!
SPEED DEMON!
AWW, YOU REMEMBERED MY NAME!
BUT DO YOU REMEMBER DOCTOR SPECTRUM? HE'S GOT THE SAME NAME AS BEFORE, BUT HE'S ALL-NEW, ALL-DIFFERENT SINCE THE LAST TIME YOU SAW HIM.
NOW, WHERE WAS I?
OH, YEAH! THE GAME!
DOC, WILL YOU DO THE HONORS?
VMM!
VMM!
THIS FACTORY IS NOT DEAD, HAWKEYE. IT'S VERY MUCH ALIVE!
AND IT LOOKS HUNGRY, THOR!
FALCON, COME IN! IT'S ANT-MAN!
YOU KNOW THE SQUADRON SUPREME BETTER THAN ANY OF US--

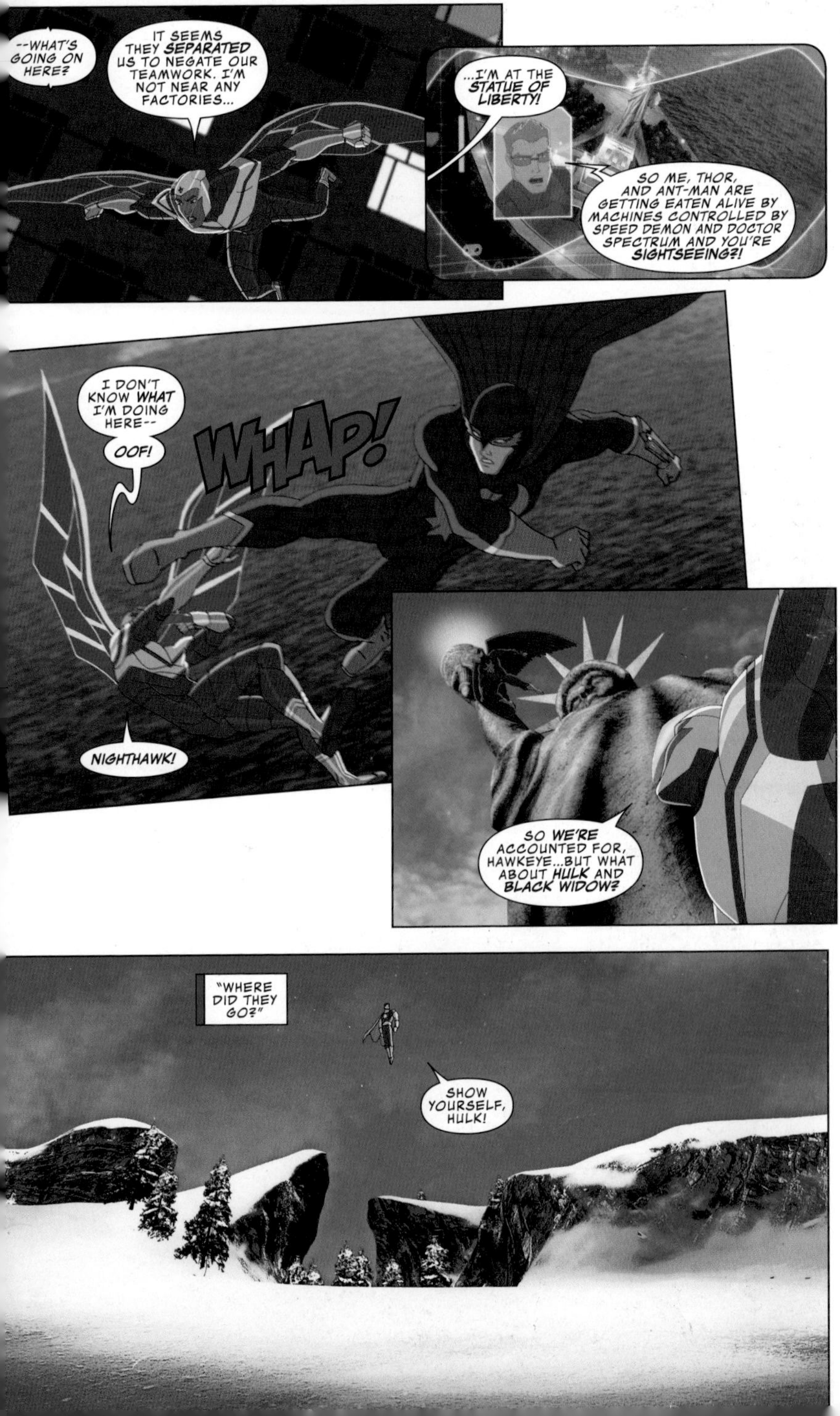
--WHAT'S GOING ON HERE?
IT SEEMS THEY SEPARATED US TO NEGATE OUR TEAMWORK. I'M NOT NEAR ANY FACTORIES...
...I'M AT THE STATUE OF LIBERTY!
SO ME, THOR, AND ANT-MAN ARE GETTING EATEN ALIVE BY MACHINES CONTROLLED BY SPEED DEMON AND DOCTOR SPECTRUM AND YOU'RE SIGHTSEEING?!
I DON'T KNOW WHAT I'M DOING HERE--
WHAP!
OOF!
NIGHTHAWK!
SO WE'RE ACCOUNTED FOR, HAWKEYE...BUT WHAT ABOUT HULK AND BLACK WIDOW?
"WHERE DID THEY GO?"
SHOW YOURSELF, HULK!

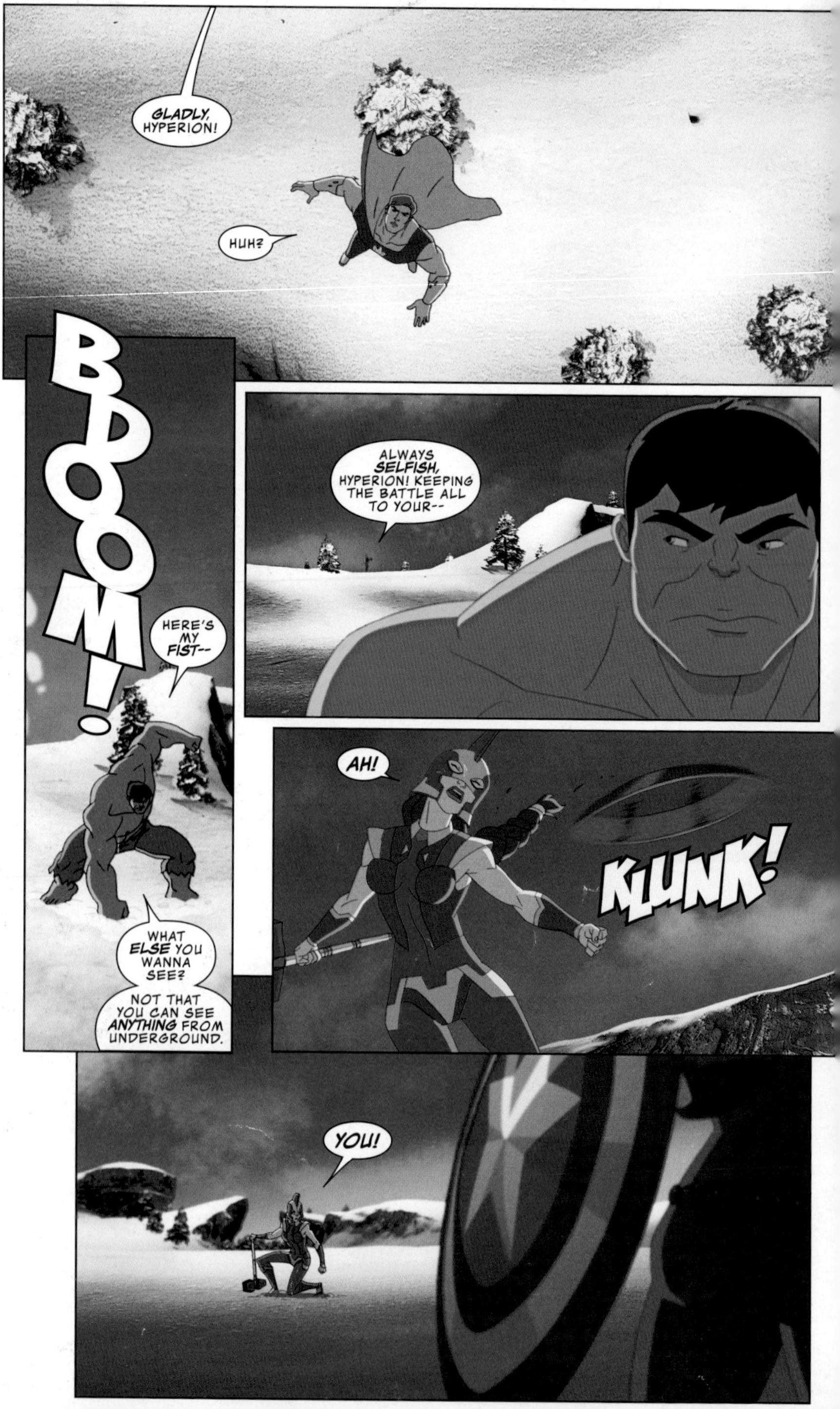
GLADLY, HYPERION!
HUH?
BDOOM!
HERE'S MY FIST--
WHAT ELSE YOU WANNA SEE?
NOT THAT YOU CAN SEE ANYTHING FROM UNDERGROUND.
ALWAYS SELFISH, HYPERION! KEEPING THE BATTLE ALL TO YOUR--
AH!
KLUNK!
YOU!

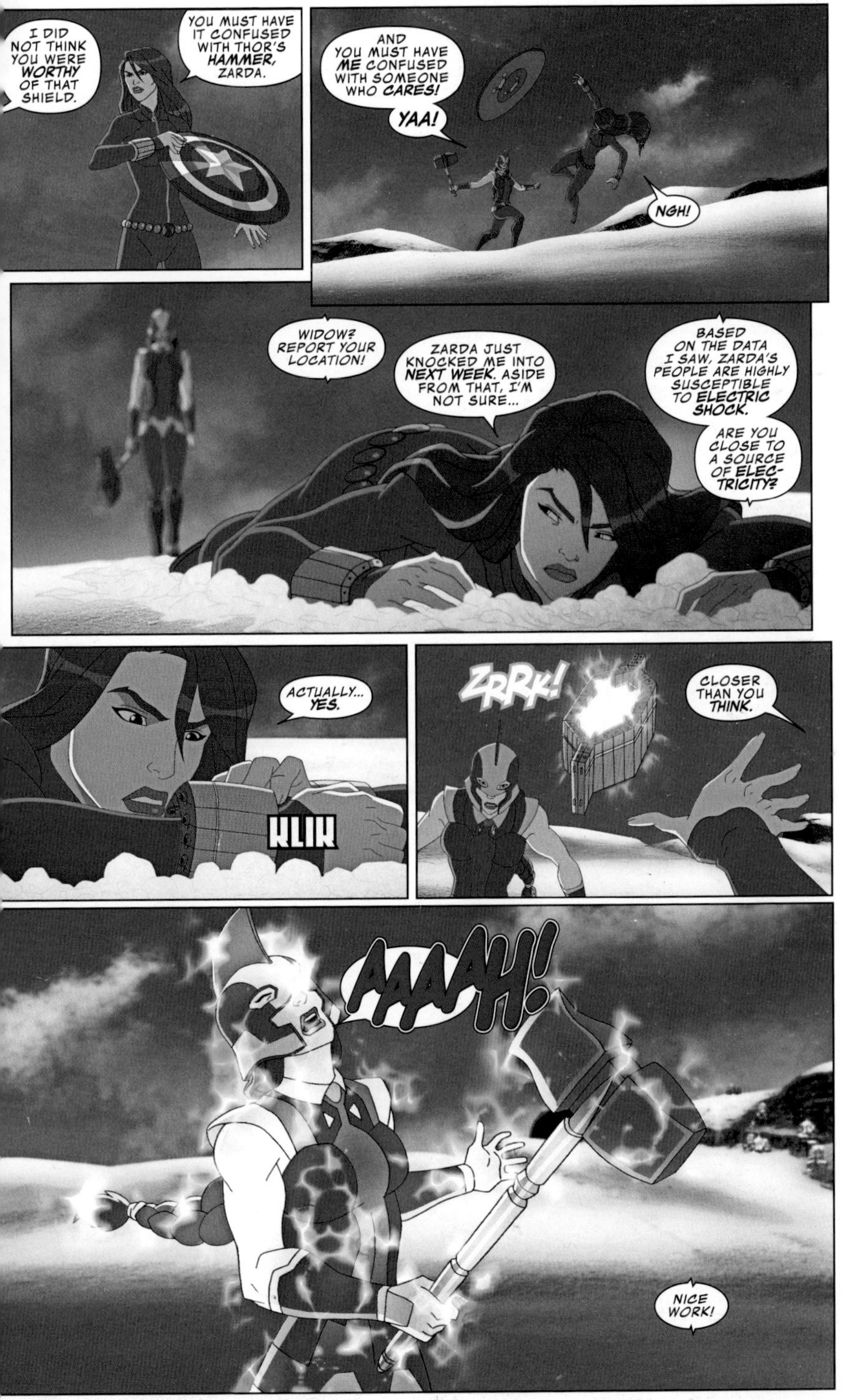

I DID NOT THINK YOU WERE WORTHY OF THAT SHIELD.
YOU MUST HAVE IT CONFUSED WITH THOR'S HAMMER, ZARDA.
AND YOU MUST HAVE ME CONFUSED WITH SOMEONE WHO CARES!
YAA!
NGH!
WIDOW? REPORT YOUR LOCATION!
ZARDA JUST KNOCKED ME INTO NEXT WEEK. ASIDE FROM THAT, I'M NOT SURE...
BASED ON THE DATA I SAW, ZARDA'S PEOPLE ARE HIGHLY SUSCEPTIBLE TO ELECTRIC SHOCK.
ARE YOU CLOSE TO A SOURCE OF ELEC-TRICITY?
ACTUALLY... YES.
KLIK
ZRRK!
CLOSER THAN YOU THINK.
AAAAH!
NICE WORK!

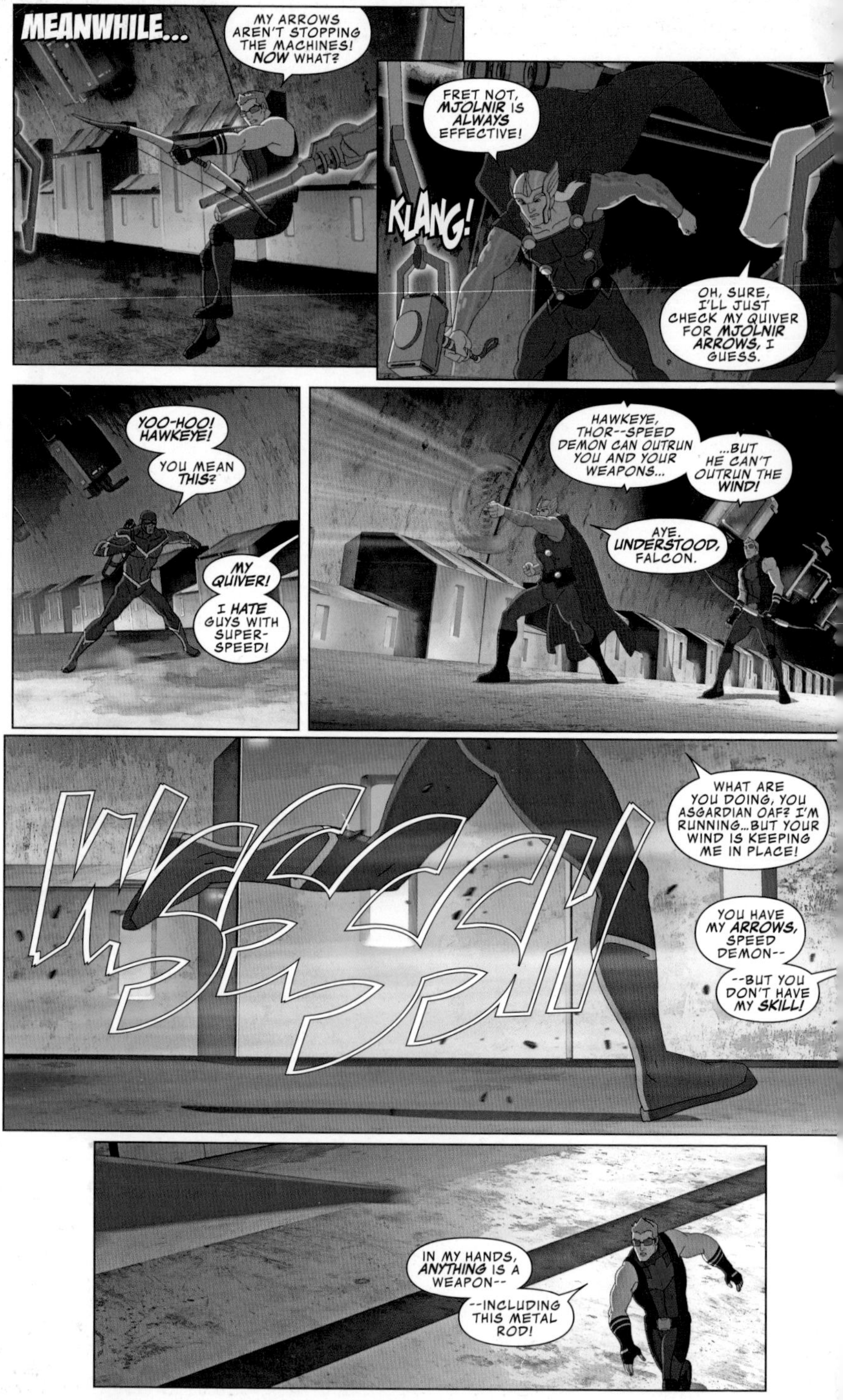
MEANWHILE...
MY ARROWS AREN'T STOPPING THE MACHINES! NOW WHAT?
FRET NOT, MJOLNIR IS ALWAYS EFFECTIVE!
KLANG!
OH, SURE, I'LL JUST CHECK MY QUIVER FOR MJOLNIR ARROWS, I GUESS.
YOO-HOO! HAWKEYE!
YOU MEAN THIS?
MY QUIVER!
I HATE GUYS WITH SUPER-SPEED!
HAWKEYE, THOR--SPEED DEMON CAN OUTRUN YOU AND YOUR WEAPONS...
...BUT HE CAN'T OUTRUN THE WIND!
AYE. UNDERSTOOD, FALCON.
WHAT ARE YOU DOING, YOU ASGARDIAN OAF? I'M RUNNING...BUT YOUR WIND IS KEEPING ME IN PLACE!
YOU HAVE MY ARROWS, SPEED DEMON--
--BUT YOU DON'T HAVE MY SKILL!
IN MY HANDS, ANYTHING IS A WEAPON--
--INCLUDING THIS METAL ROD!

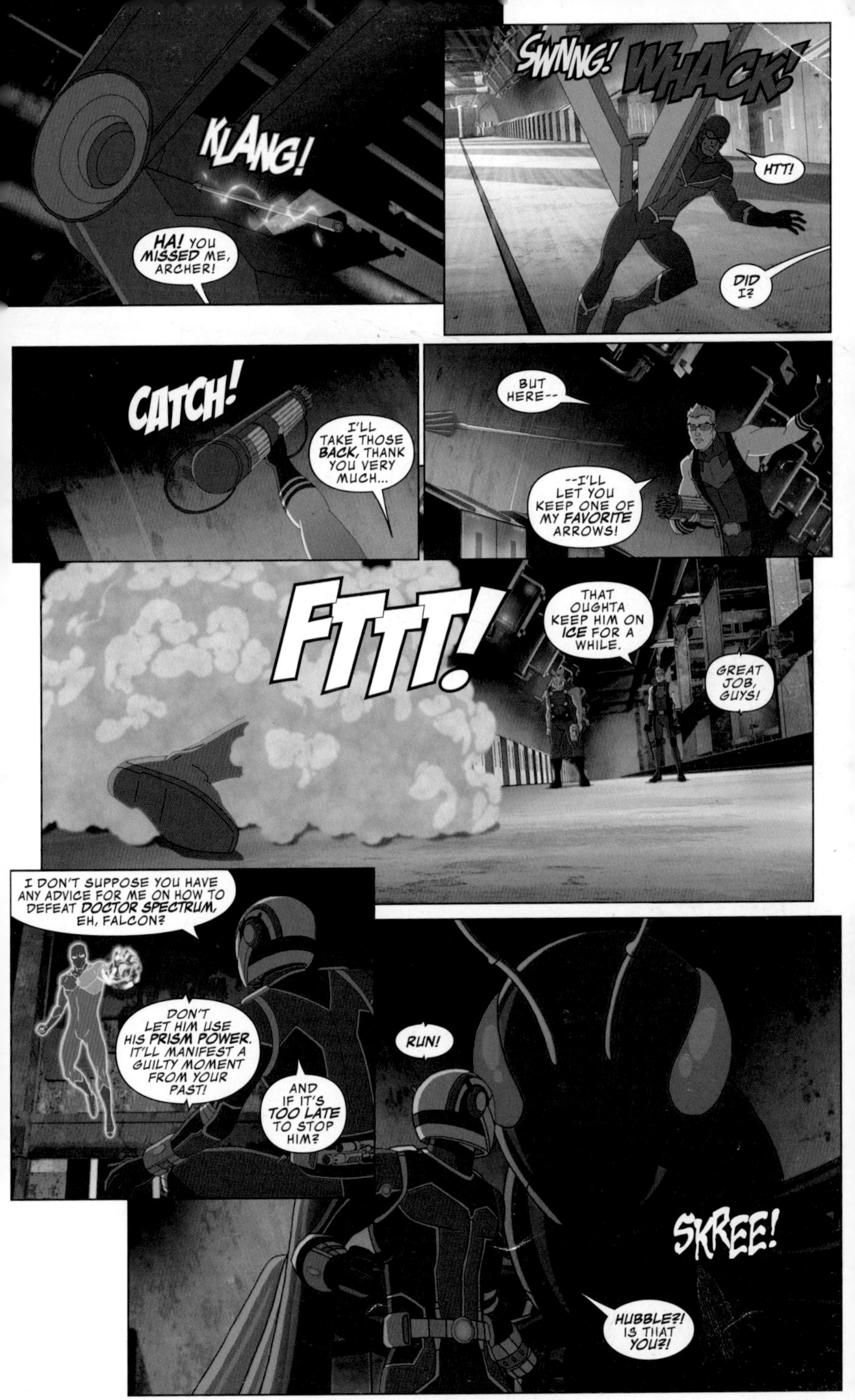
KLANG!
HA! YOU MISSED ME, ARCHER!
SWNNG! WHACK!
HTT!
DID I?
CATCH!
I'LL TAKE THOSE BACK, THANK YOU VERY MUCH...
BUT HERE--
--I'LL LET YOU KEEP ONE OF MY FAVORITE ARROWS!
FTTT!
THAT OUGHTA KEEP HIM ON ICE FOR A WHILE.
GREAT JOB, GUYS!
I DON'T SUPPOSE YOU HAVE ANY ADVICE FOR ME ON HOW TO DEFEAT DOCTOR SPECTRUM, EH, FALCON?
DON'T LET HIM USE HIS PRISM POWER. IT'LL MANIFEST A GUILTY MOMENT FROM YOUR PAST!
AND IF IT'S TOO LATE TO STOP HIM?
RUN!
SKREE!
HUBBLE?! IS THAT YOU?!

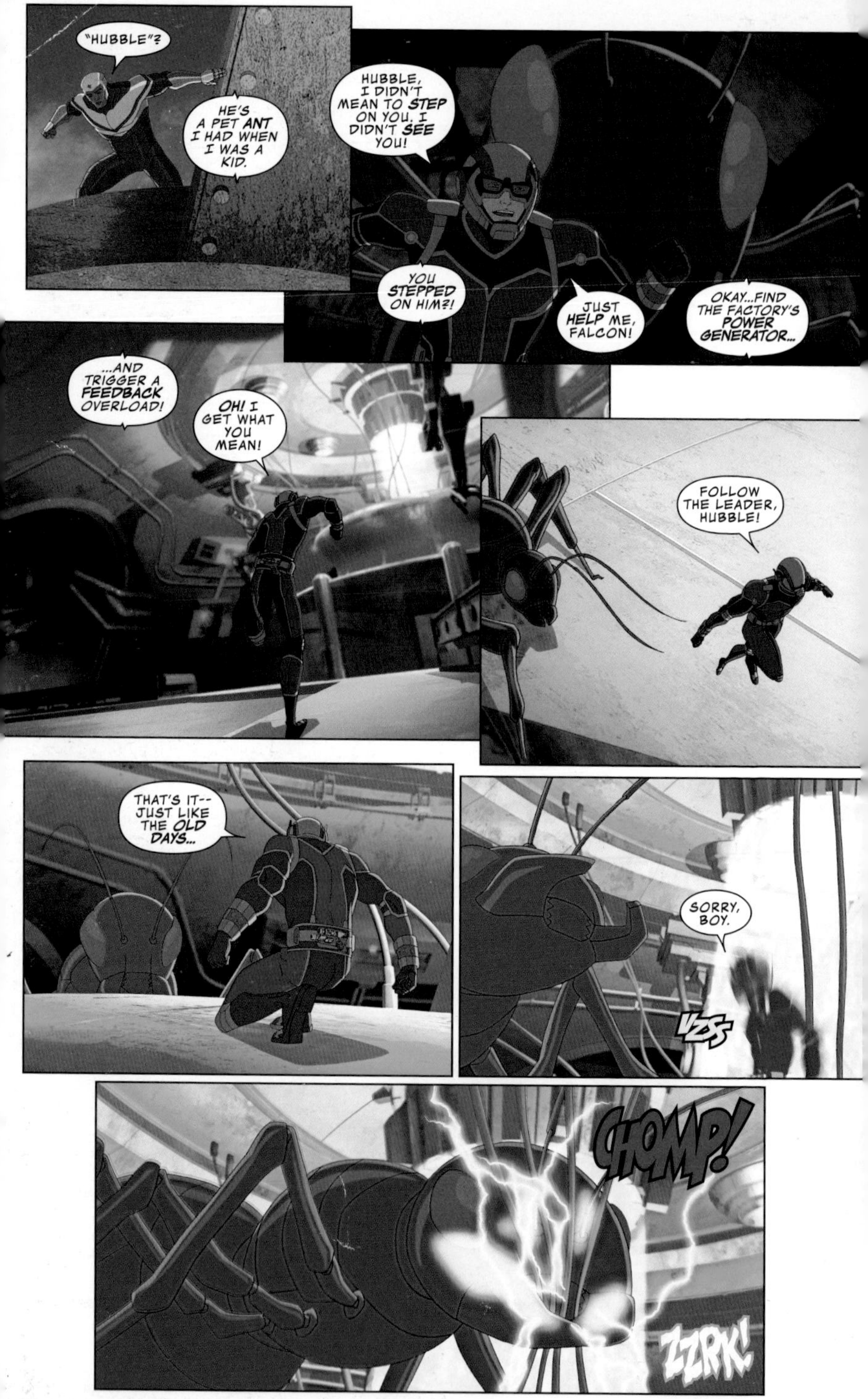
"HUBBLE"?
HE'S A PET ANT I HAD WHEN I WAS A KID.
HUBBLE, I DIDN'T MEAN TO STEP ON YOU. I DIDN'T SEE YOU!
YOU STEPPED ON HIM?!
JUST HELP ME, FALCON!
OKAY...FIND THE FACTORY'S POWER GENERATOR...
...AND TRIGGER A FEEDBACK OVERLOAD!
OH! I GET WHAT YOU MEAN!
FOLLOW THE LEADER, HUBBLE!
THAT'S IT--JUST LIKE THE OLD DAYS...
SORRY, BOY.
VZSS
CHOMP!
ZZRK!

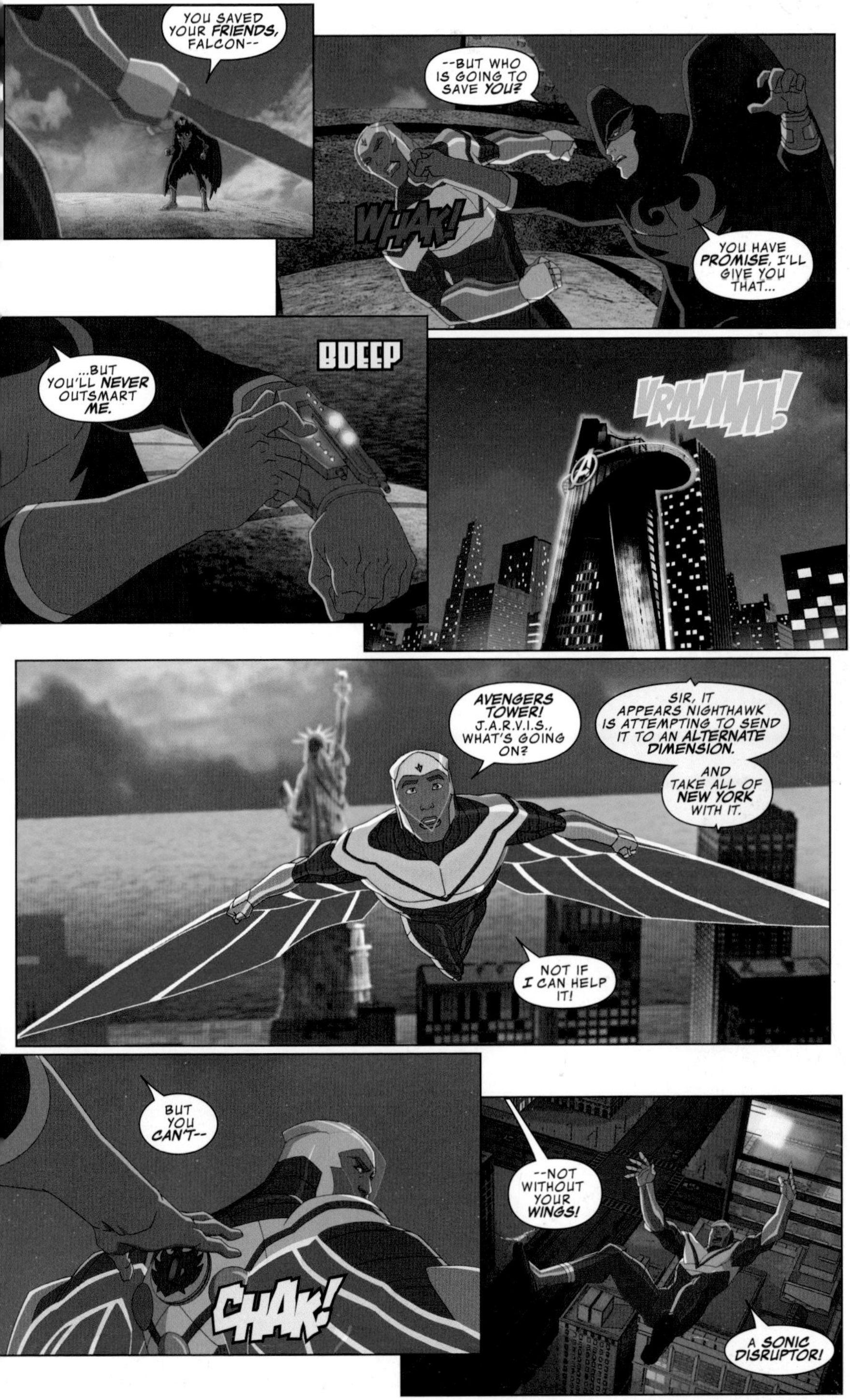
YOU SAVED YOUR FRIENDS, FALCON--
--BUT WHO IS GOING TO SAVE YOU?
WHAK!
YOU HAVE PROMISE, I'LL GIVE YOU THAT...
...BUT YOU'LL NEVER OUTSMART ME.
BDEEP
VRMMMM!
AVENGERS TOWER! J.A.R.V.I.S., WHAT'S GOING ON?
SIR, IT APPEARS NIGHTHAWK IS ATTEMPTING TO SEND IT TO AN ALTERNATE DIMENSION.
AND TAKE ALL OF NEW YORK WITH IT.
NOT IF I CAN HELP IT!
BUT YOU CAN'T--
CHAK!
--NOT WITHOUT YOUR WINGS!
A SONIC DISRUPTOR!

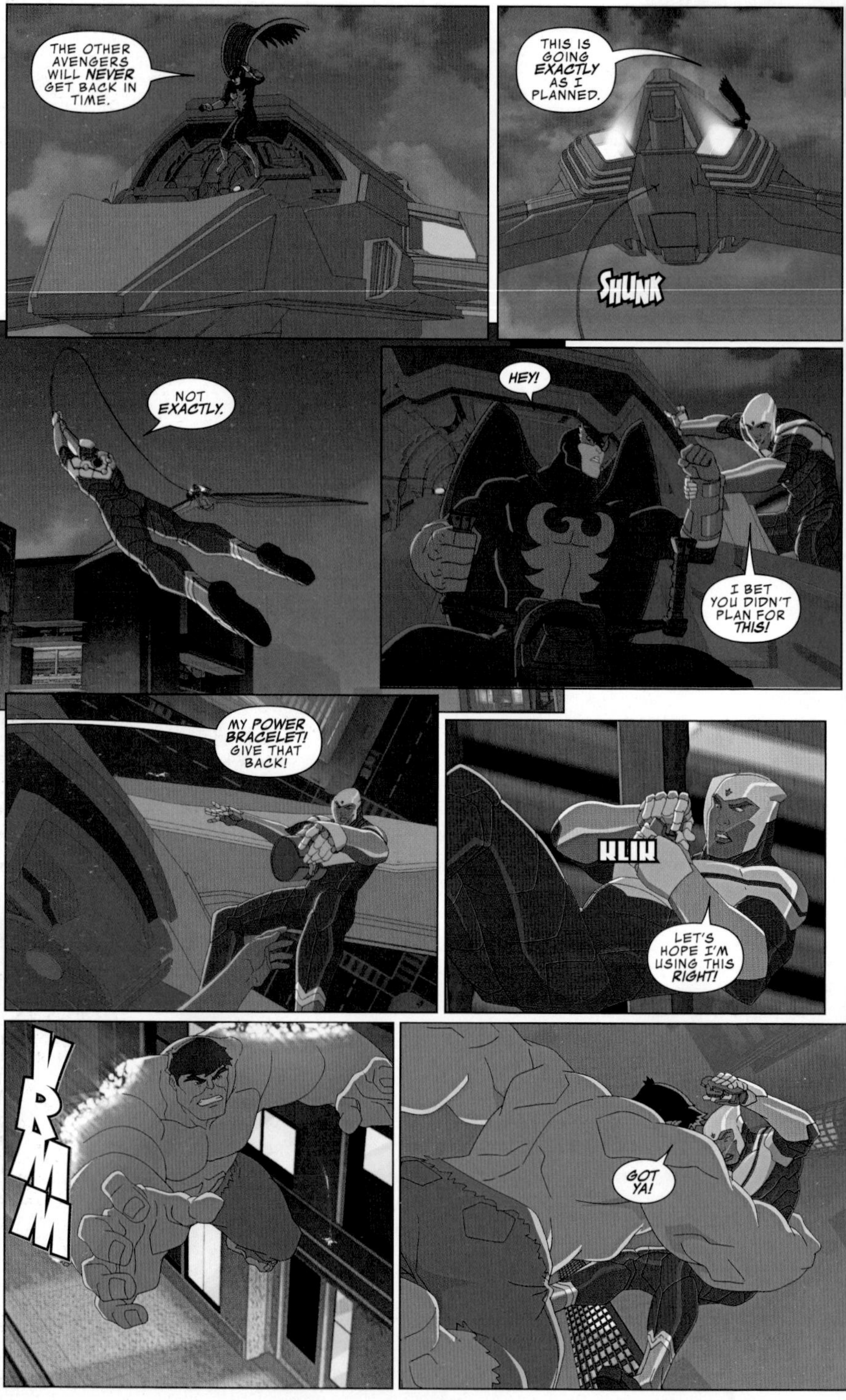

THE OTHER AVENGERS WILL NEVER GET BACK IN TIME.
THIS IS GOING EXACTLY AS I PLANNED.
SHUNK
NOT EXACTLY.
HEY!
I BET YOU DIDN'T PLAN FOR THIS!
MY POWER BRACELET! GIVE THAT BACK!
KLIK
LET'S HOPE I'M USING THIS RIGHT!
VRMM
GOT YA!

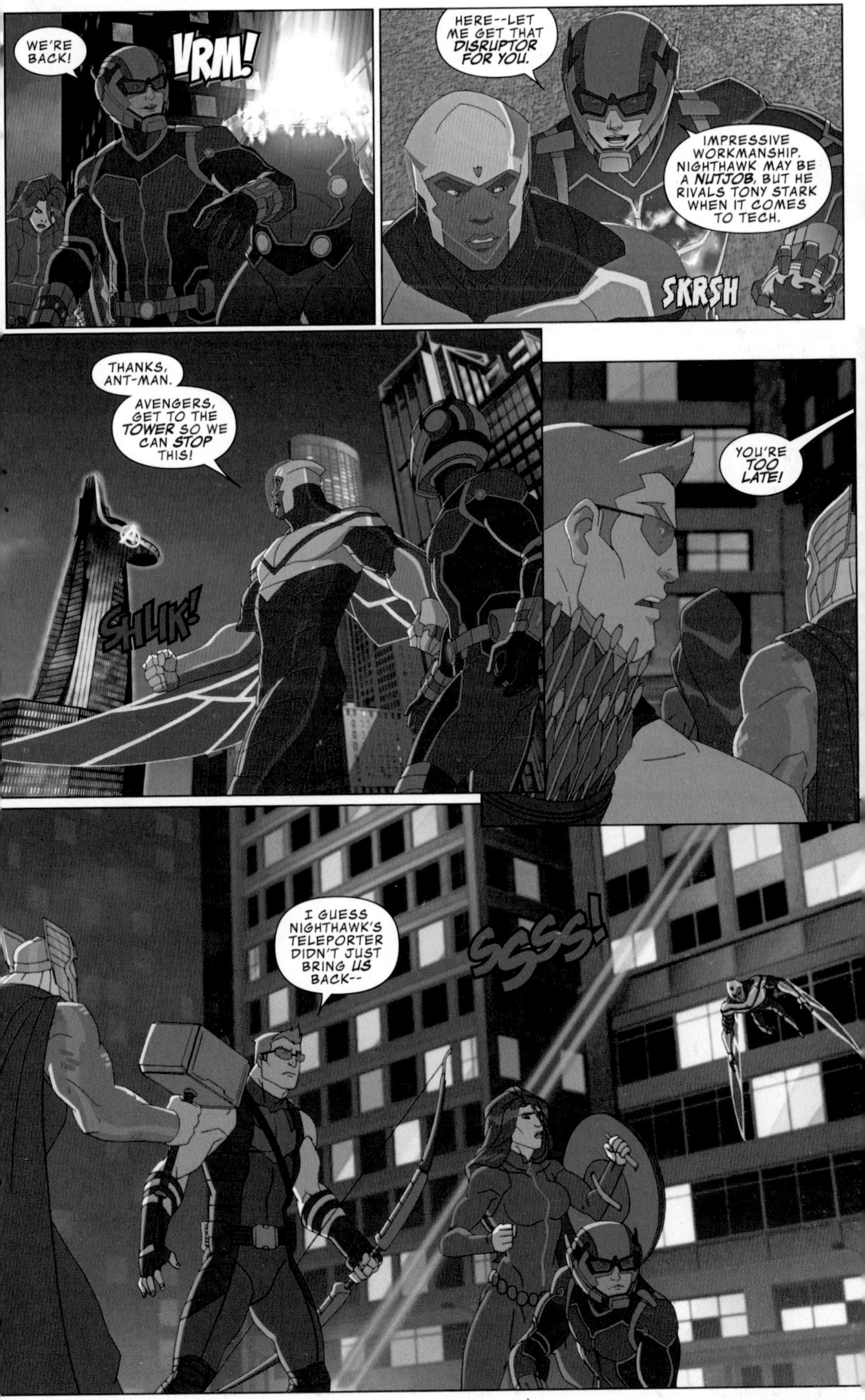
WE'RE BACK!
VRM!
HERE--LET ME GET THAT DISRUPTOR FOR YOU.
IMPRESSIVE WORKMANSHIP. NIGHTHAWK MAY BE A NUTJOB, BUT HE RIVALS TONY STARK WHEN IT COMES TO TECH.
SKRSH
THANKS, ANT-MAN.
AVENGERS, GET TO THE TOWER SO WE CAN STOP THIS!
SHLIK!
YOU'RE TOO LATE!
I GUESS NIGHTHAWK'S TELEPORTER DIDN'T JUST BRING US BACK--
SSSS!

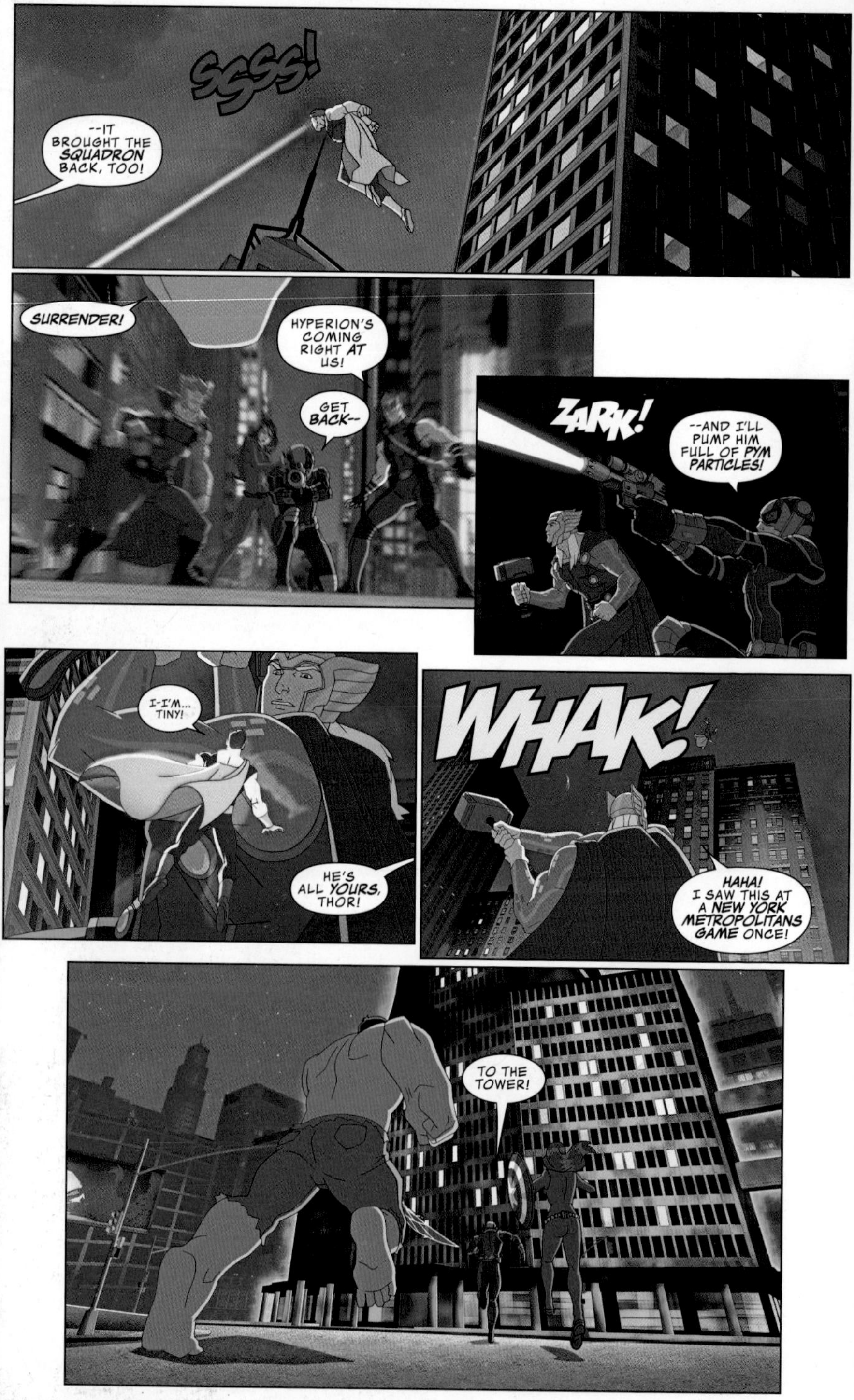
SSSS!
--IT BROUGHT THE SQUADRON BACK, TOO!
SURRENDER!
HYPERION'S COMING RIGHT AT US!
GET BACK--
ZARK!
--AND I'LL PUMP HIM FULL OF PYM PARTICLES!
I-I'M... TINY!
HE'S ALL YOURS, THOR!
WHAK!
HAHA! I SAW THIS AT A NEW YORK METROPOLITANS GAME ONCE!
TO THE TOWER!

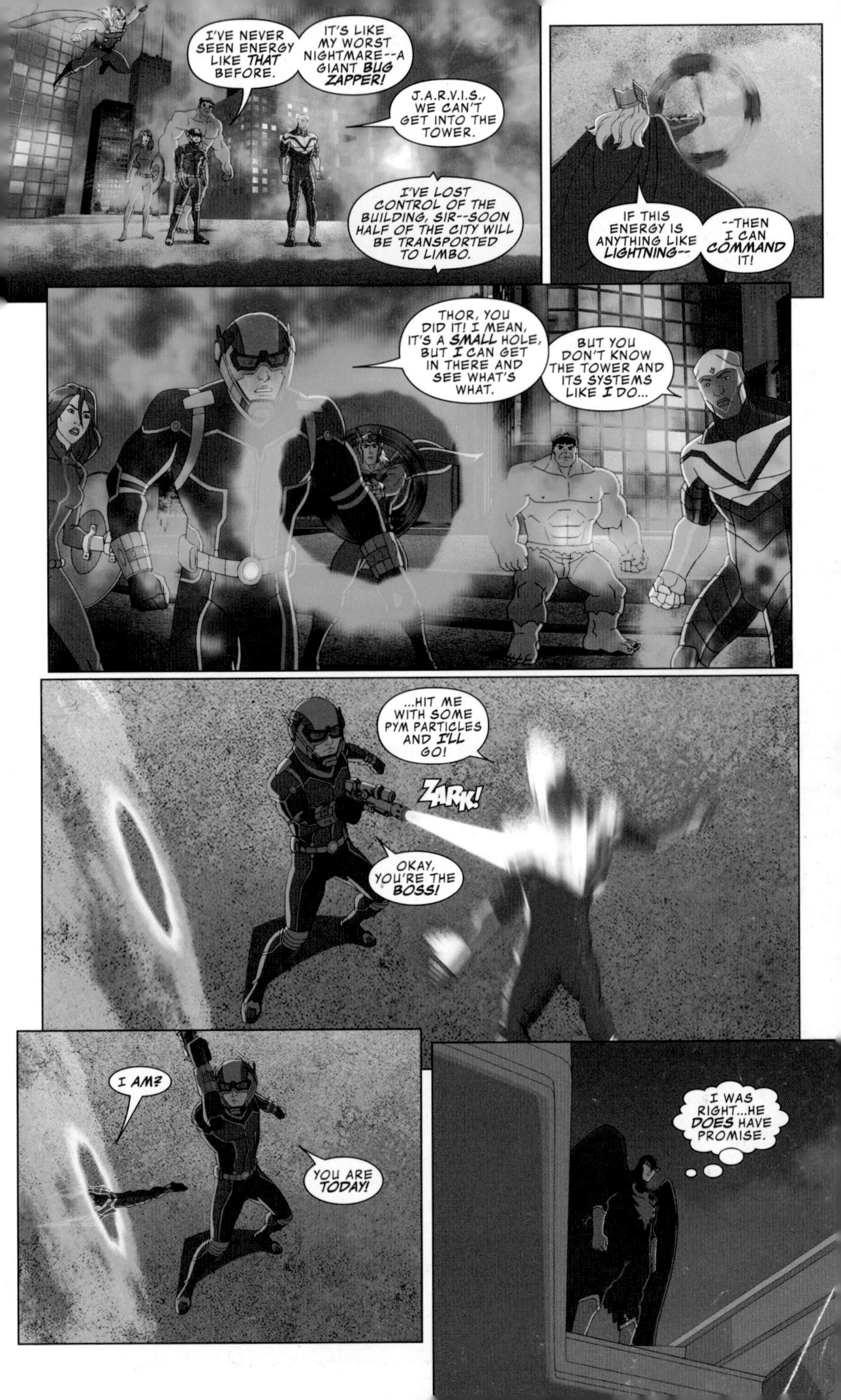

I'VE NEVER SEEN ENERGY LIKE THAT BEFORE.
IT'S LIKE MY WORST NIGHTMARE--A GIANT BUG ZAPPER!
J.A.R.V.I.S., WE CAN'T GET INTO THE TOWER.
I'VE LOST CONTROL OF THE BUILDING, SIR--SOON HALF OF THE CITY WILL BE TRANSPORTED TO LIMBO.
IF THIS ENERGY IS ANYTHING LIKE LIGHTNING--
--THEN I CAN COMMAND IT!
THOR, YOU DID IT! I MEAN, IT'S A SMALL HOLE, BUT I CAN GET IN THERE AND SEE WHAT'S WHAT.
BUT YOU DON'T KNOW THE TOWER AND ITS SYSTEMS LIKE I DO...
...HIT ME WITH SOME PYM PARTICLES AND I'LL GO!
ZARK!
OKAY, YOU'RE THE BOSS!
I AM?
YOU ARE TODAY!
I WAS RIGHT...HE DOES HAVE PROMISE.

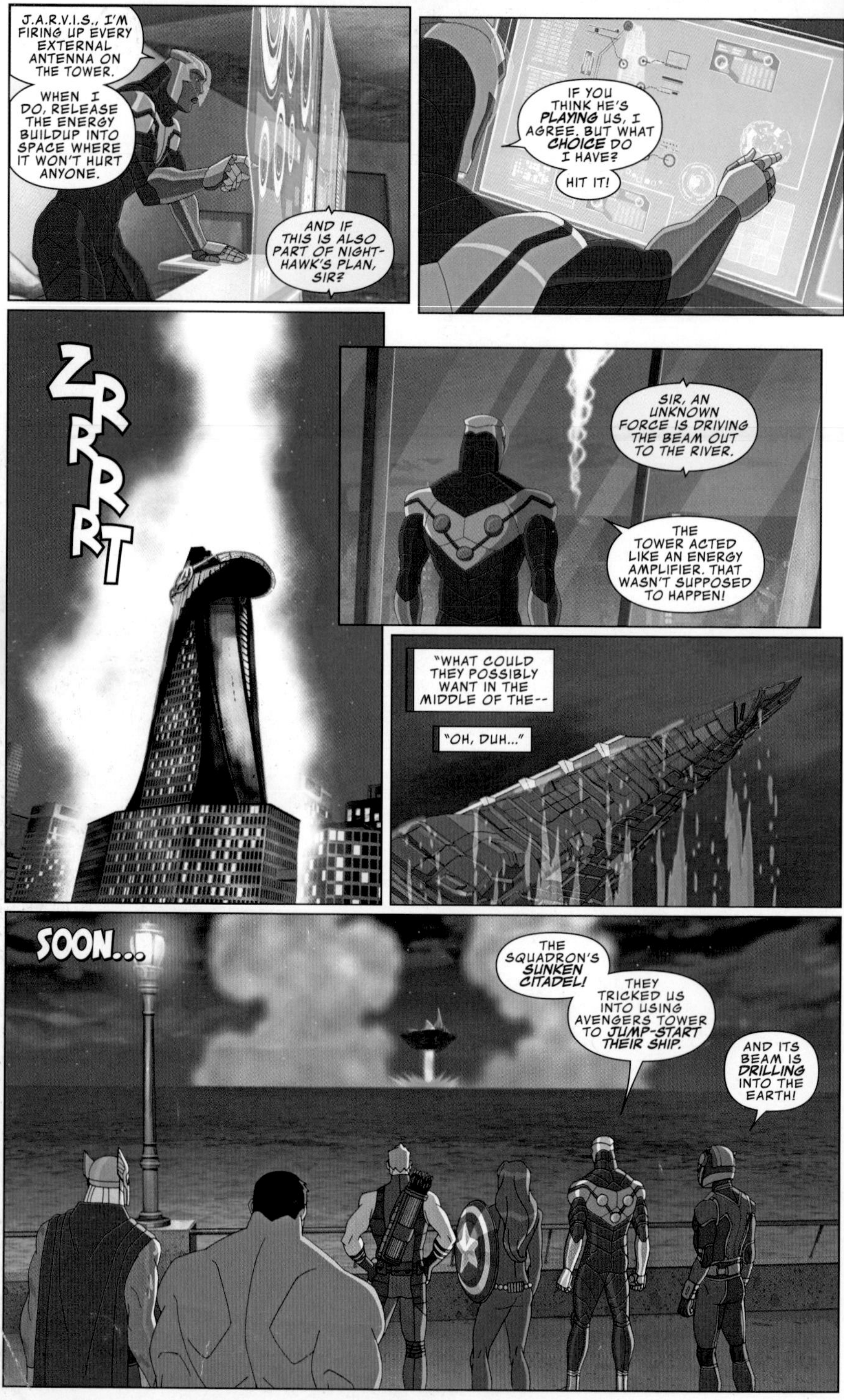
J.A.R.V.I.S., I'M FIRING UP EVERY EXTERNAL ANTENNA ON THE TOWER.
WHEN I DO, RELEASE THE ENERGY BUILDUP INTO SPACE WHERE IT WON'T HURT ANYONE.
AND IF THIS IS ALSO PART OF NIGHT-HAWK'S PLAN, SIR?
IF YOU THINK HE'S PLAYING US, I AGREE. BUT WHAT CHOICE DO I HAVE?
HIT IT!
ZRRRRT
SIR, AN UNKNOWN FORCE IS DRIVING THE BEAM OUT TO THE RIVER.
THE TOWER ACTED LIKE AN ENERGY AMPLIFIER. THAT WASN'T SUPPOSED TO HAPPEN!
"WHAT COULD THEY POSSIBLY WANT IN THE MIDDLE OF THE--
"OH, DUH..."
SOON...
THE SQUADRON'S SUNKEN CITADEL!
THEY TRICKED US INTO USING AVENGERS TOWER TO JUMP-START THEIR SHIP.
AND ITS BEAM IS DRILLING INTO THE EARTH!

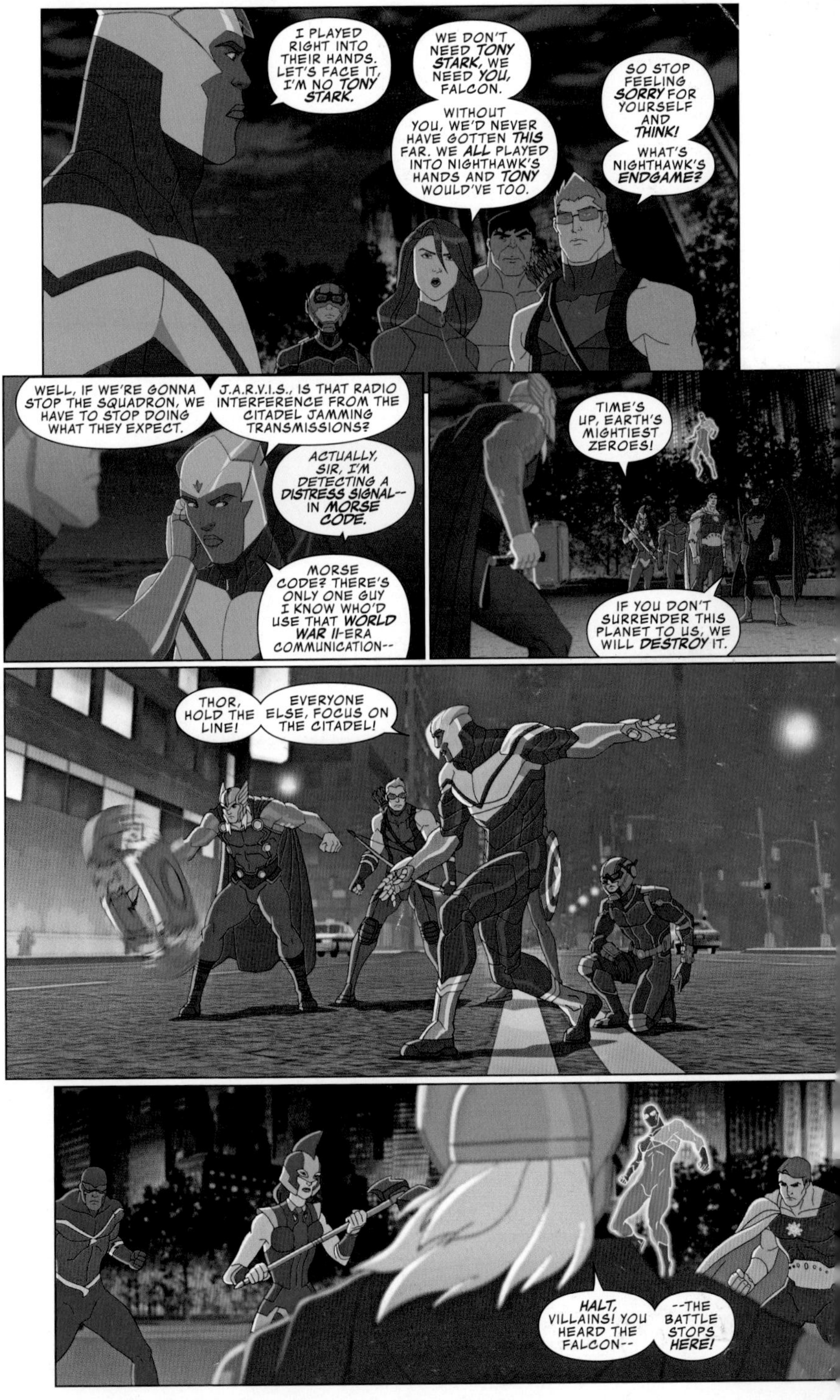
I PLAYED RIGHT INTO THEIR HANDS. LET'S FACE IT, I'M NO TONY STARK.
WE DON'T NEED TONY STARK, WE NEED YOU, FALCON.
WITHOUT YOU, WE'D NEVER HAVE GOTTEN THIS FAR. WE ALL PLAYED INTO NIGHTHAWK'S HANDS AND TONY WOULD'VE TOO.
SO STOP FEELING SORRY FOR YOURSELF AND THINK!
WHAT'S NIGHTHAWK'S ENDGAME?
WELL, IF WE'RE GONNA STOP THE SQUADRON, WE HAVE TO STOP DOING WHAT THEY EXPECT.
J.A.R.V.I.S., IS THAT RADIO INTERFERENCE FROM THE CITADEL JAMMING TRANSMISSIONS?
ACTUALLY, SIR, I'M DETECTING A DISTRESS SIGNAL-- IN MORSE CODE.
MORSE CODE? THERE'S ONLY ONE GUY I KNOW WHO'D USE THAT WORLD WAR II-ERA COMMUNICATION--
TIME'S UP, EARTH'S MIGHTIEST ZEROES!
IF YOU DON'T SURRENDER THIS PLANET TO US, WE WILL DESTROY IT.
THOR, HOLD THE LINE!
EVERYONE ELSE, FOCUS ON THE CITADEL!
HALT, VILLAINS! YOU HEARD THE FALCON--
--THE BATTLE STOPS HERE!

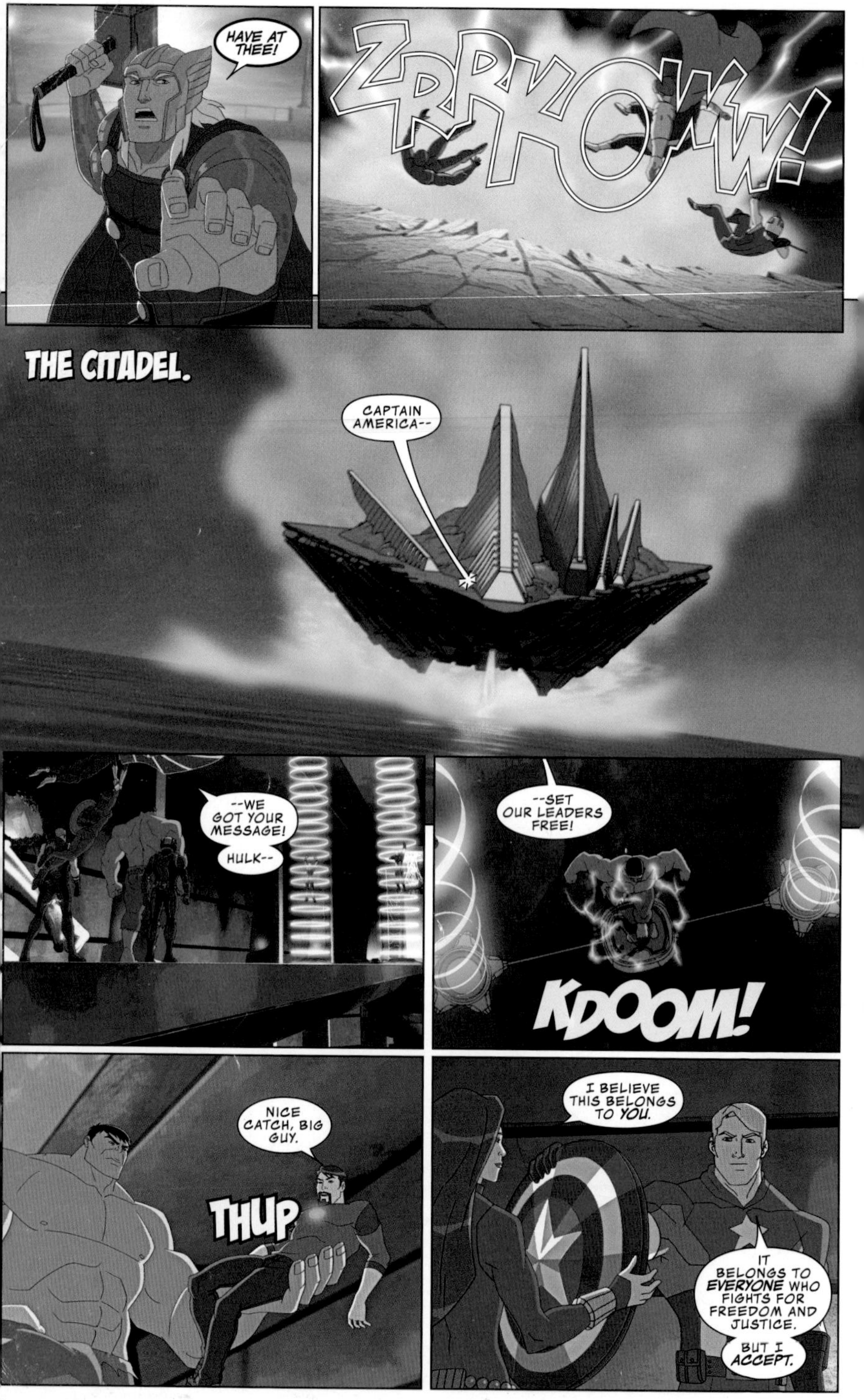
HAVE AT THEE!
ZRRKOWW!
THE CITADEL.
CAPTAIN AMERICA--
--WE GOT YOUR MESSAGE!
HULK--
--SET OUR LEADERS FREE!
KDOOM!
NICE CATCH, BIG GUY.
THUP
I BELIEVE THIS BELONGS TO YOU.
IT BELONGS TO EVERYONE WHO FIGHTS FOR FREEDOM AND JUSTICE.
BUT I ACCEPT.

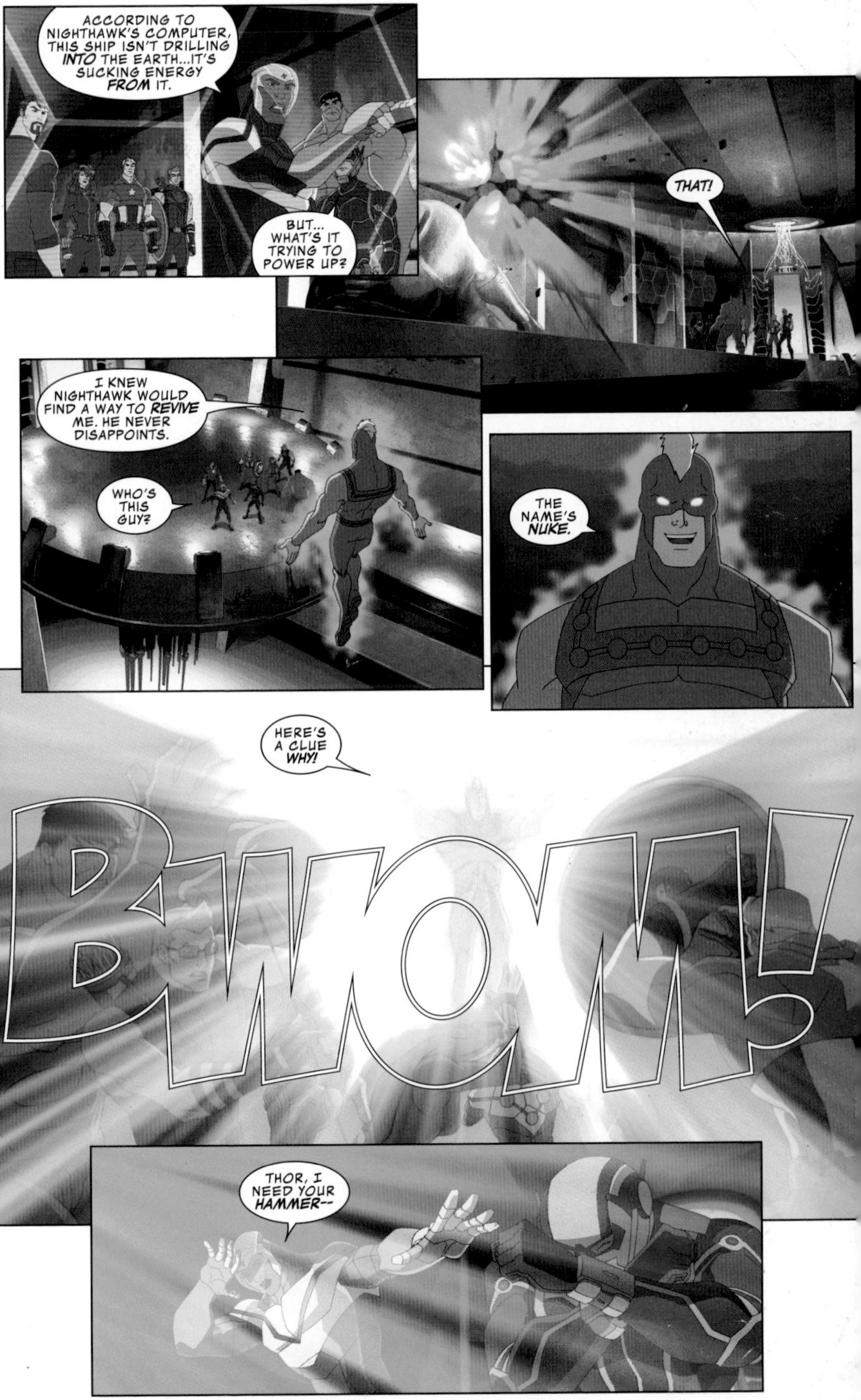
ACCORDING TO NIGHTHAWK'S COMPUTER, THIS SHIP ISN'T DRILLING INTO THE EARTH...IT'S SUCKING ENERGY FROM IT.
BUT... WHAT'S IT TRYING TO POWER UP?
THAT!
I KNEW NIGHTHAWK WOULD FIND A WAY TO REVIVE ME. HE NEVER DISAPPOINTS.
WHO'S THIS GUY?
THE NAME'S NUKE.
HERE'S A CLUE WHY!
BWOM!
THOR, I NEED YOUR HAMMER--

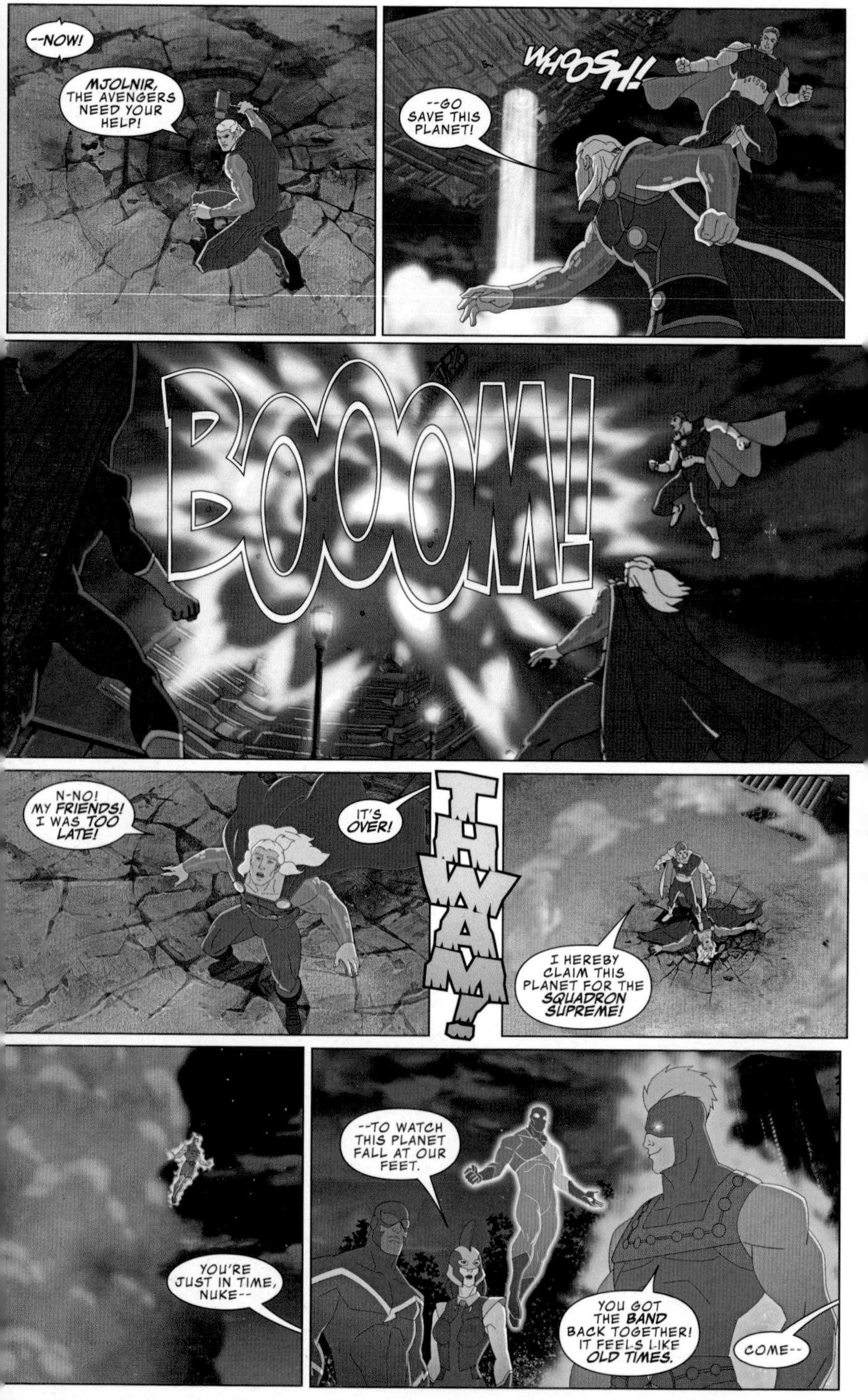
--NOW!
MJOLNIR, THE AVENGERS NEED YOUR HELP!
WHOOSH!
--GO SAVE THIS PLANET!
BOOOM!
N-NO! MY FRIENDS! I WAS TOO LATE!
IT'S OVER!
THWAM!
I HEREBY CLAIM THIS PLANET FOR THE SQUADRON SUPREME!
YOU'RE JUST IN TIME, NUKE--
--TO WATCH THIS PLANET FALL AT OUR FEET.
YOU GOT THE BAND BACK TOGETHER! IT FEELS LIKE OLD TIMES.
COME--

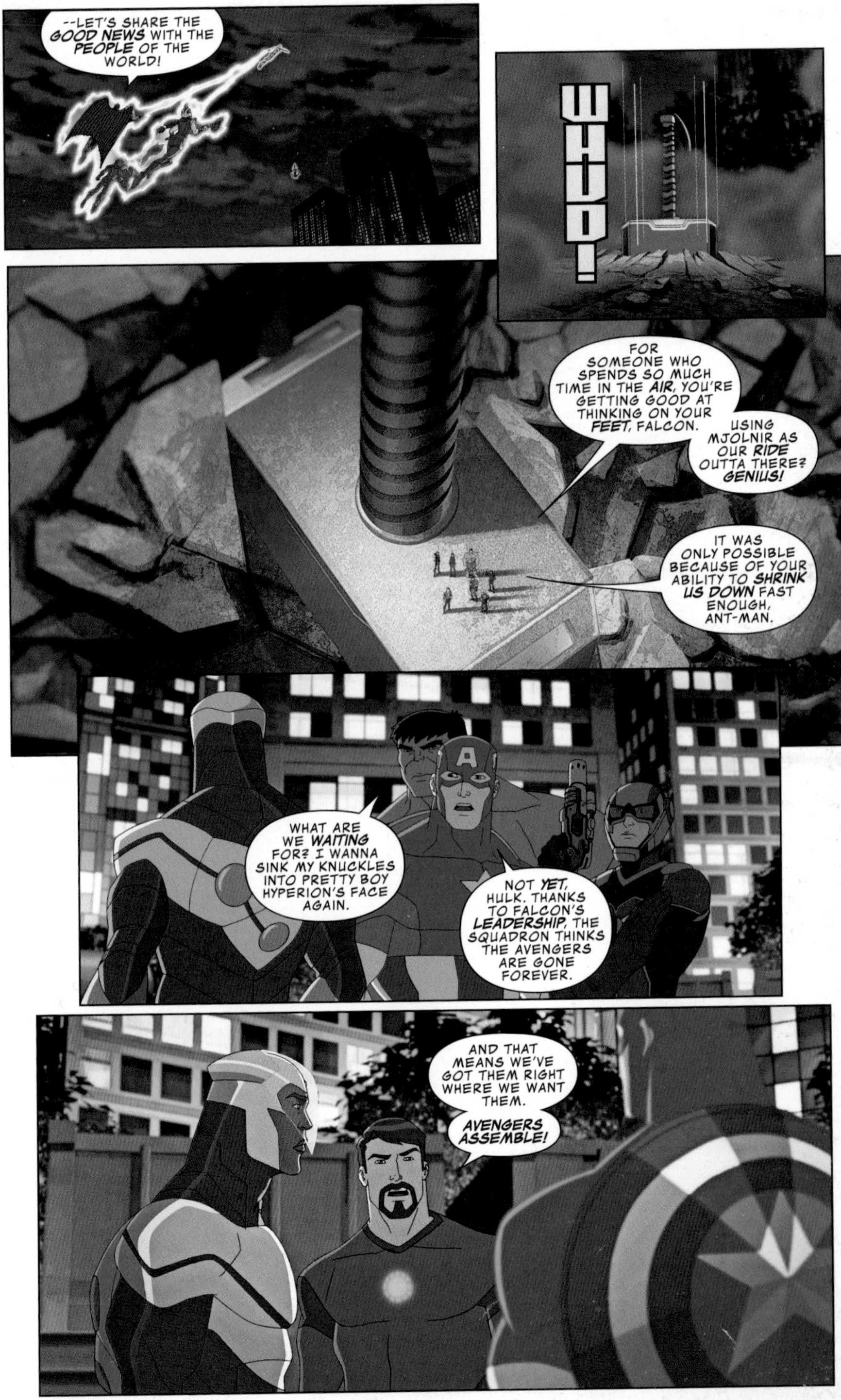
--LET'S SHARE THE GOOD NEWS WITH THE PEOPLE OF THE WORLD!
WHUD!
FOR SOMEONE WHO SPENDS SO MUCH TIME IN THE AIR, YOU'RE GETTING GOOD AT THINKING ON YOUR FEET, FALCON.
USING MJOLNIR AS OUR RIDE OUTTA THERE? GENIUS!
IT WAS ONLY POSSIBLE BECAUSE OF YOUR ABILITY TO SHRINK US DOWN FAST ENOUGH, ANT-MAN.
WHAT ARE WE WAITING FOR? I WANNA SINK MY KNUCKLES INTO PRETTY BOY HYPERION'S FACE AGAIN.
NOT YET, HULK. THANKS TO FALCON'S LEADERSHIP, THE SQUADRON THINKS THE AVENGERS ARE GONE FOREVER.
AND THAT MEANS WE'VE GOT THEM RIGHT WHERE WE WANT THEM.
AVENGERS ASSEMBLE!

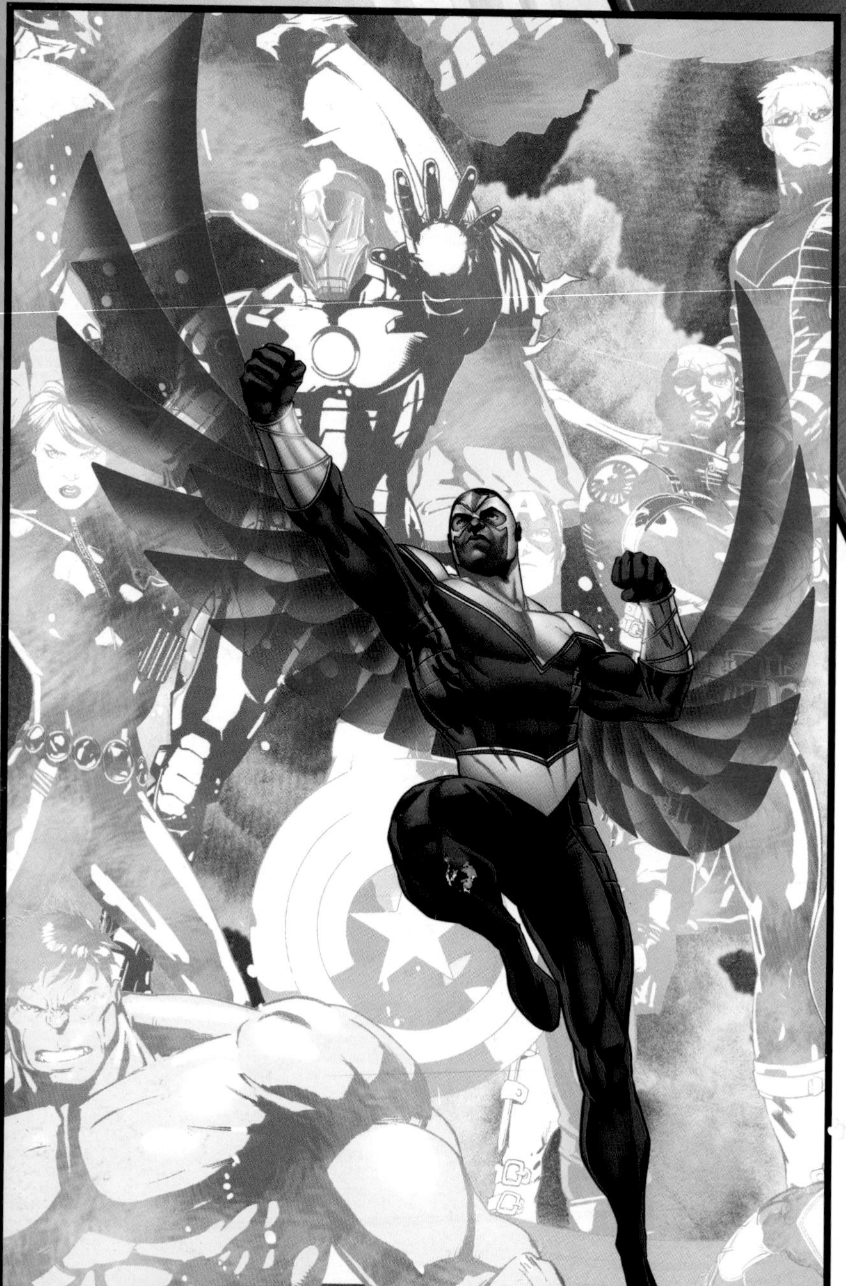

#14 BASED ON "AVENGERS UNDERGROUND"

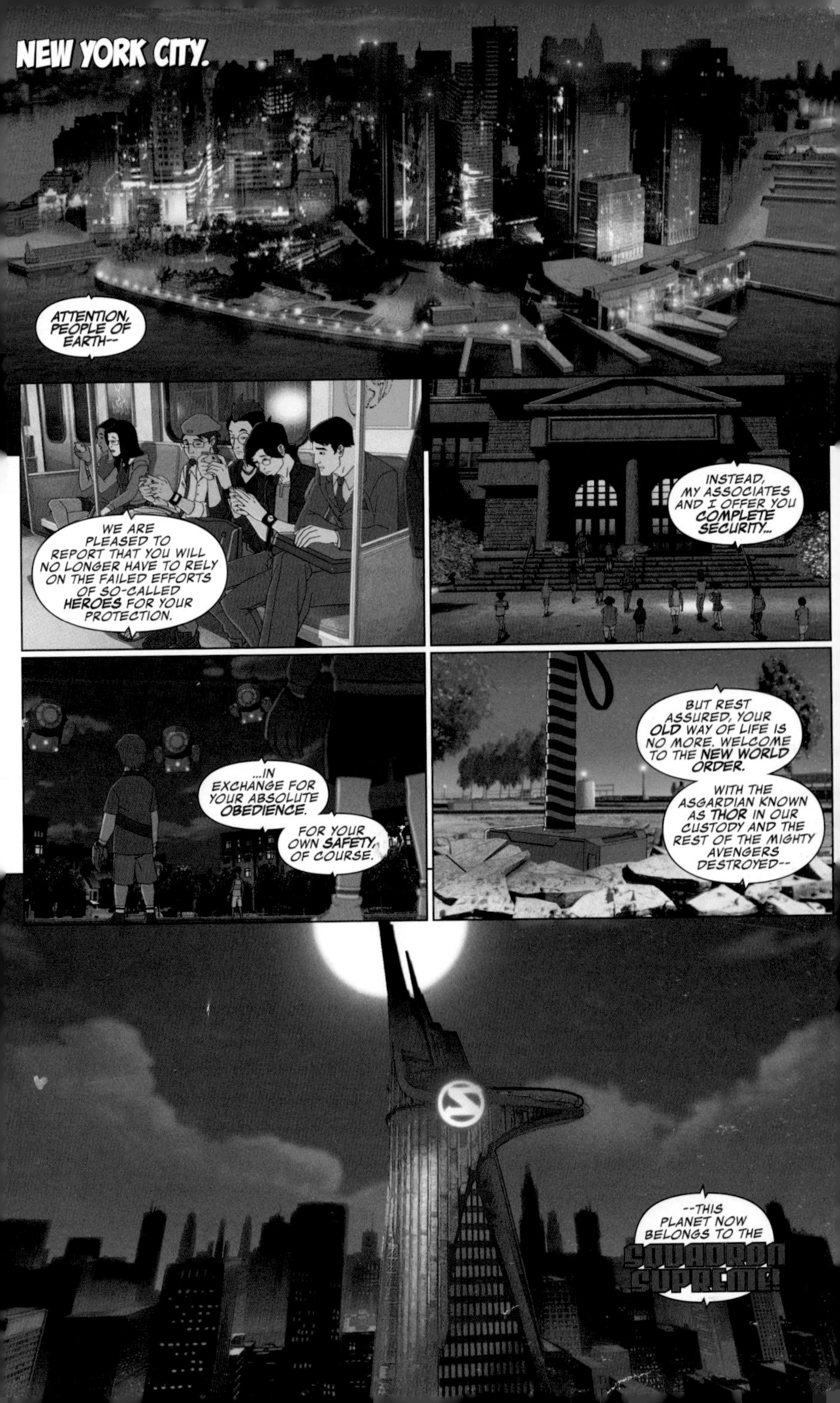
NEW YORK CITY.
ATTENTION, PEOPLE OF EARTH--
WE ARE PLEASED TO REPORT THAT YOU WILL NO LONGER HAVE TO RELY ON THE FAILED EFFORTS OF SO-CALLED HEROES FOR YOUR PROTECTION.
INSTEAD, MY ASSOCIATES AND I OFFER YOU COMPLETE SECURITY...
...IN EXCHANGE FOR YOUR ABSOLUTE OBEDIENCE.
FOR YOUR OWN SAFETY, OF COURSE.
BUT REST ASSURED, YOUR OLD WAY OF LIFE IS NO MORE. WELCOME TO THE NEW WORLD ORDER.
WITH THE ASGARDIAN KNOWN AS THOR IN OUR CUSTODY AND THE REST OF THE MIGHTY AVENGERS DESTROYED--
--THIS PLANET NOW BELONGS TO THE SQUADRON SUPREME!

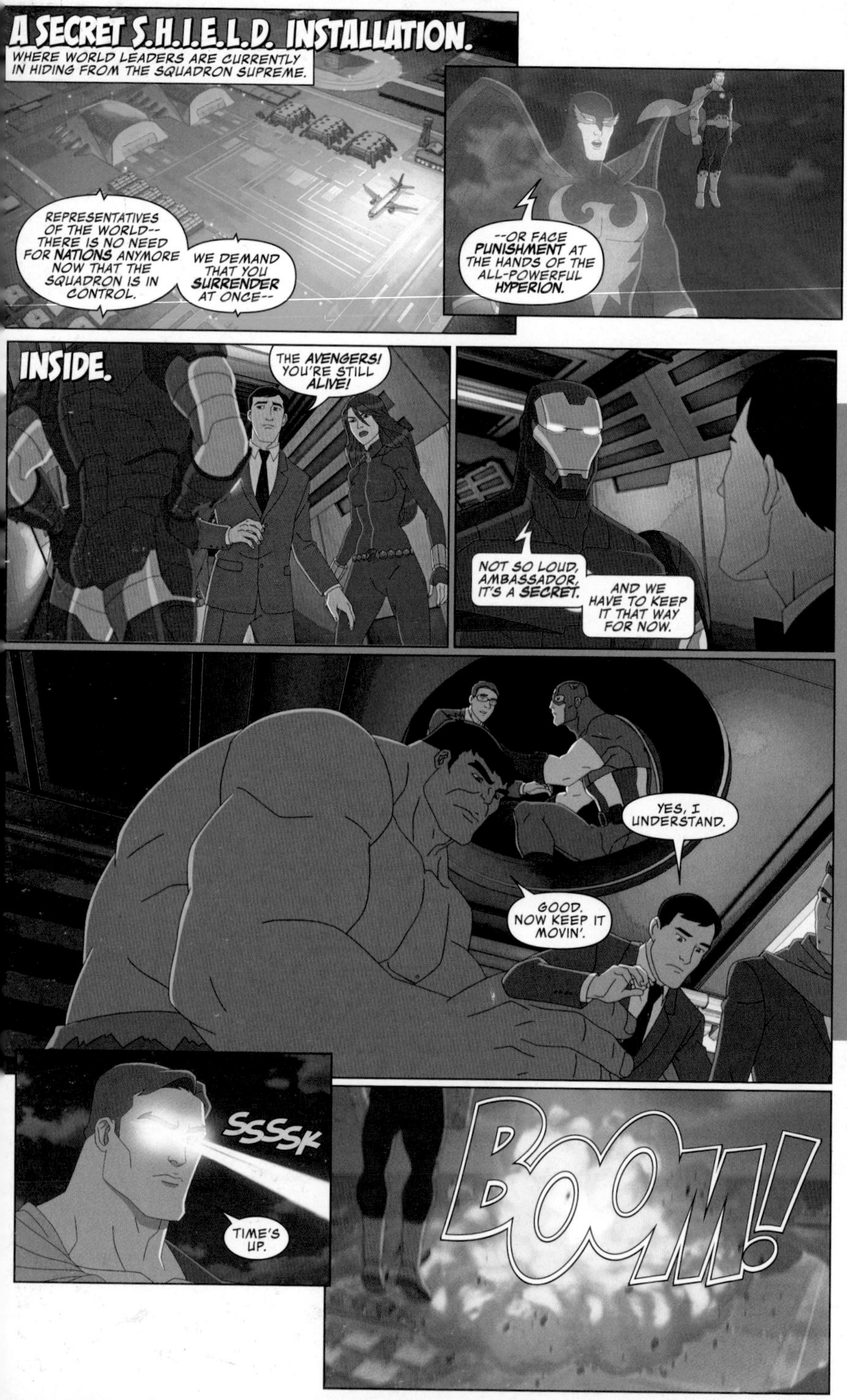
A SECRET S.H.I.E.L.D. INSTALLATION.
WHERE WORLD LEADERS ARE CURRENTLY IN HIDING FROM THE SQUADRON SUPREME.
REPRESENTATIVES OF THE WORLD-- THERE IS NO NEED FOR NATIONS ANYMORE NOW THAT THE SQUADRON IS IN CONTROL.
WE DEMAND THAT YOU SURRENDER AT ONCE--
--OR FACE PUNISHMENT AT THE HANDS OF THE ALL-POWERFUL HYPERION.
INSIDE.
THE AVENGERS! YOU'RE STILL ALIVE!
NOT SO LOUD, AMBASSADOR, IT'S A SECRET.
AND WE HAVE TO KEEP IT THAT WAY FOR NOW.
YES, I UNDERSTAND.
GOOD. NOW KEEP IT MOVIN'.
SSSSK
TIME'S UP.
BOOM!

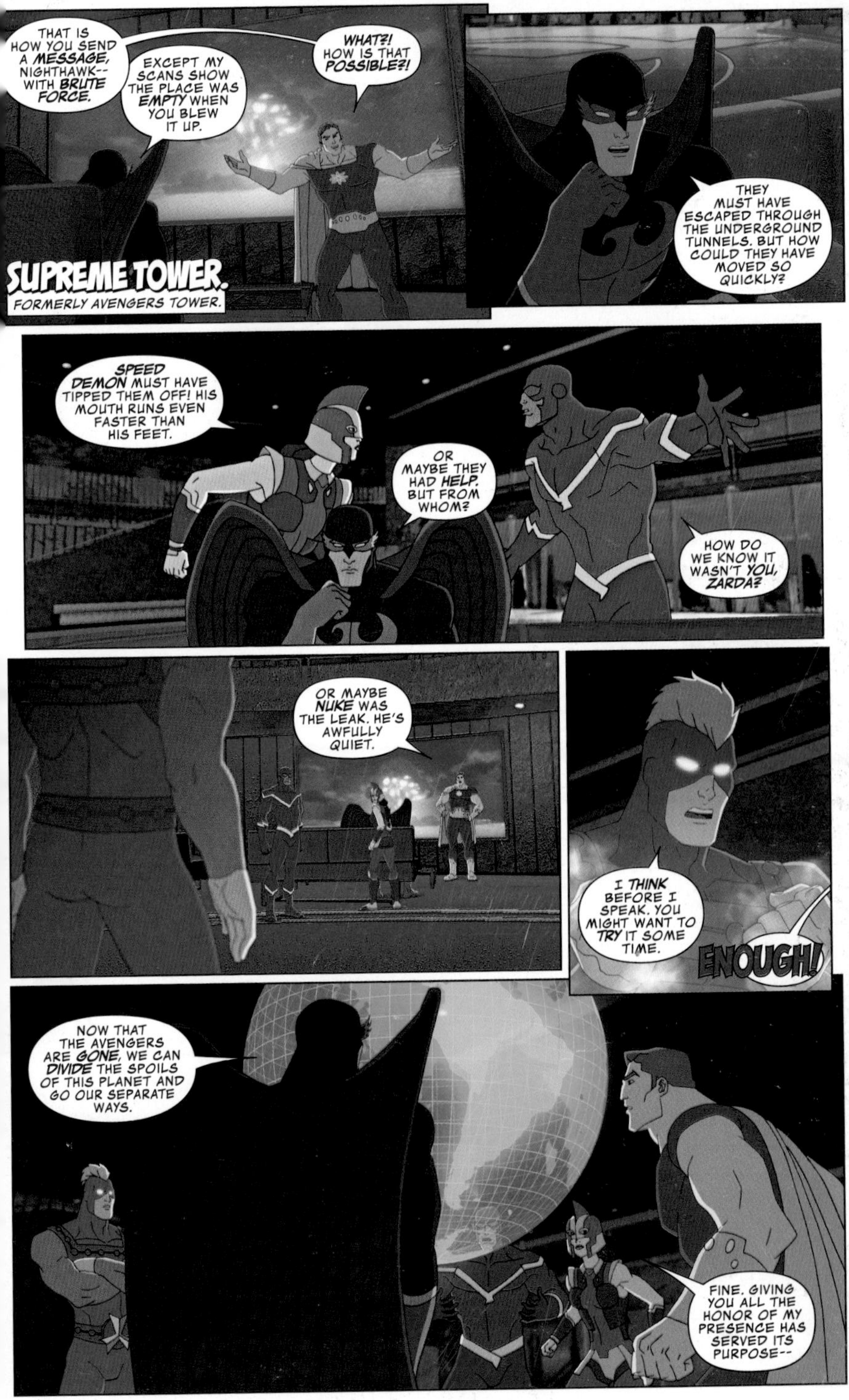

THAT IS HOW YOU SEND A MESSAGE, NIGHTHAWK-- WITH BRUTE FORCE.
EXCEPT MY SCANS SHOW THE PLACE WAS EMPTY WHEN YOU BLEW IT UP.
WHAT?! HOW IS THAT POSSIBLE?!
SUPREME TOWER.
FORMERLY AVENGERS TOWER.
THEY MUST HAVE ESCAPED THROUGH THE UNDERGROUND TUNNELS. BUT HOW COULD THEY HAVE MOVED SO QUICKLY?
SPEED DEMON MUST HAVE TIPPED THEM OFF! HIS MOUTH RUNS EVEN FASTER THAN HIS FEET.
OR MAYBE THEY HAD HELP. BUT FROM WHOM?
HOW DO WE KNOW IT WASN'T YOU, ZARDA?
OR MAYBE NUKE WAS THE LEAK. HE'S AWFULLY QUIET.
I THINK BEFORE I SPEAK. YOU MIGHT WANT TO TRY IT SOME TIME.
ENOUGH!
NOW THAT THE AVENGERS ARE GONE, WE CAN DIVIDE THE SPOILS OF THIS PLANET AND GO OUR SEPARATE WAYS.
FINE. GIVING YOU ALL THE HONOR OF MY PRESENCE HAS SERVED ITS PURPOSE--

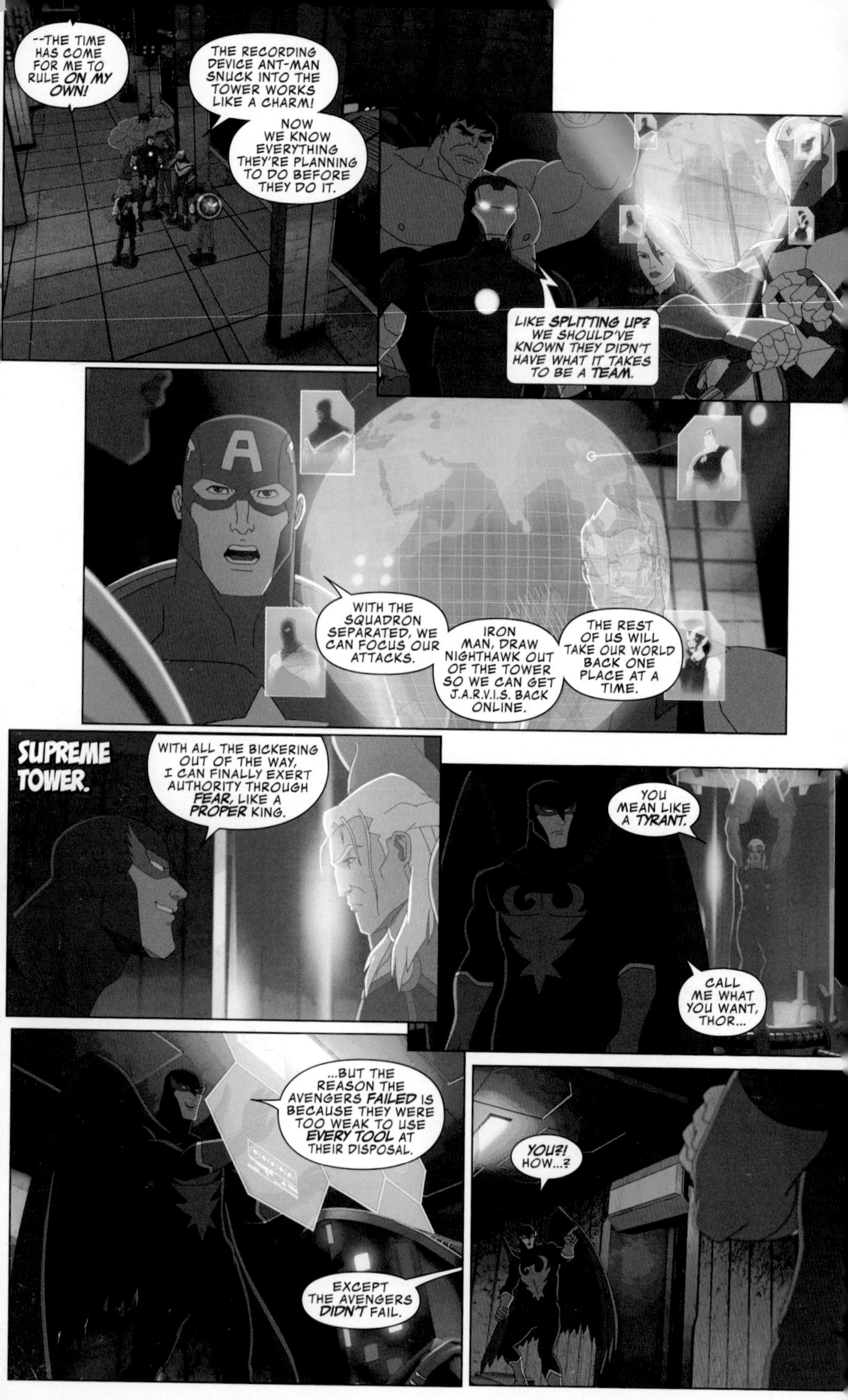
--THE TIME HAS COME FOR ME TO RULE ON MY OWN!
THE RECORDING DEVICE ANT-MAN SNUCK INTO THE TOWER WORKS LIKE A CHARM!
NOW WE KNOW EVERYTHING THEY'RE PLANNING TO DO BEFORE THEY DO IT.
LIKE SPLITTING UP? WE SHOULD'VE KNOWN THEY DIDN'T HAVE WHAT IT TAKES TO BE A TEAM.
WITH THE SQUADRON SEPARATED, WE CAN FOCUS OUR ATTACKS.
IRON MAN, DRAW NIGHTHAWK OUT OF THE TOWER SO WE CAN GET J.A.R.V.I.S. BACK ONLINE.
THE REST OF US WILL TAKE OUR WORLD BACK ONE PLACE AT A TIME.
SUPREME TOWER.
WITH ALL THE BICKERING OUT OF THE WAY, I CAN FINALLY EXERT AUTHORITY THROUGH FEAR, LIKE A PROPER KING.
YOU MEAN LIKE A TYRANT.
CALL ME WHAT YOU WANT, THOR...
...BUT THE REASON THE AVENGERS FAILED IS BECAUSE THEY WERE TOO WEAK TO USE EVERY TOOL AT THEIR DISPOSAL.
EXCEPT THE AVENGERS DIDN'T FAIL.
YOU?! HOW...?

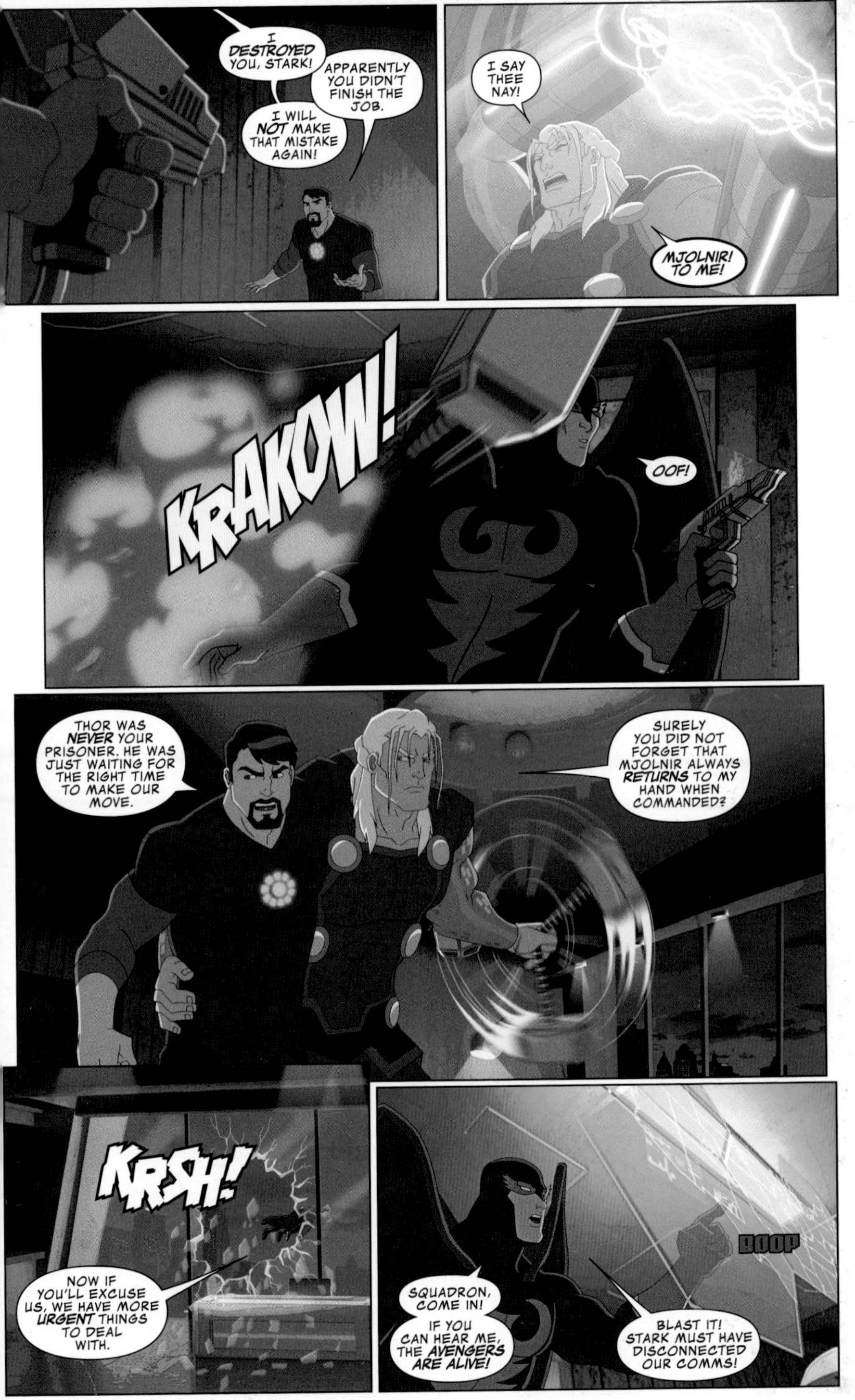
I DESTROYED YOU, STARK!
I WILL NOT MAKE THAT MISTAKE AGAIN!
APPARENTLY YOU DIDN'T FINISH THE JOB.
I SAY THEE NAY!
MJOLNIR! TO ME!
KRAKOW!
OOF!
THOR WAS NEVER YOUR PRISONER. HE WAS JUST WAITING FOR THE RIGHT TIME TO MAKE OUR MOVE.
SURELY YOU DID NOT FORGET THAT MJOLNIR ALWAYS RETURNS TO MY HAND WHEN COMMANDED?
KRSH!
NOW IF YOU'LL EXCUSE US, WE HAVE MORE URGENT THINGS TO DEAL WITH.
BOOP
SQUADRON, COME IN!
IF YOU CAN HEAR ME, THE AVENGERS ARE ALIVE!
BLAST IT! STARK MUST HAVE DISCONNECTED OUR COMMS!

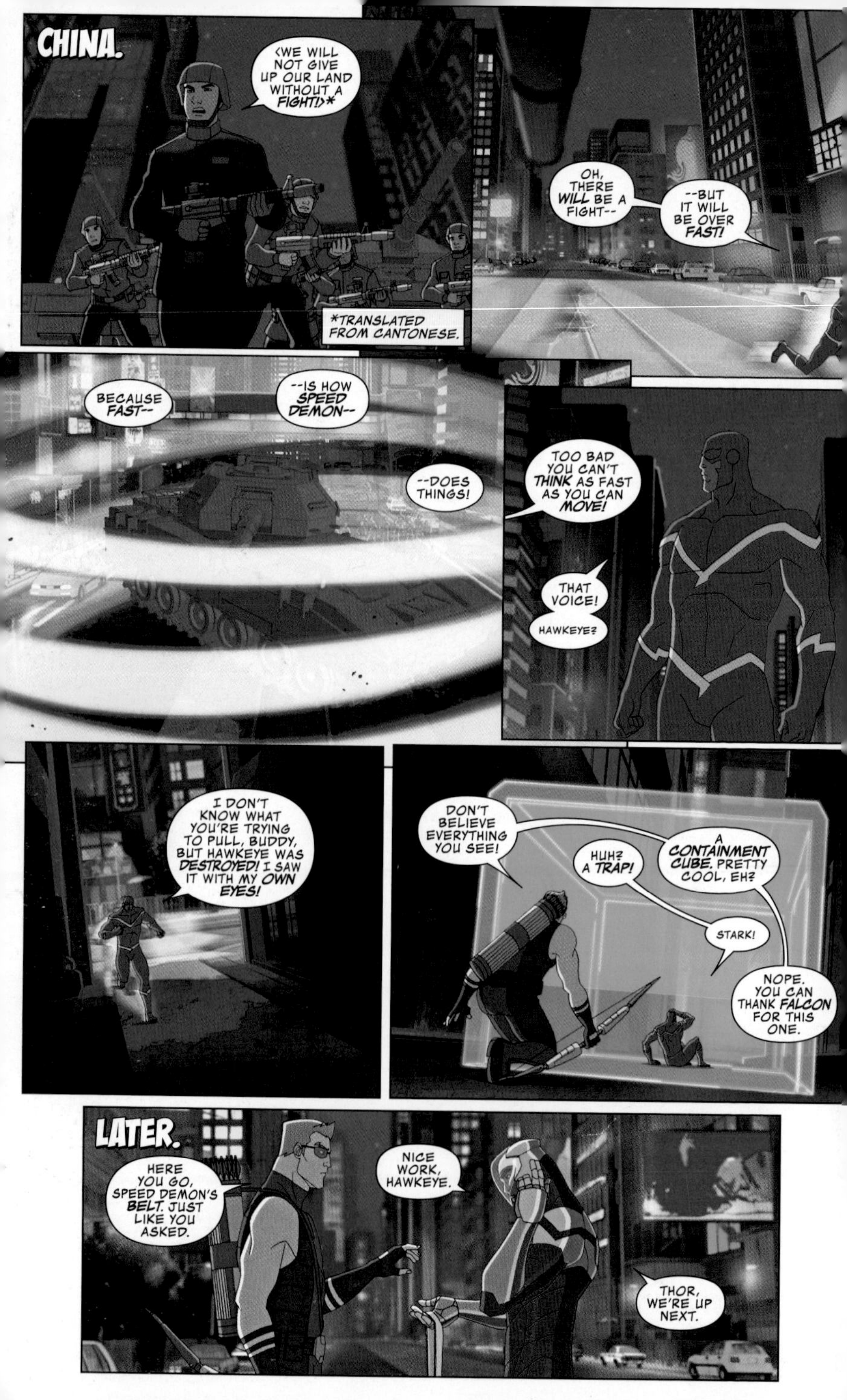
CHINA.
<WE WILL NOT GIVE UP OUR LAND WITHOUT A FIGHT!>*
*TRANSLATED FROM CANTONESE.
OH, THERE WILL BE A FIGHT--
--BUT IT WILL BE OVER FAST!
BECAUSE FAST--
--IS HOW SPEED DEMON--
--DOES THINGS!
TOO BAD YOU CAN'T THINK AS FAST AS YOU CAN MOVE!
THAT VOICE!
HAWKEYE?
I DON'T KNOW WHAT YOU'RE TRYING TO PULL, BUDDY, BUT HAWKEYE WAS DESTROYED! I SAW IT WITH MY OWN EYES!
DON'T BELIEVE EVERYTHING YOU SEE!
A CONTAINMENT CUBE. PRETTY COOL, EH?
HUH? A TRAP!
STARK!
NOPE. YOU CAN THANK FALCON FOR THIS ONE.
LATER.
HERE YOU GO, SPEED DEMON'S BELT. JUST LIKE YOU ASKED.
NICE WORK, HAWKEYE.
THOR, WE'RE UP NEXT.

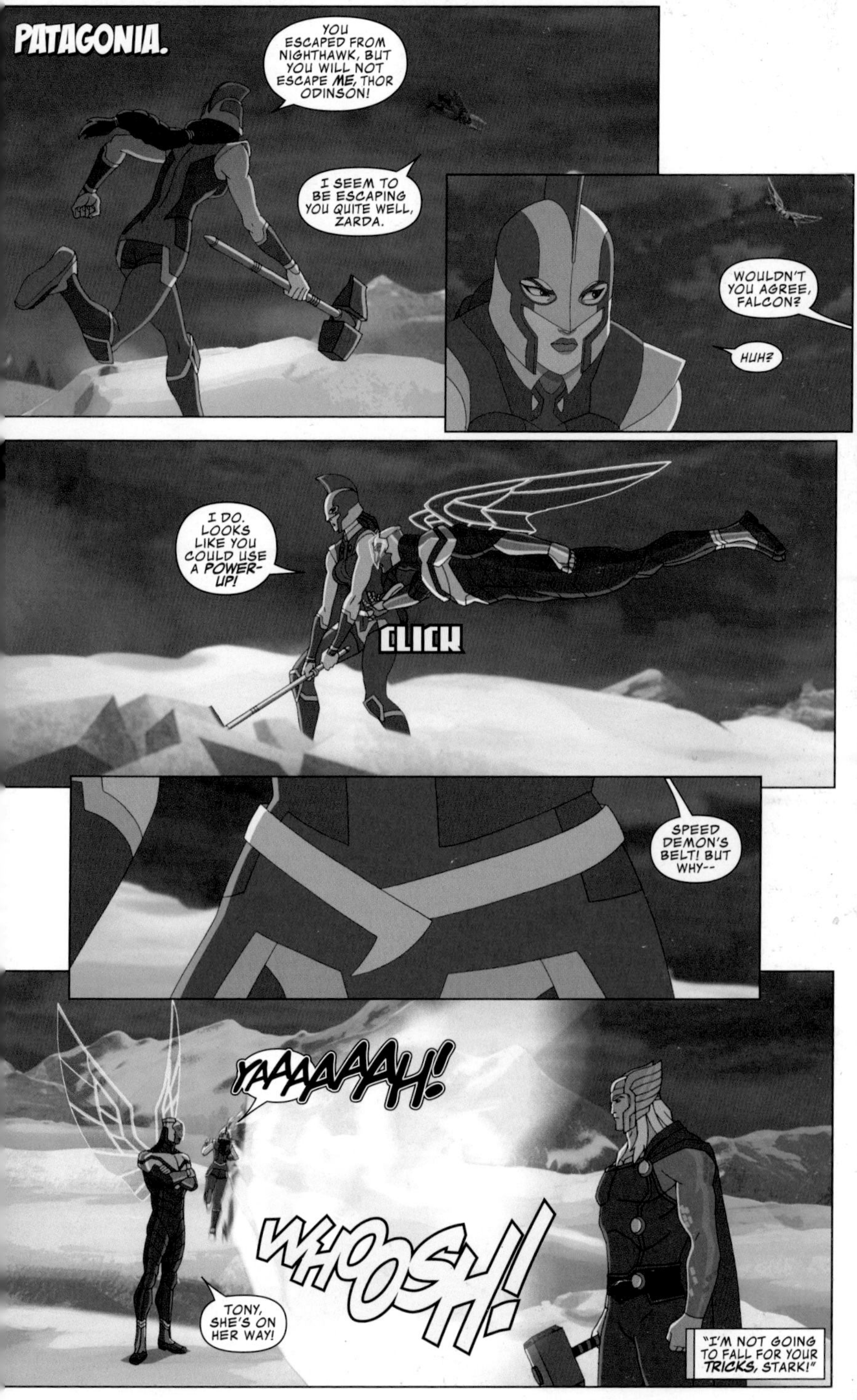

PATAGONIA.
YOU ESCAPED FROM NIGHTHAWK, BUT YOU WILL NOT ESCAPE ME, THOR ODINSON!
I SEEM TO BE ESCAPING YOU QUITE WELL, ZARDA.
WOULDN'T YOU AGREE, FALCON?
HUH?
I DO. LOOKS LIKE YOU COULD USE A POWER-UP!
CLICK
SPEED DEMON'S BELT! BUT WHY--
YAAAAAAH!
WHOOSH!
TONY, SHE'S ON HER WAY!
"I'M NOT GOING TO FALL FOR YOUR TRICKS, STARK!"

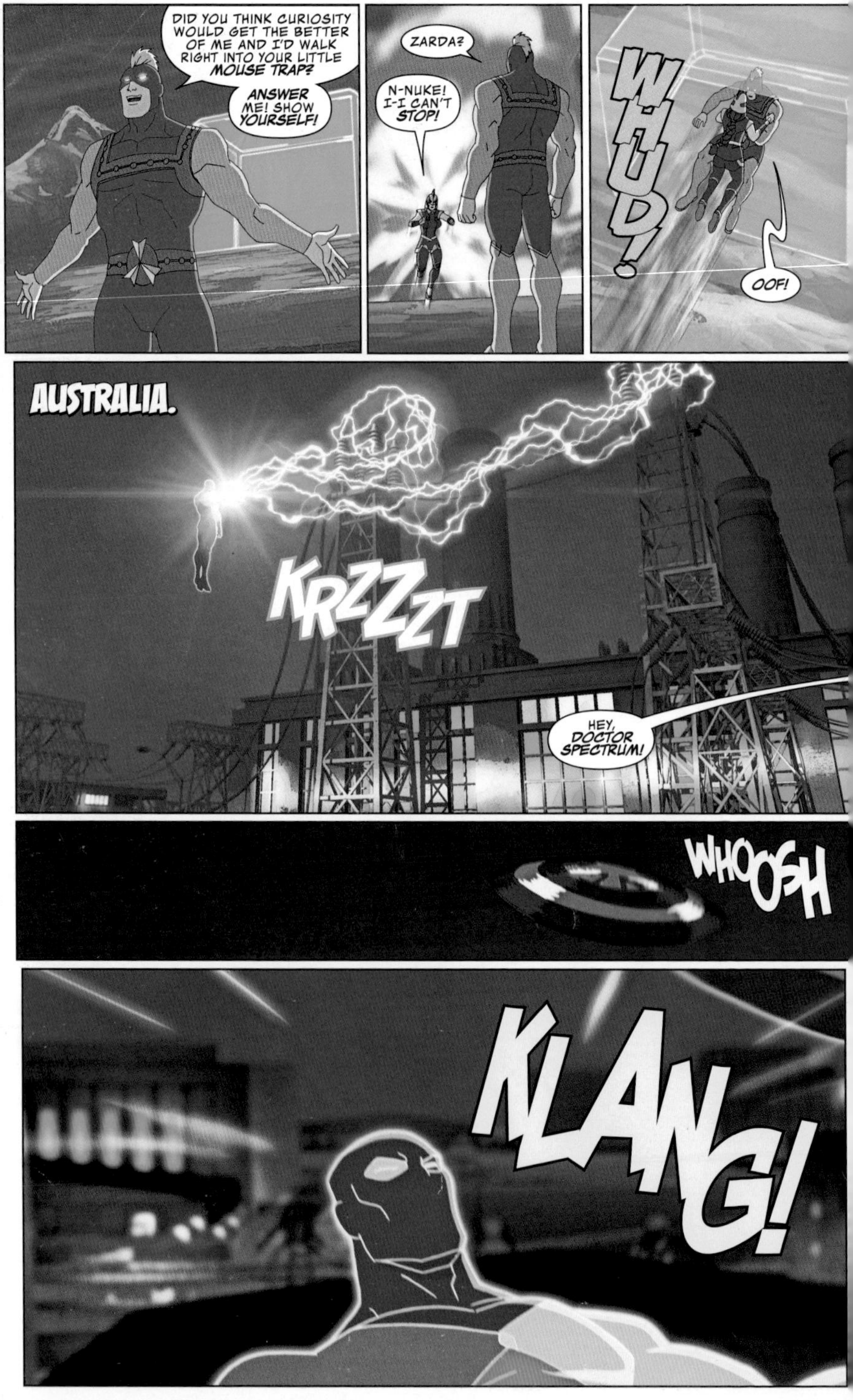
DID YOU THINK CURIOSITY WOULD GET THE BETTER OF ME AND I'D WALK RIGHT INTO YOUR LITTLE MOUSE TRAP?
ANSWER ME! SHOW YOURSELF!
ZARDA?
N-NUKE! I-I CAN'T STOP!
WHUD!
OOF!
AUSTRALIA.
KRZZZT
HEY, DOCTOR SPECTRUM!
WHOOSH
KLANG!

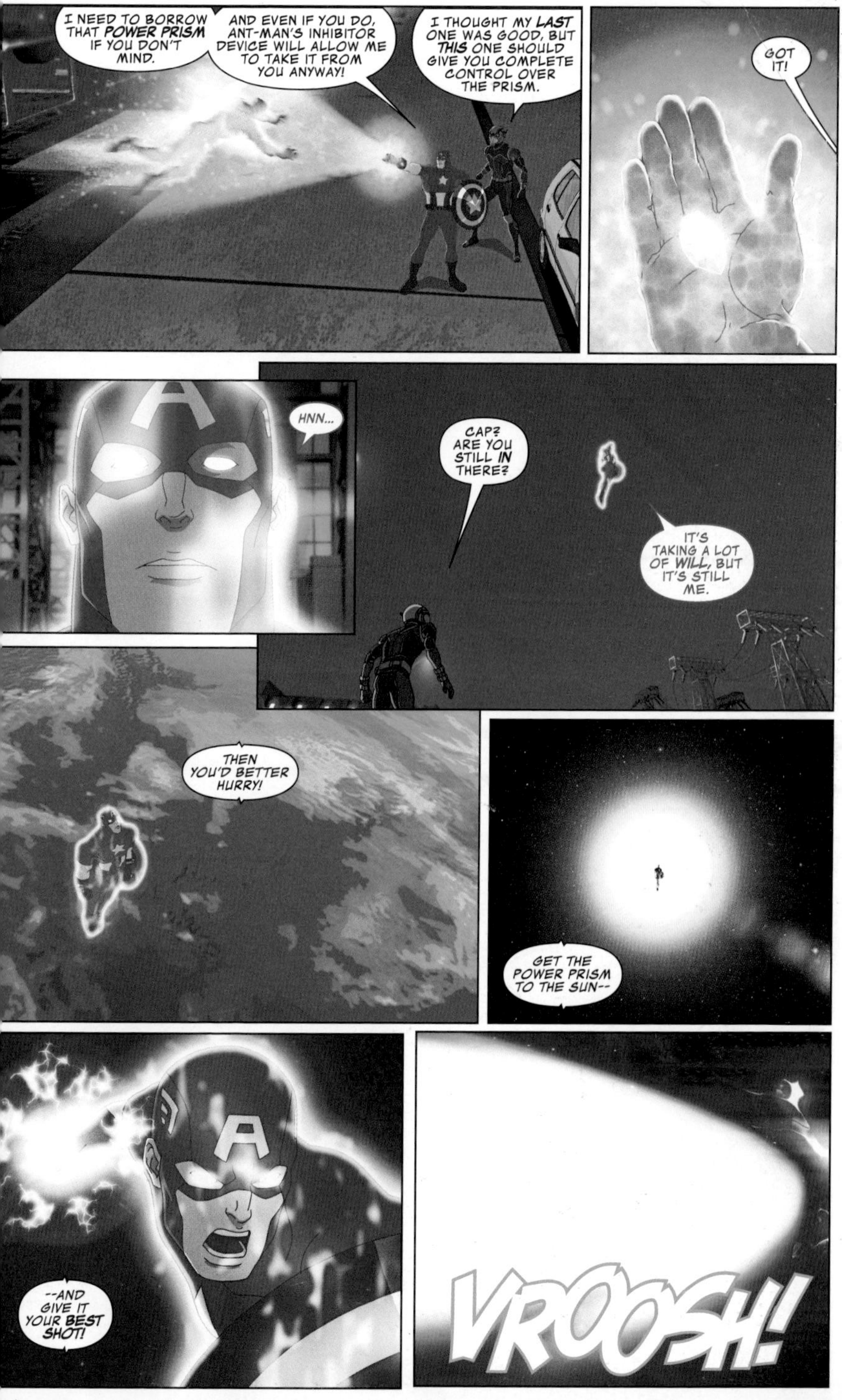

I NEED TO BORROW THAT POWER PRISM IF YOU DON'T MIND.
AND EVEN IF YOU DO, ANT-MAN'S INHIBITOR DEVICE WILL ALLOW ME TO TAKE IT FROM YOU ANYWAY!
I THOUGHT MY LAST ONE WAS GOOD, BUT THIS ONE SHOULD GIVE YOU COMPLETE CONTROL OVER THE PRISM.
GOT IT!
HNN...
CAP? ARE YOU STILL IN THERE?
IT'S TAKING A LOT OF WILL, BUT IT'S STILL ME.
THEN YOU'D BETTER HURRY!
GET THE POWER PRISM TO THE SUN--
--AND GIVE IT YOUR BEST SHOT!
VROOSH!

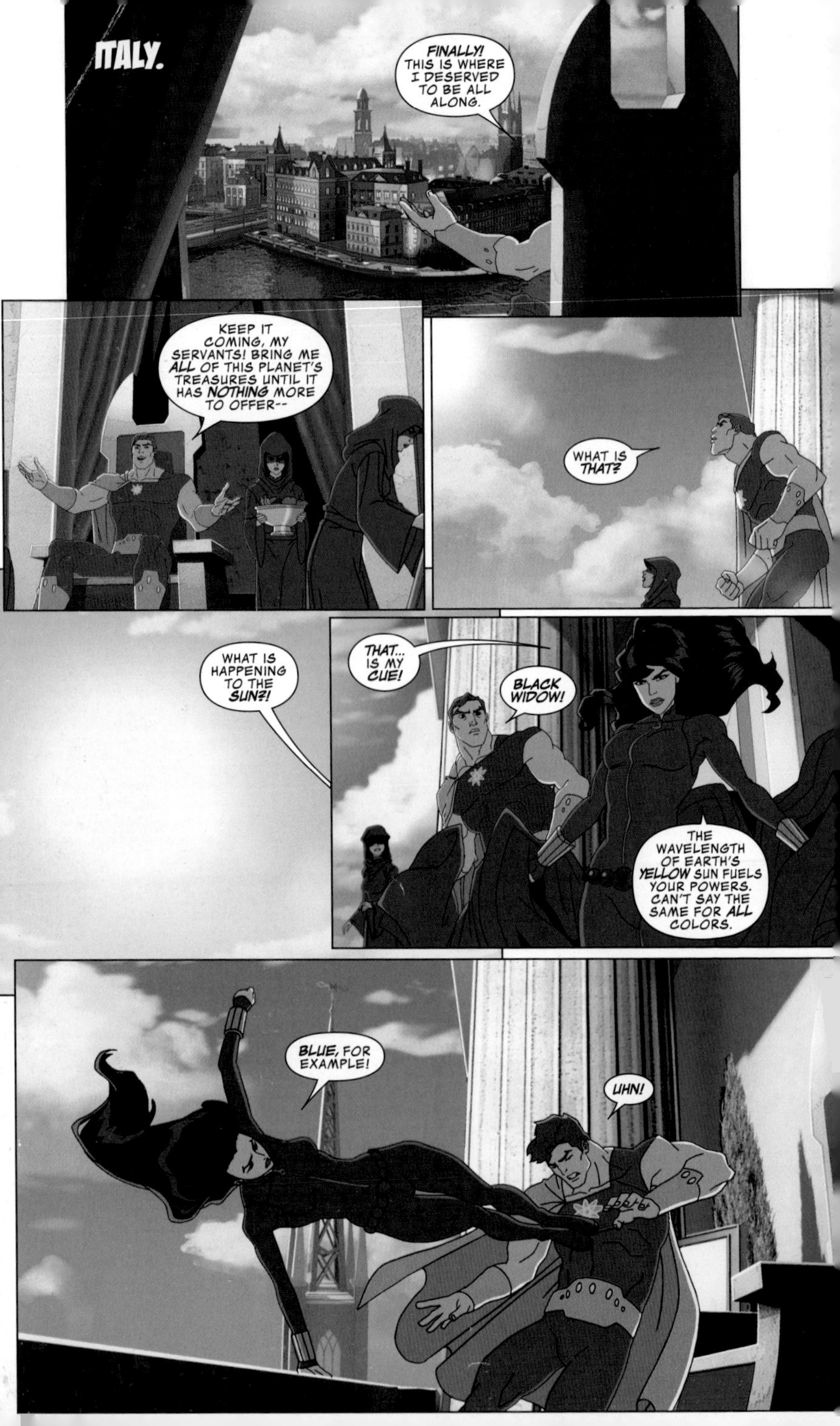

ITALY.
FINALLY! THIS IS WHERE I DESERVED TO BE ALL ALONG.
KEEP IT COMING, MY SERVANTS! BRING ME ALL OF THIS PLANET'S TREASURES UNTIL IT HAS NOTHING MORE TO OFFER--
WHAT IS THAT?
WHAT IS HAPPENING TO THE SUN?!
THAT... IS MY CUE!
BLACK WIDOW!
THE WAVELENGTH OF EARTH'S YELLOW SUN FUELS YOUR POWERS. CAN'T SAY THE SAME FOR ALL COLORS.
BLUE, FOR EXAMPLE!
UHN!

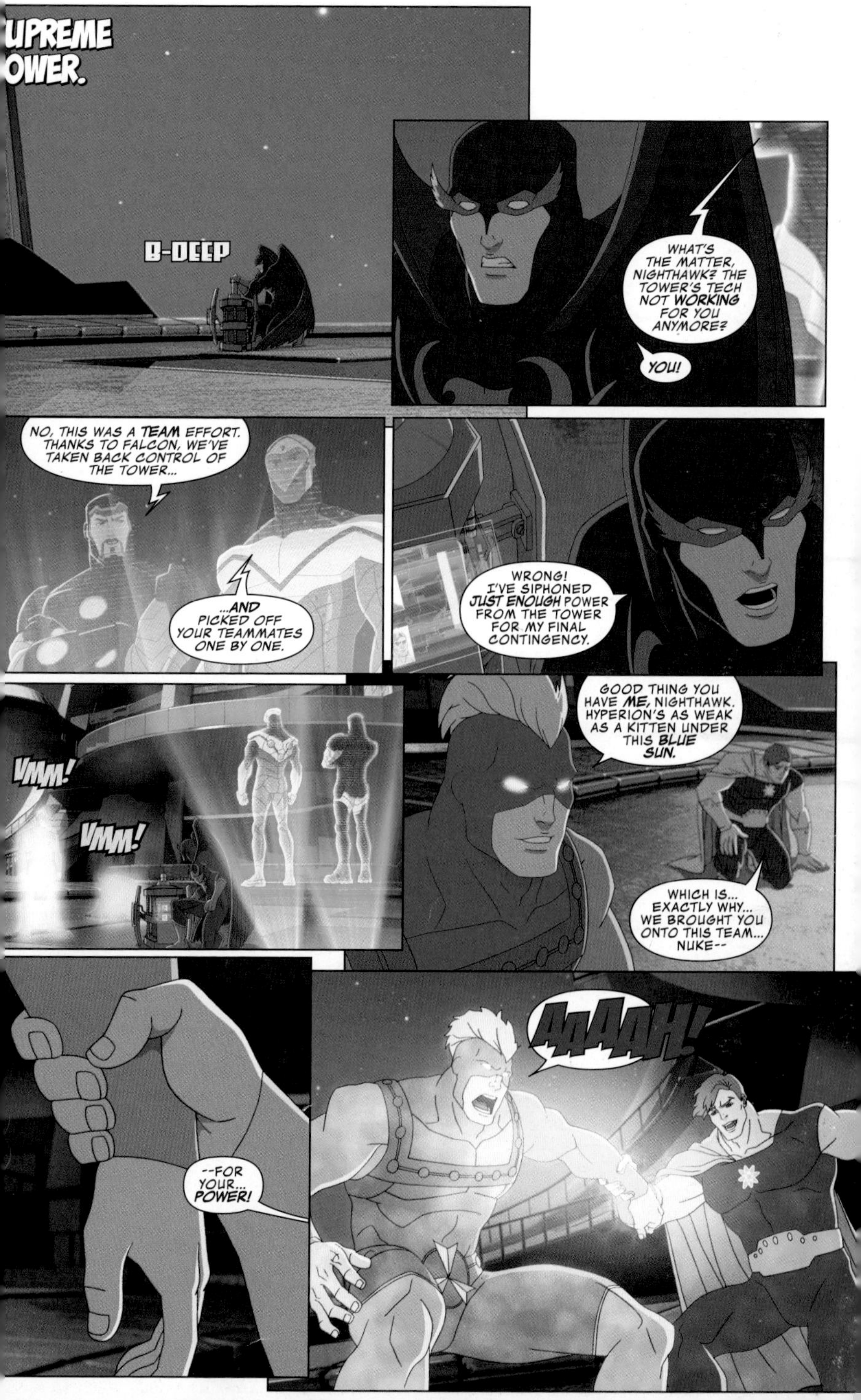

UPREME
OWER.
B-DEEP
WHAT'S THE MATTER, NIGHTHAWK? THE TOWER'S TECH NOT WORKING FOR YOU ANYMORE?
YOU!
NO, THIS WAS A TEAM EFFORT. THANKS TO FALCON, WE'VE TAKEN BACK CONTROL OF THE TOWER...
...AND PICKED OFF YOUR TEAMMATES ONE BY ONE.
WRONG! I'VE SIPHONED JUST ENOUGH POWER FROM THE TOWER FOR MY FINAL CONTINGENCY.
VMM!
VMM!
GOOD THING YOU HAVE ME, NIGHTHAWK. HYPERION'S AS WEAK AS A KITTEN UNDER THIS BLUE SUN.
WHICH IS... EXACTLY WHY... WE BROUGHT YOU ONTO THIS TEAM... NUKE--
--FOR YOUR... POWER!
AAAAH!

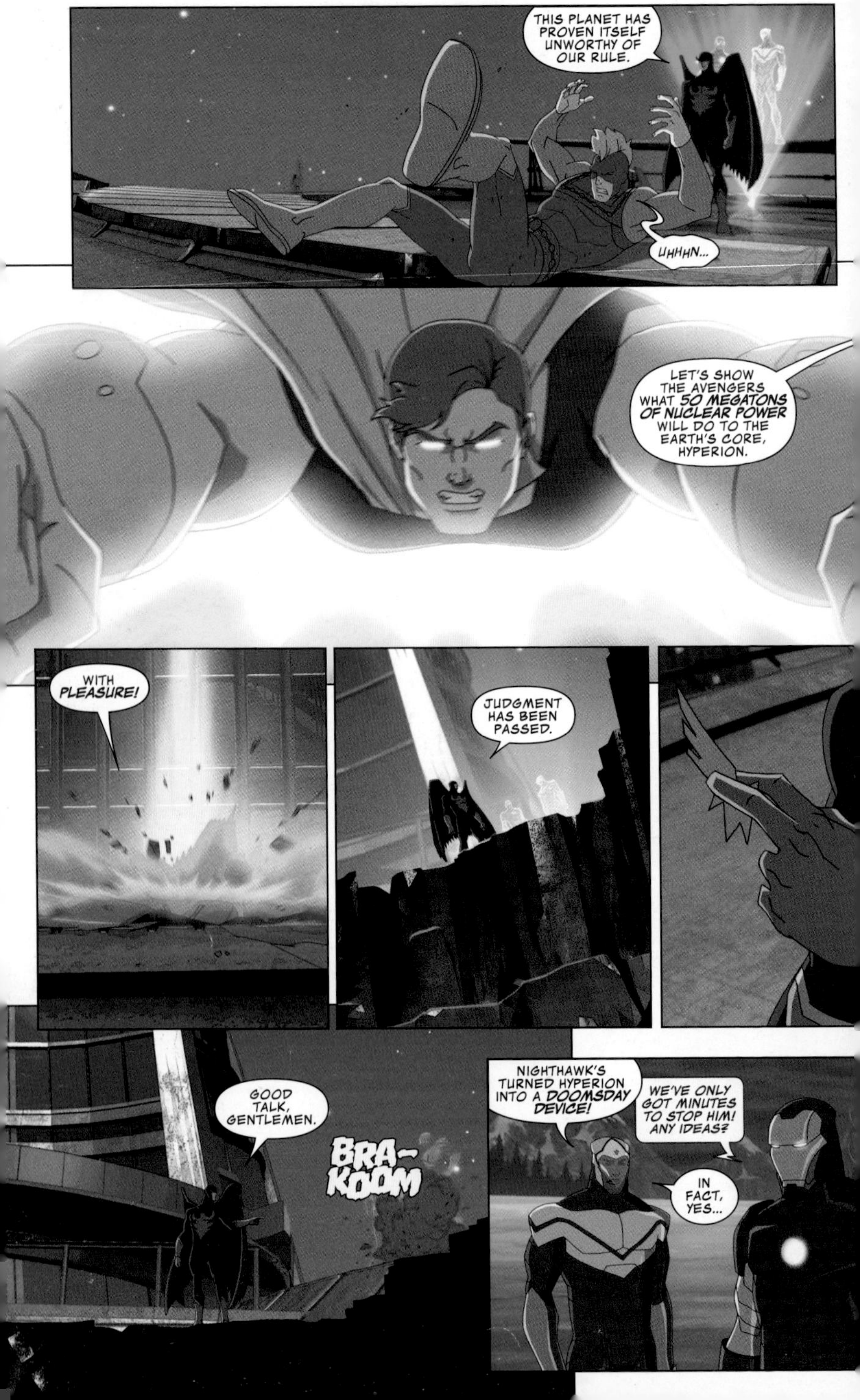

THIS PLANET HAS PROVEN ITSELF UNWORTHY OF OUR RULE.
UHHHN...
LET'S SHOW THE AVENGERS WHAT 50 MEGATONS OF NUCLEAR POWER WILL DO TO THE EARTH'S CORE, HYPERION.
WITH PLEASURE!
JUDGMENT HAS BEEN PASSED.
GOOD TALK, GENTLEMEN.
BRA-KOOM
NIGHTHAWK'S TURNED HYPERION INTO A DOOMSDAY DEVICE!
WE'VE ONLY GOT MINUTES TO STOP HIM! ANY IDEAS?
IN FACT, YES...

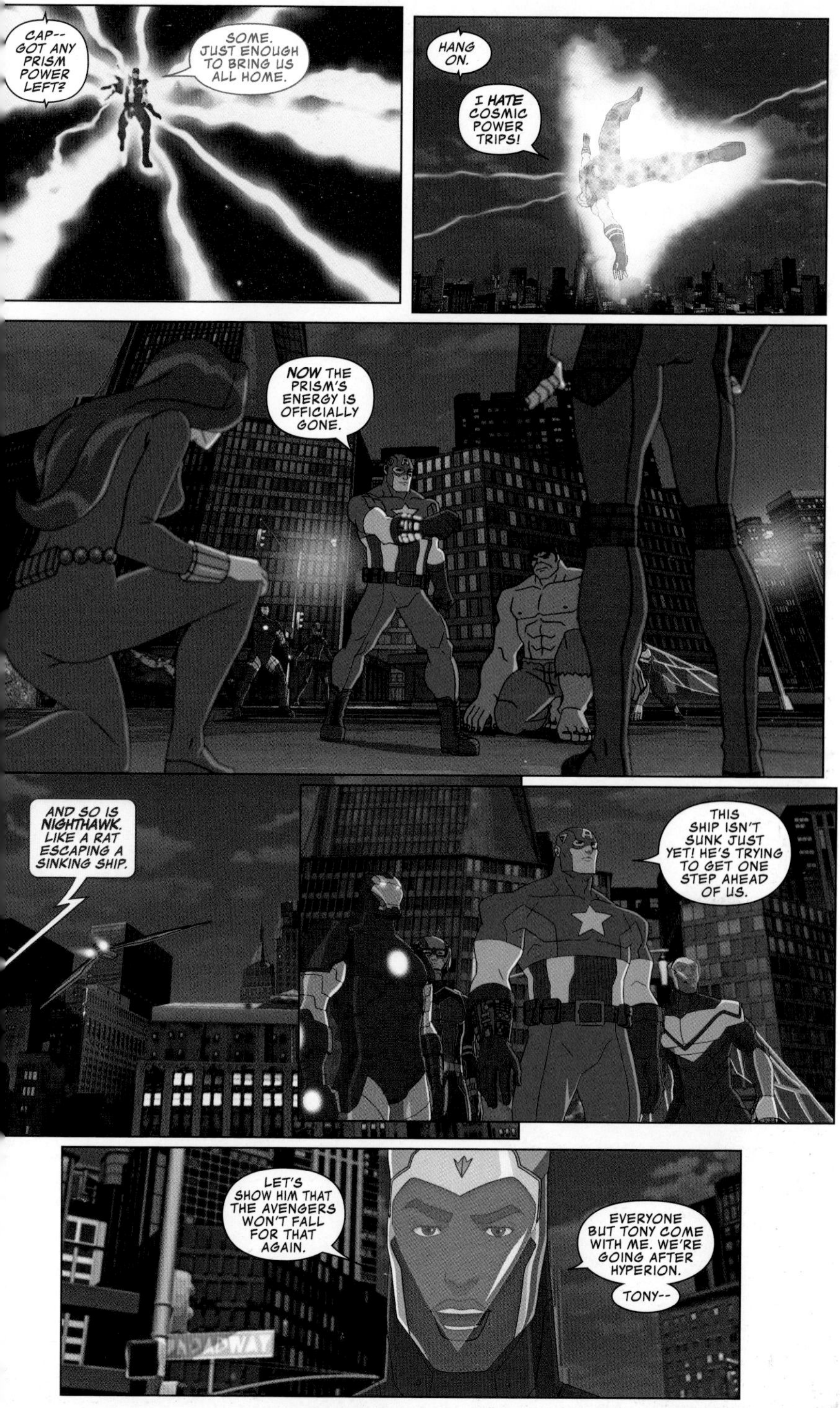
CAP-- GOT ANY PRISM POWER LEFT?
SOME. JUST ENOUGH TO BRING US ALL HOME.
HANG ON.
I HATE COSMIC POWER TRIPS!
NOW THE PRISM'S ENERGY IS OFFICIALLY GONE.
AND SO IS NIGHTHAWK. LIKE A RAT ESCAPING A SINKING SHIP.
THIS SHIP ISN'T SUNK JUST YET! HE'S TRYING TO GET ONE STEP AHEAD OF US.
LET'S SHOW HIM THAT THE AVENGERS WON'T FALL FOR THAT AGAIN.
EVERYONE BUT TONY COME WITH ME. WE'RE GOING AFTER HYPERION.
TONY--

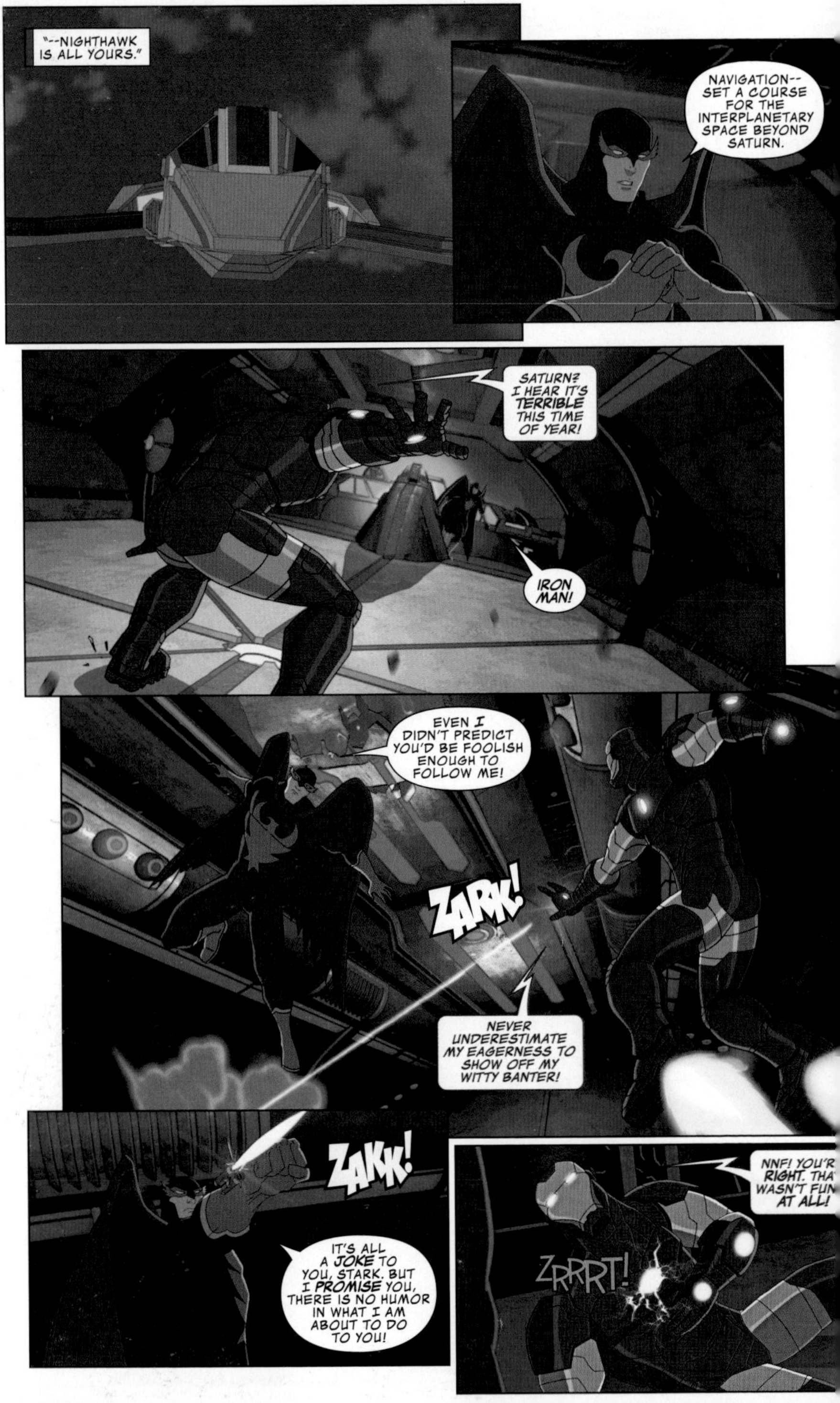
"--NIGHTHAWK IS ALL YOURS."
NAVIGATION-- SET A COURSE FOR THE INTERPLANETARY SPACE BEYOND SATURN.
SATURN? I HEAR IT'S TERRIBLE THIS TIME OF YEAR!
IRON MAN!
EVEN I DIDN'T PREDICT YOU'D BE FOOLISH ENOUGH TO FOLLOW ME!
ZARK!
NEVER UNDERESTIMATE MY EAGERNESS TO SHOW OFF MY WITTY BANTER!
ZAKK!
IT'S ALL A JOKE TO YOU, STARK. BUT I PROMISE YOU, THERE IS NO HUMOR IN WHAT I AM ABOUT TO DO TO YOU!
NNF! YOU'R RIGHT. THA WASN'T FUN AT ALL!
ZRRRRT!

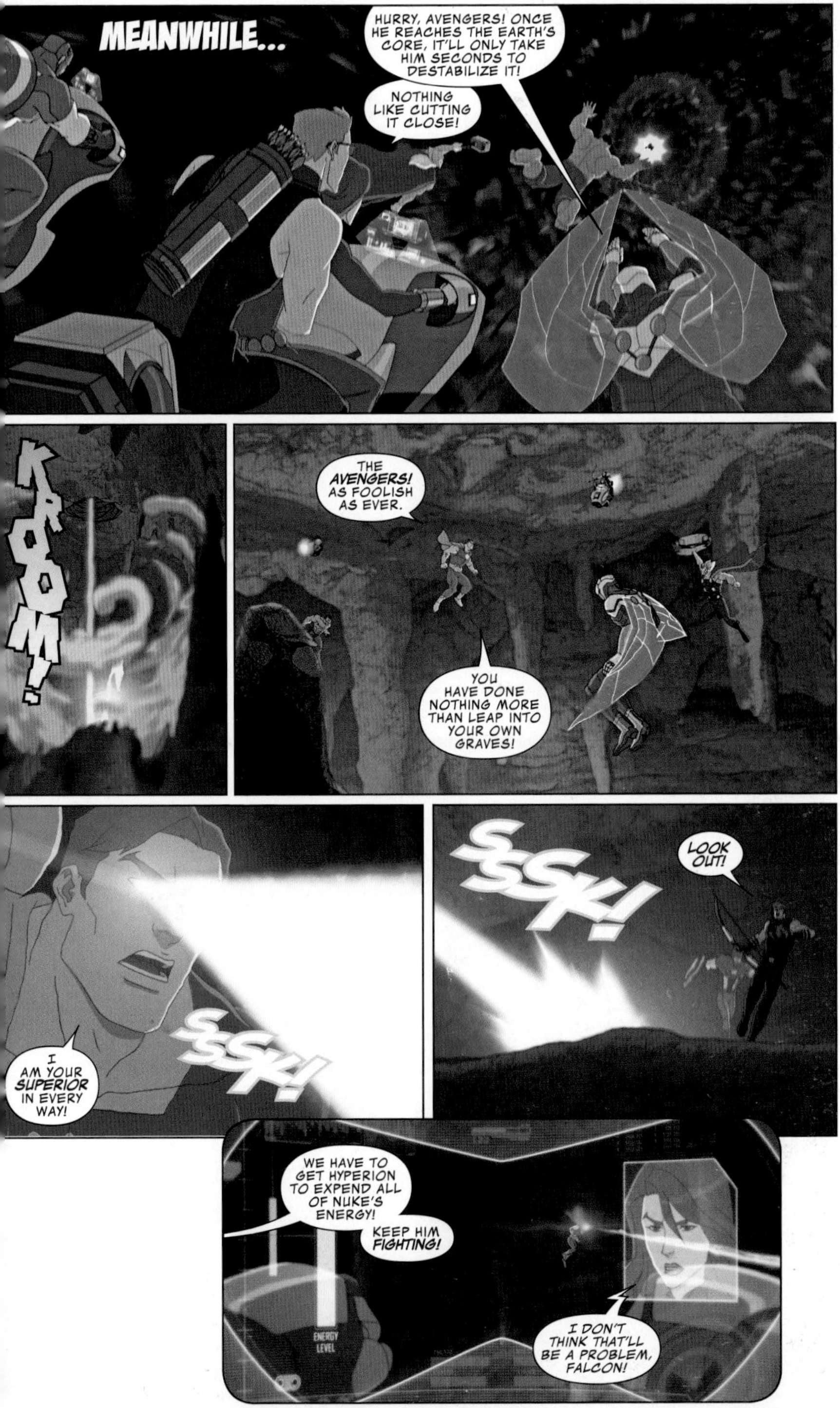
MEANWHILE...
HURRY, AVENGERS! ONCE HE REACHES THE EARTH'S CORE, IT'LL ONLY TAKE HIM SECONDS TO DESTABILIZE IT!
NOTHING LIKE CUTTING IT CLOSE!
KRROOM!
THE AVENGERS! AS FOOLISH AS EVER.
YOU HAVE DONE NOTHING MORE THAN LEAP INTO YOUR OWN GRAVES!
I AM YOUR SUPERIOR IN EVERY WAY!
SSSK!
SSSK!
LOOK OUT!
WE HAVE TO GET HYPERION TO EXPEND ALL OF NUKE'S ENERGY!
KEEP HIM FIGHTING!
ENERGY LEVEL
I DON'T THINK THAT'LL BE A PROBLEM, FALCON!

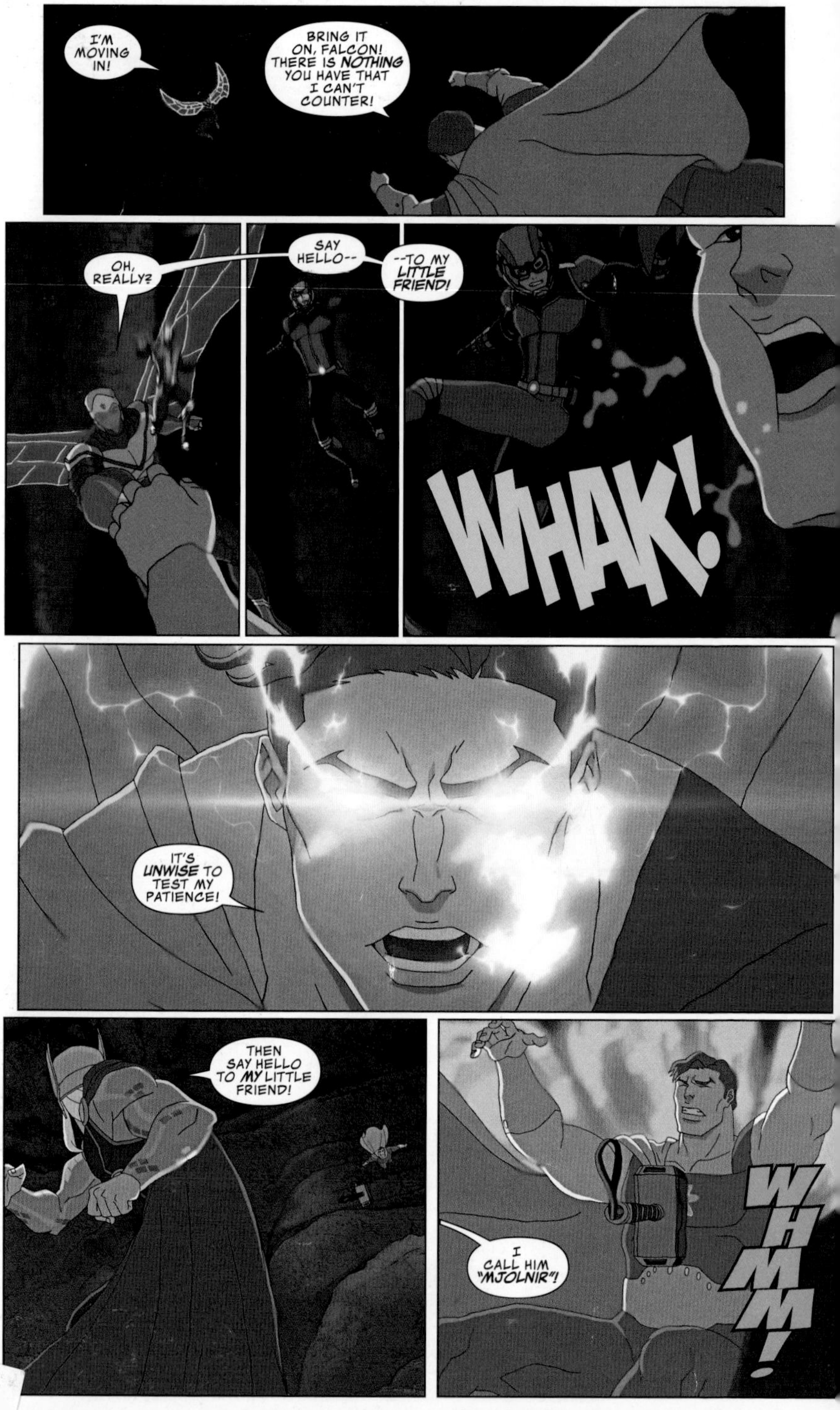

I'M MOVING IN!
BRING IT ON, FALCON! THERE IS NOTHING YOU HAVE THAT I CAN'T COUNTER!
OH, REALLY?
SAY HELLO--
--TO MY LITTLE FRIEND!
WHAK!
IT'S UNWISE TO TEST MY PATIENCE!
THEN SAY HELLO TO MY LITTLE FRIEND!
I CALL HIM "MJOLNIR"!
WHMM!

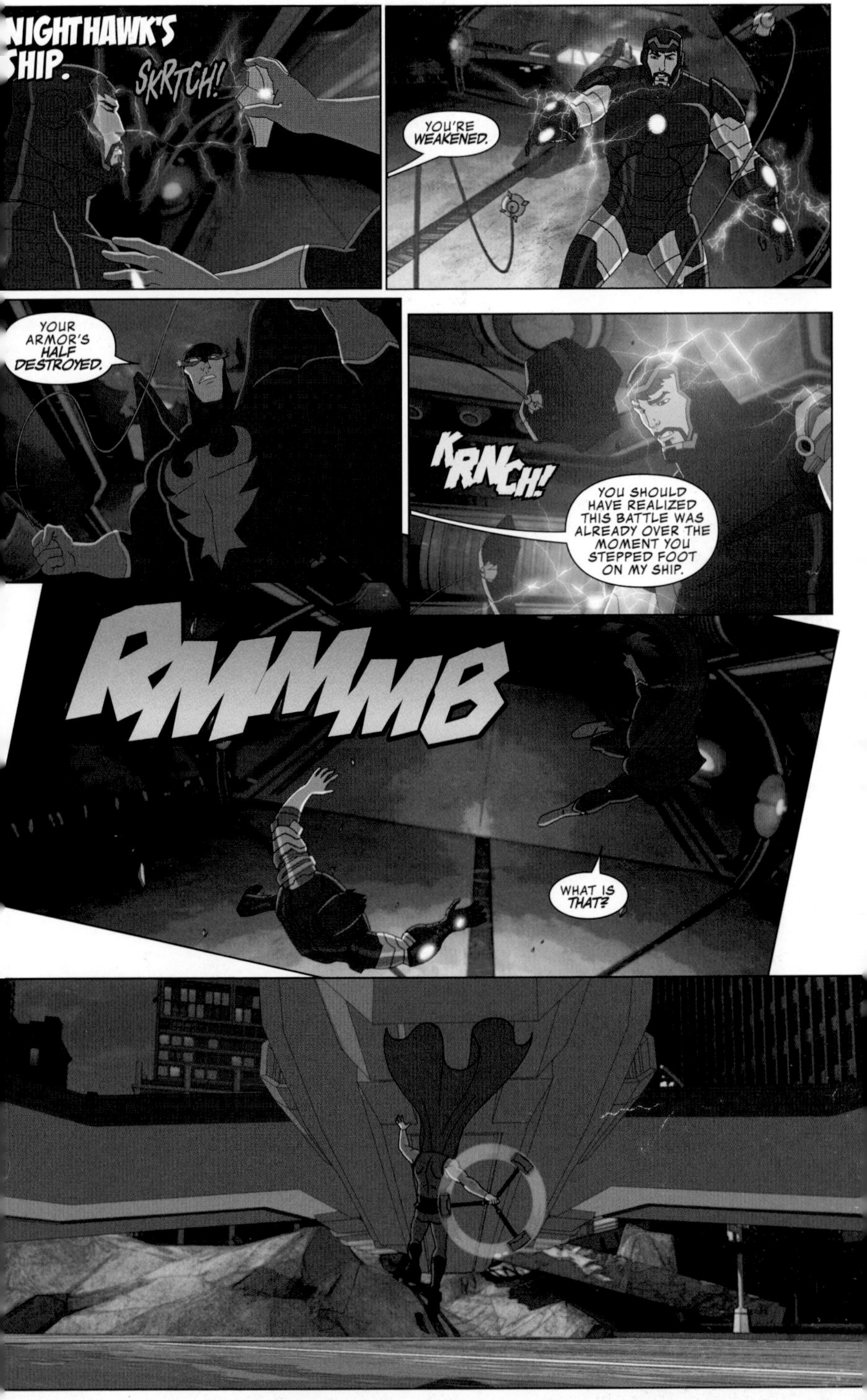
NIGHTHAWK'S SHIP.
SKRTCH!
YOU'RE WEAKENED.
YOUR ARMOR'S HALF DESTROYED.
KRNCH!
YOU SHOULD HAVE REALIZED THIS BATTLE WAS ALREADY OVER THE MOMENT YOU STEPPED FOOT ON MY SHIP.
RMMMB
WHAT IS THAT?

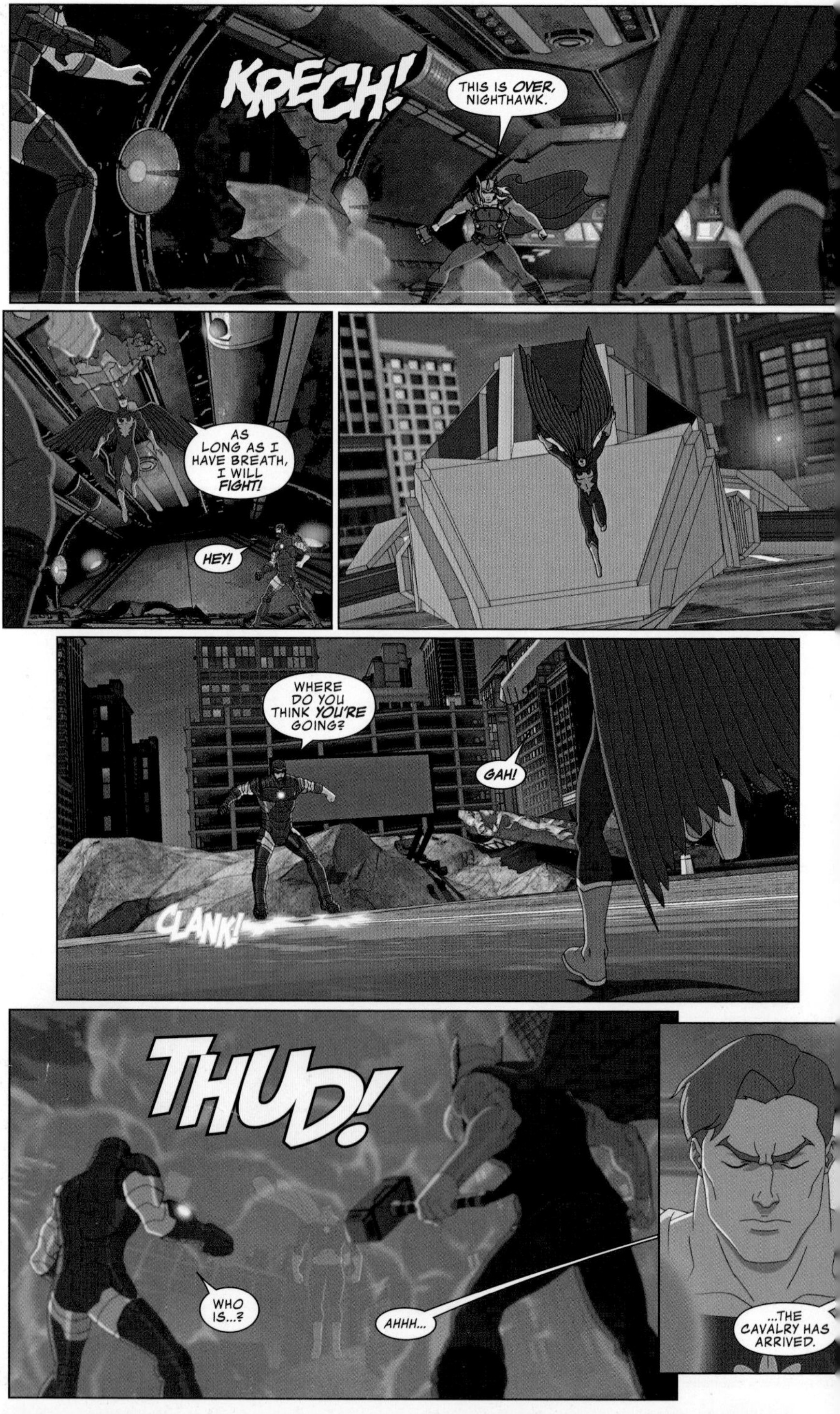
KRECH!
THIS IS OVER, NIGHTHAWK.
AS LONG AS I HAVE BREATH, I WILL FIGHT!
HEY!
WHERE DO YOU THINK YOU'RE GOING?
GAH!
CLANK!
THUD!
WHO IS...?
AHHH...
...THE CAVALRY HAS ARRIVED.

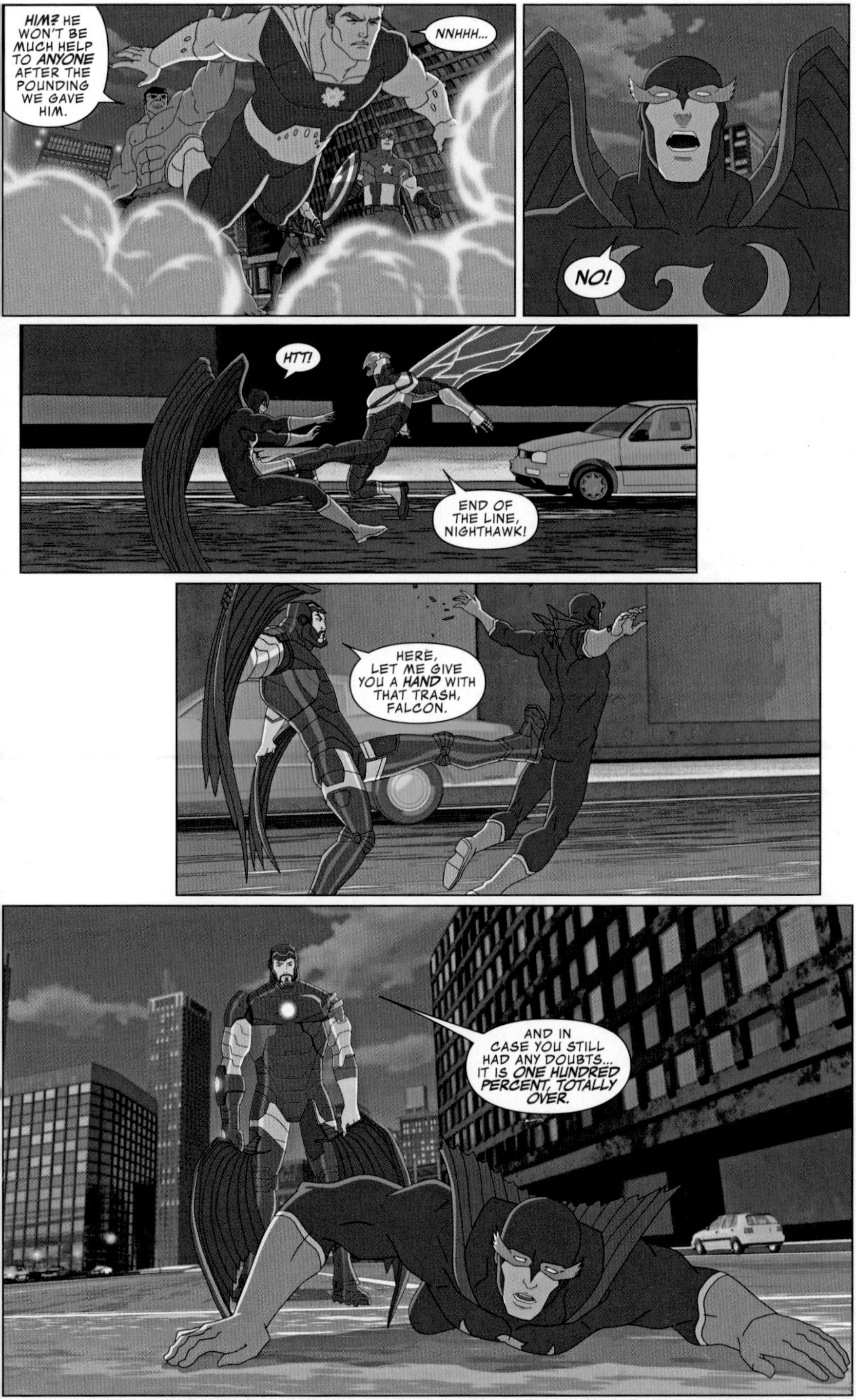
HIM? HE WON'T BE MUCH HELP TO ANYONE AFTER THE POUNDING WE GAVE HIM.
NNHHH...
NO!
HTT!
END OF THE LINE, NIGHTHAWK!
HERE, LET ME GIVE YOU A HAND WITH THAT TRASH, FALCON.
AND IN CASE YOU STILL HAD ANY DOUBTS... IT IS ONE HUNDRED PERCENT, TOTALLY OVER.

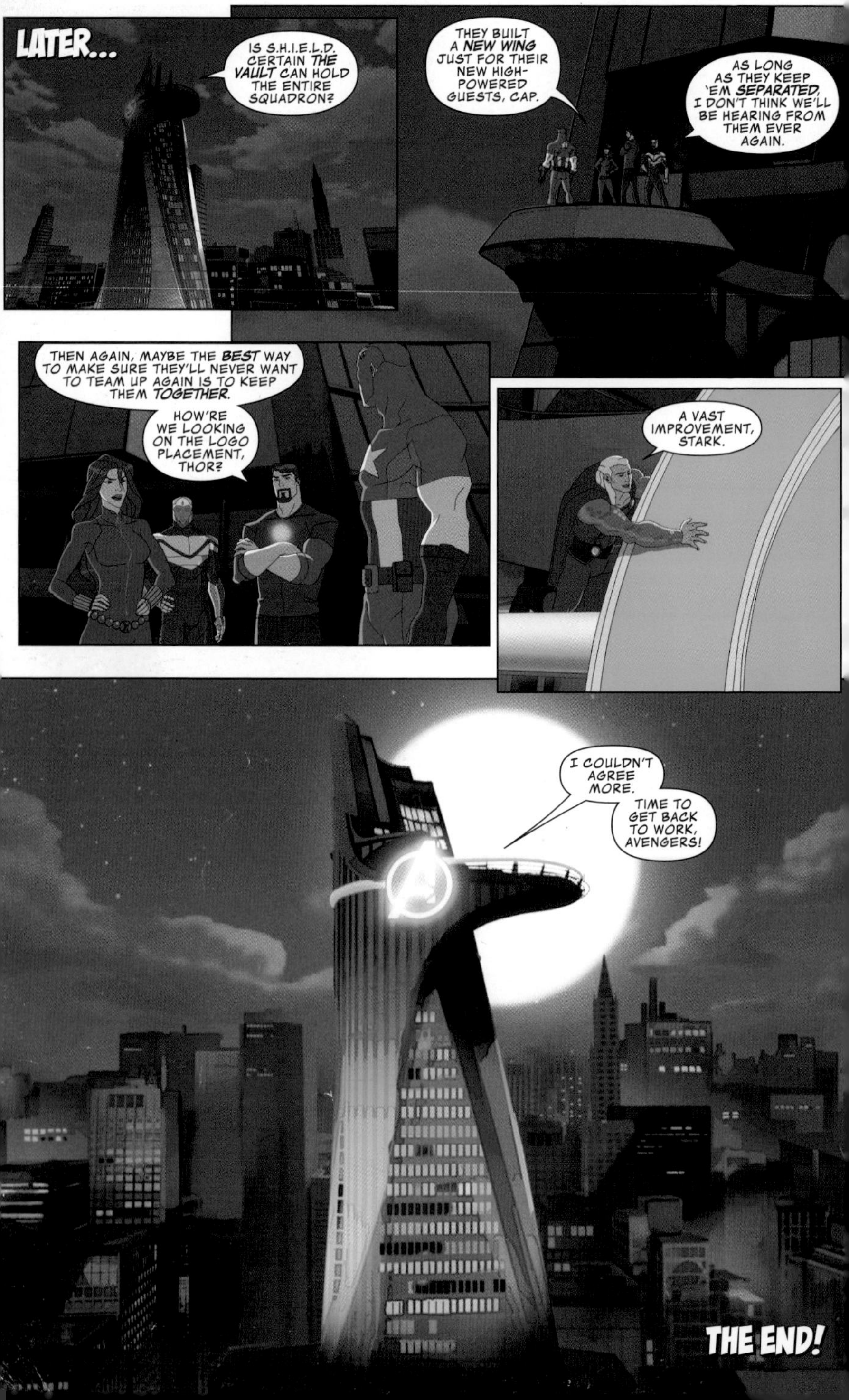

LATER...
IS S.H.I.E.L.D. CERTAIN THE VAULT CAN HOLD THE ENTIRE SQUADRON?
THEY BUILT A NEW WING JUST FOR THEIR NEW HIGH-POWERED GUESTS, CAP.
AS LONG AS THEY KEEP 'EM SEPARATED, I DON'T THINK WE'LL BE HEARING FROM THEM EVER AGAIN.
THEN AGAIN, MAYBE THE BEST WAY TO MAKE SURE THEY'LL NEVER WANT TO TEAM UP AGAIN IS TO KEEP THEM TOGETHER.
HOW'RE WE LOOKING ON THE LOGO PLACEMENT, THOR?
A VAST IMPROVEMENT, STARK.
I COULDN'T AGREE MORE.
TIME TO GET BACK TO WORK, AVENGERS!
THE END!

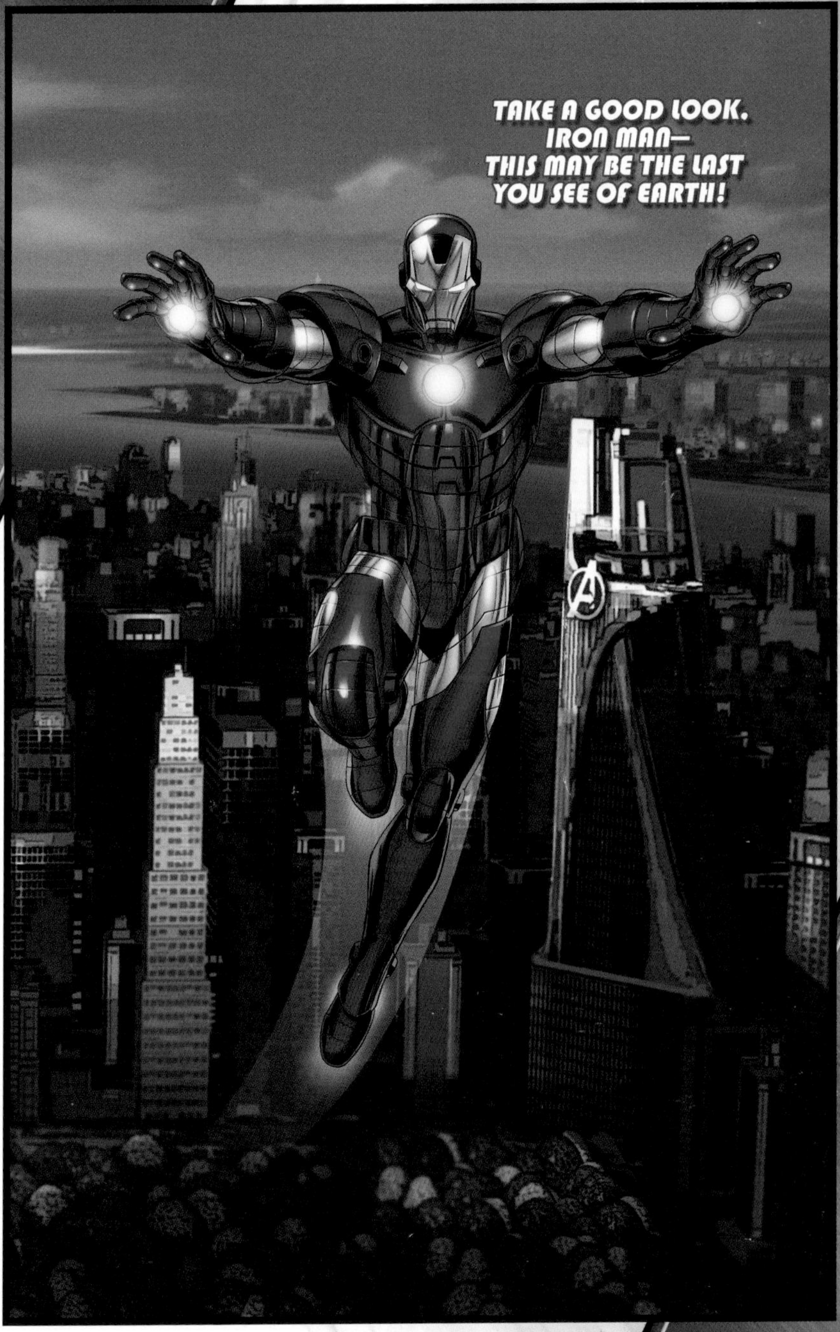
TAKE A GOOD LOOK.
IRON MAN—
THIS MAY BE THE LAST
YOU SEE OF EARTH!

BASED ON "NEW FRONTIERS" #15

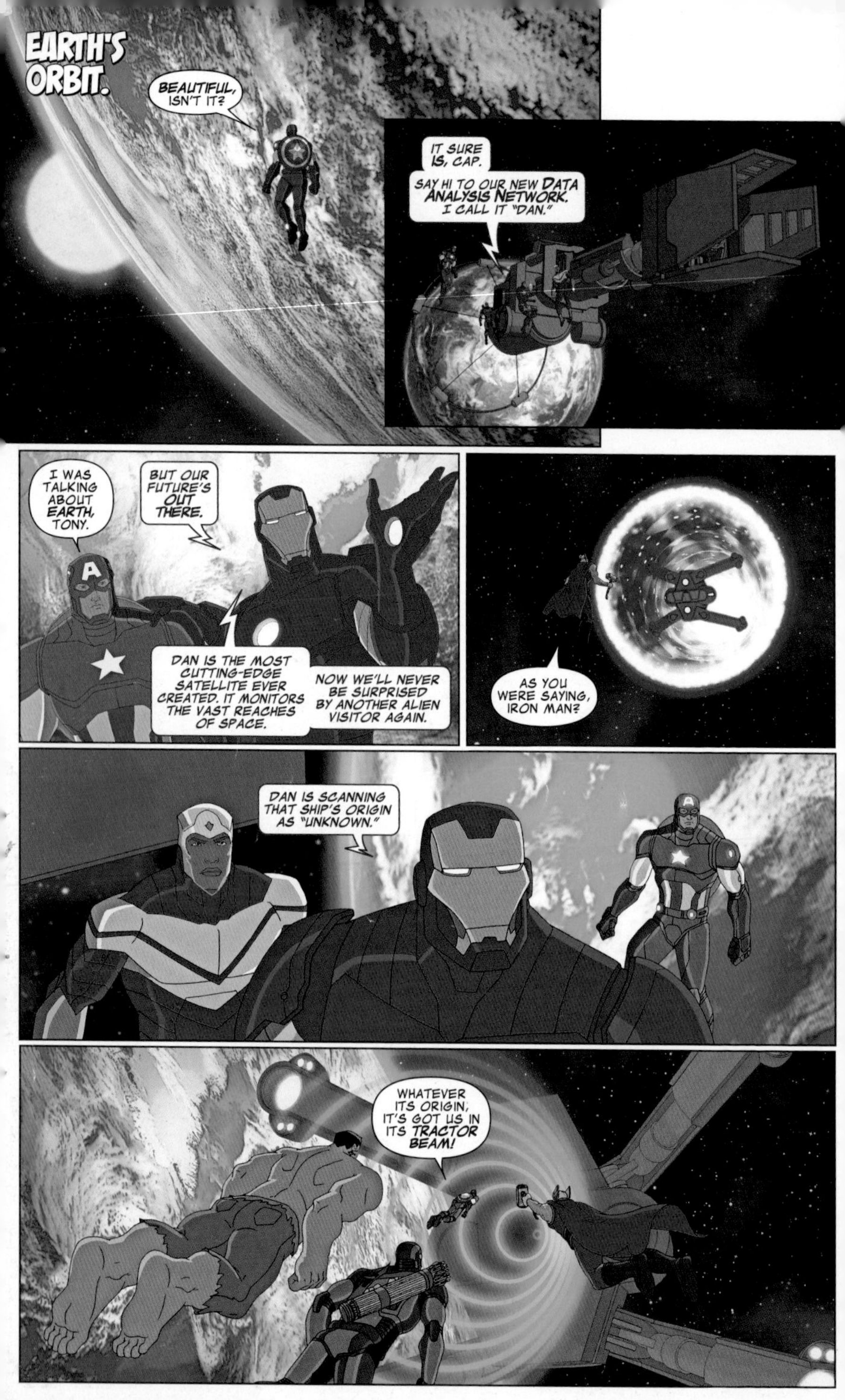
EARTH'S ORBIT.
BEAUTIFUL, ISN'T IT?
IT SURE IS, CAP.
SAY HI TO OUR NEW DATA ANALYSIS NETWORK. I CALL IT "DAN."
I WAS TALKING ABOUT EARTH, TONY.
BUT OUR FUTURE'S OUT THERE.
DAN IS THE MOST CUTTING-EDGE SATELLITE EVER CREATED. IT MONITORS THE VAST REACHES OF SPACE.
NOW WE'LL NEVER BE SURPRISED BY ANOTHER ALIEN VISITOR AGAIN.
AS YOU WERE SAYING, IRON MAN?
DAN IS SCANNING THAT SHIP'S ORIGIN AS "UNKNOWN."
WHATEVER ITS ORIGIN, IT'S GOT US IN ITS TRACTOR BEAM!

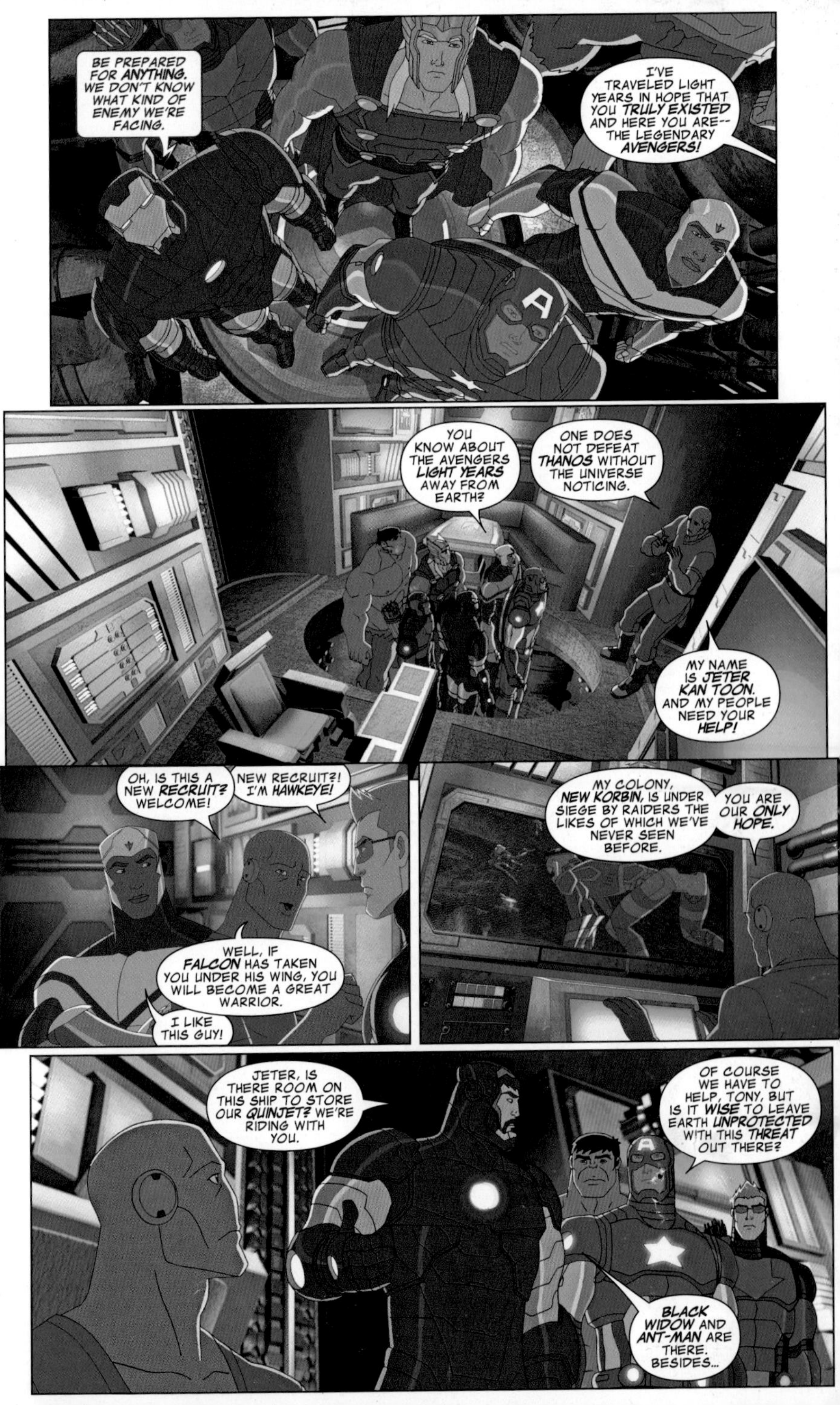
BE PREPARED FOR ANYTHING. WE DON'T KNOW WHAT KIND OF ENEMY WE'RE FACING.
I'VE TRAVELED LIGHT YEARS IN HOPE THAT YOU TRULY EXISTED AND HERE YOU ARE-- THE LEGENDARY AVENGERS!
YOU KNOW ABOUT THE AVENGERS LIGHT YEARS AWAY FROM EARTH?
ONE DOES NOT DEFEAT THANOS WITHOUT THE UNIVERSE NOTICING.
MY NAME IS JETER KAN TOON. AND MY PEOPLE NEED YOUR HELP!
OH, IS THIS A NEW RECRUIT? WELCOME!
NEW RECRUIT?! I'M HAWKEYE!
WELL, IF FALCON HAS TAKEN YOU UNDER HIS WING, YOU WILL BECOME A GREAT WARRIOR.
I LIKE THIS GUY!
MY COLONY, NEW KORBIN, IS UNDER SIEGE BY RAIDERS THE LIKES OF WHICH WE'VE NEVER SEEN BEFORE.
YOU ARE OUR ONLY HOPE.
JETER, IS THERE ROOM ON THIS SHIP TO STORE OUR QUINJET? WE'RE RIDING WITH YOU.
OF COURSE WE HAVE TO HELP, TONY, BUT IS IT WISE TO LEAVE EARTH UNPROTECTED WITH THIS THREAT OUT THERE?
BLACK WIDOW AND ANT-MAN ARE THERE. BESIDES...

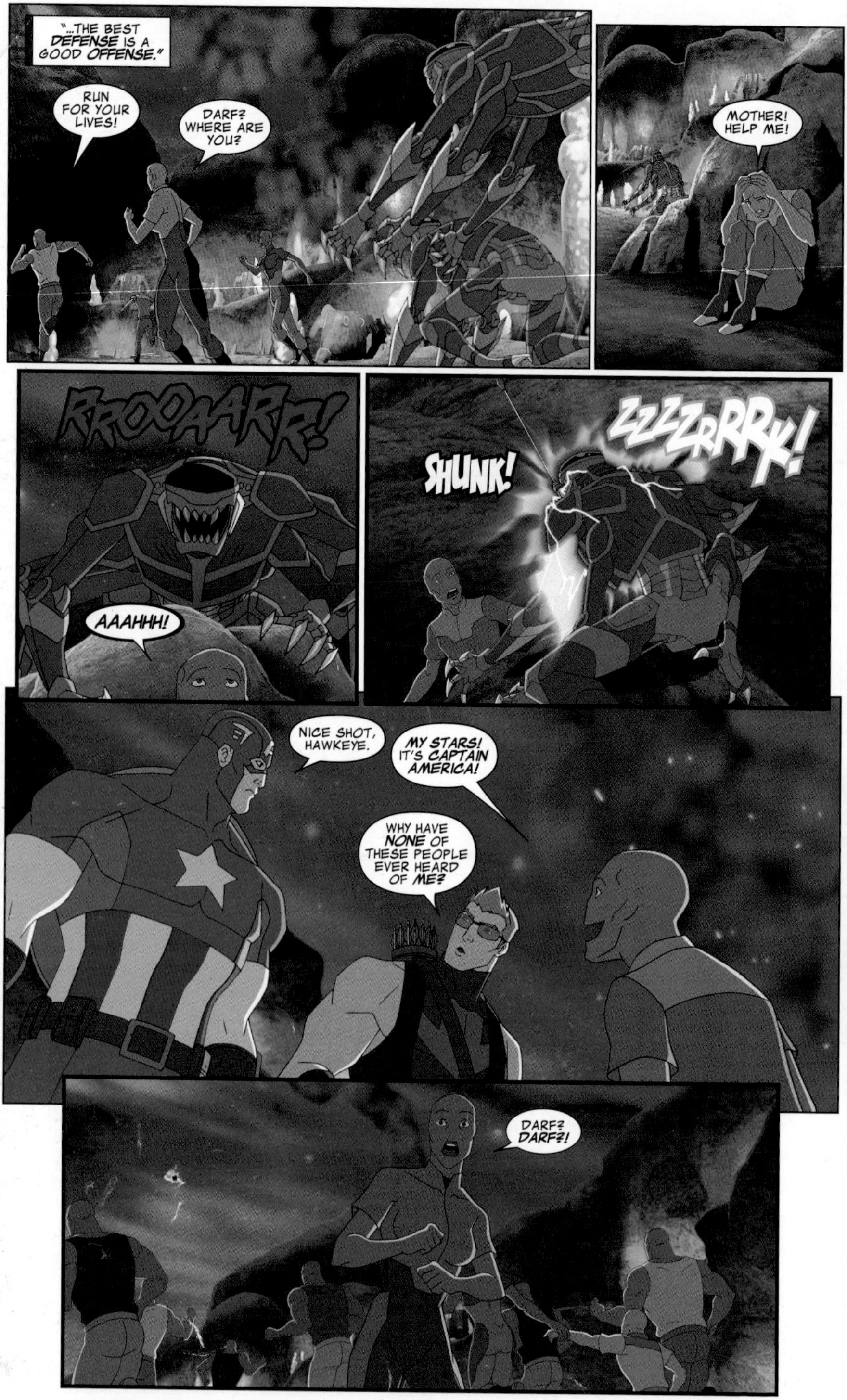
"...THE BEST DEFENSE IS A GOOD OFFENSE."
RUN FOR YOUR LIVES!
DARF? WHERE ARE YOU?
MOTHER! HELP ME!
RROOAARR!
AAAHHH!
SHUNK!
ZZZZRRRRK!
NICE SHOT, HAWKEYE.
MY STARS! IT'S CAPTAIN AMERICA!
WHY HAVE NONE OF THESE PEOPLE EVER HEARD OF ME?
DARF? DARF?!

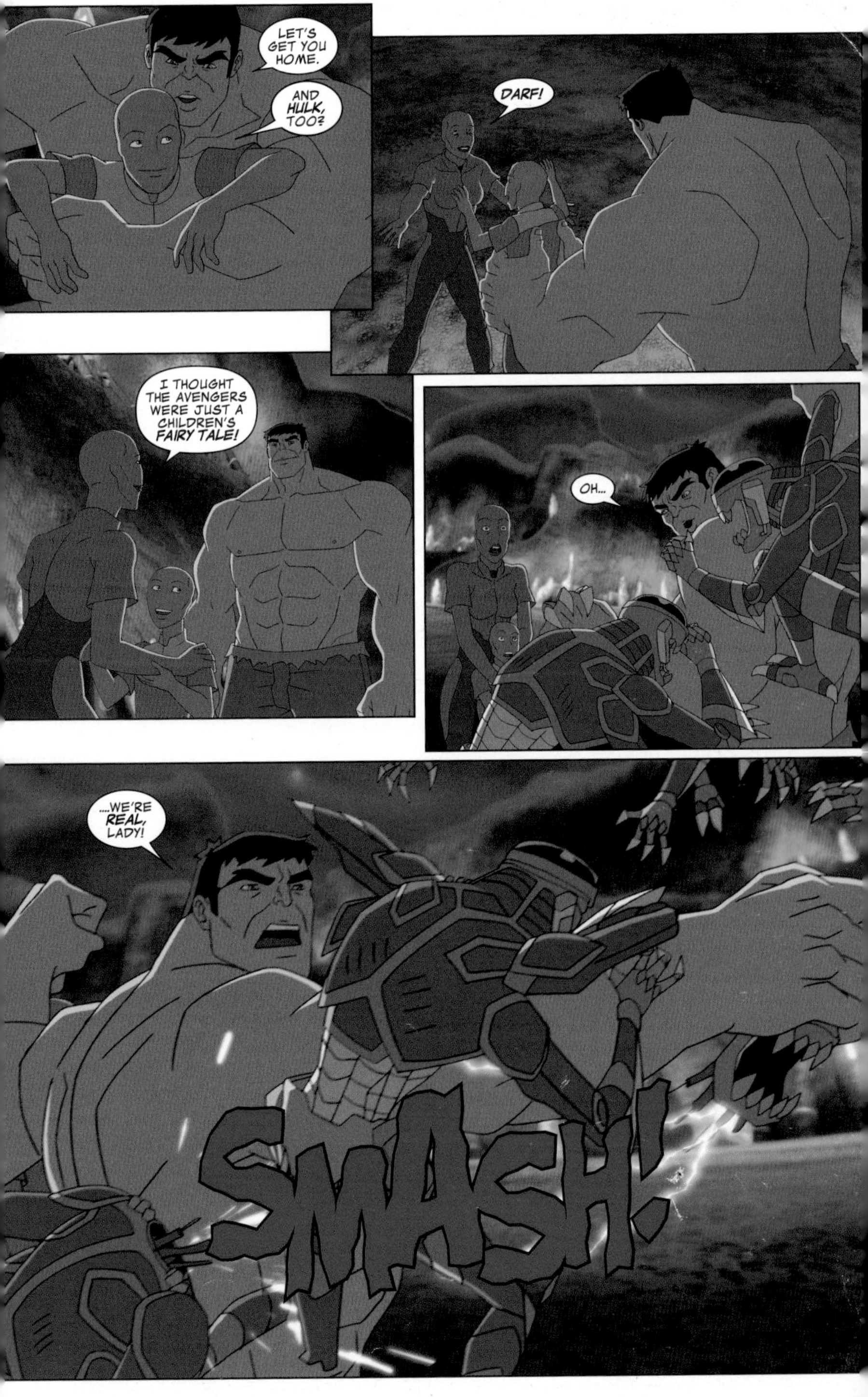
LET'S GET YOU HOME.
AND HULK, TOO?
DARF!
I THOUGHT THE AVENGERS WERE JUST A CHILDREN'S FAIRY TALE!
OH...
...WE'RE REAL, LADY!
SMASH!

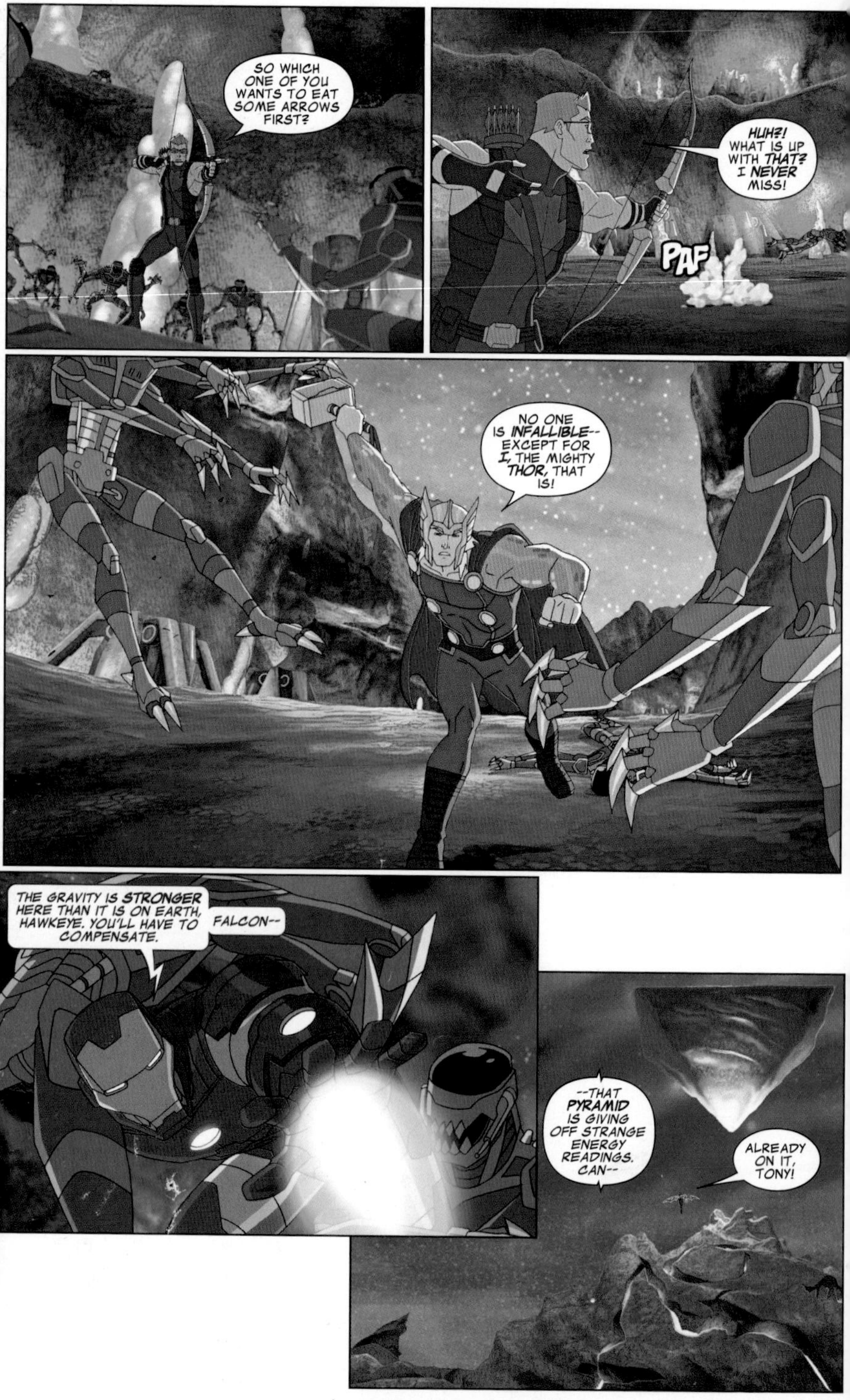
SO WHICH ONE OF YOU WANTS TO EAT SOME ARROWS FIRST?
HUH?! WHAT IS UP WITH THAT? I NEVER MISS!
PAF
NO ONE IS INFALLIBLE-- EXCEPT FOR I, THE MIGHTY THOR, THAT IS!
THE GRAVITY IS STRONGER HERE THAN IT IS ON EARTH, HAWKEYE. YOU'LL HAVE TO COMPENSATE.
FALCON--
--THAT PYRAMID IS GIVING OFF STRANGE ENERGY READINGS. CAN--
ALREADY ON IT, TONY!

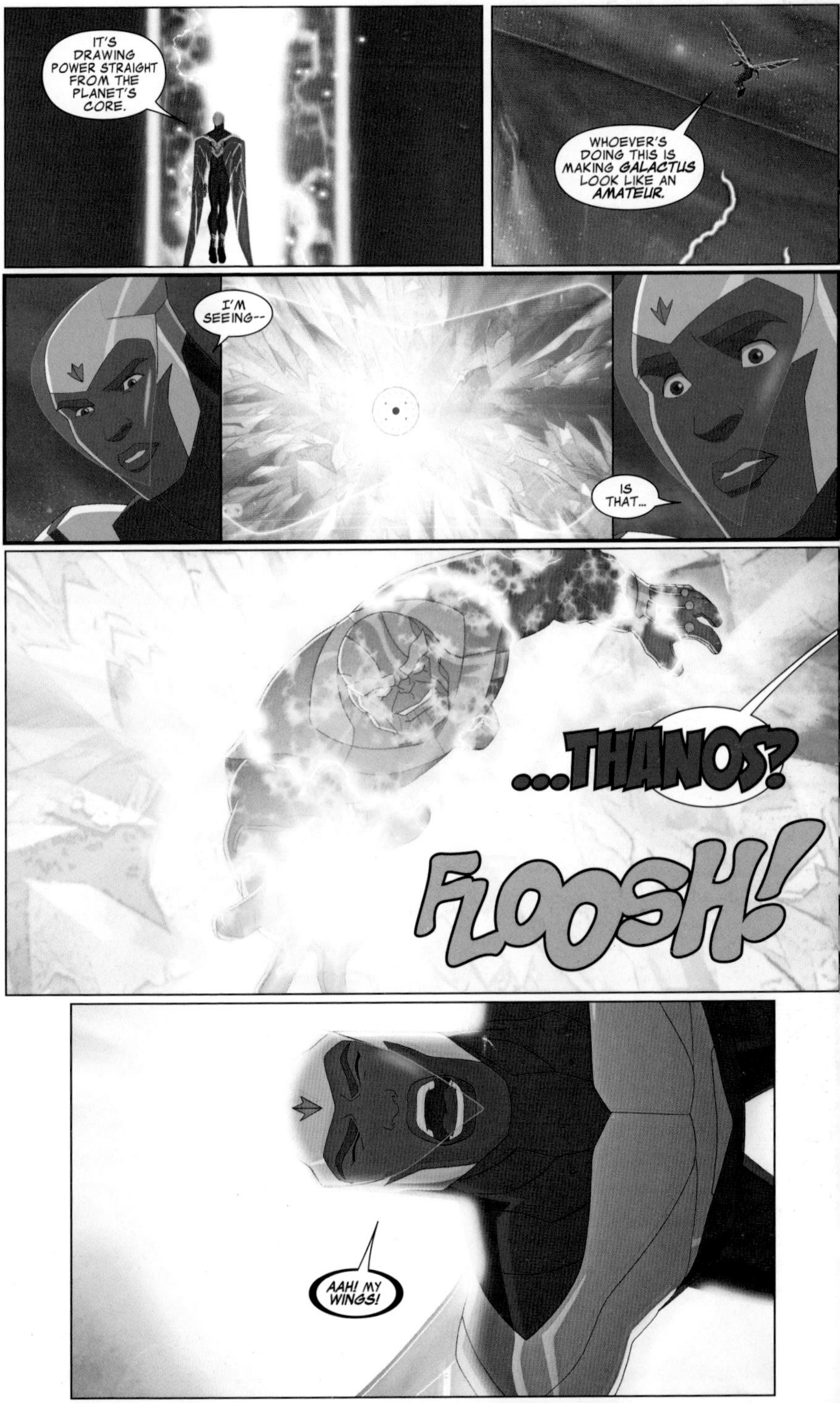
IT'S DRAWING POWER STRAIGHT FROM THE PLANET'S CORE.
WHOEVER'S DOING THIS IS MAKING GALACTUS LOOK LIKE AN AMATEUR.
I'M SEEING--
IS THAT...
...THANOS?
FLOOSH!
AAH! MY WINGS!

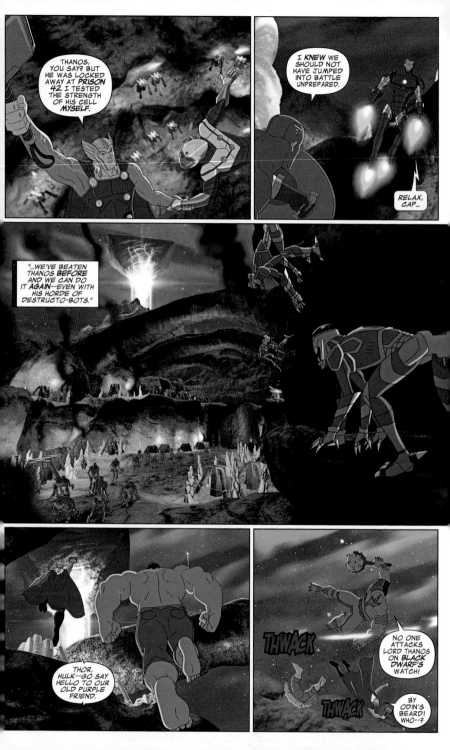

THANOS, YOU SAY? BUT HE WAS LOCKED AWAY AT *PRISON 42.* I TESTED THE STRENGTH OF HIS CELL *MYSELF.*

I *KNEW* WE SHOULD NOT HAVE JUMPED INTO BATTLE UNPREPARED.

RELAX, CAP...

"...WE'VE BEATEN THANOS *BEFORE* AND WE CAN DO IT *AGAIN*--EVEN WITH HIS HORDE OF DESTRUCTO-BOTS."

THOR, HULK--GO SAY HELLO TO OUR OLD PURPLE FRIEND.

THWACK

NO ONE ATTACKS LORD THANOS ON *BLACK DWARF'S* WATCH!

THWACK

BY ODIN'S BEARD! WHO--?

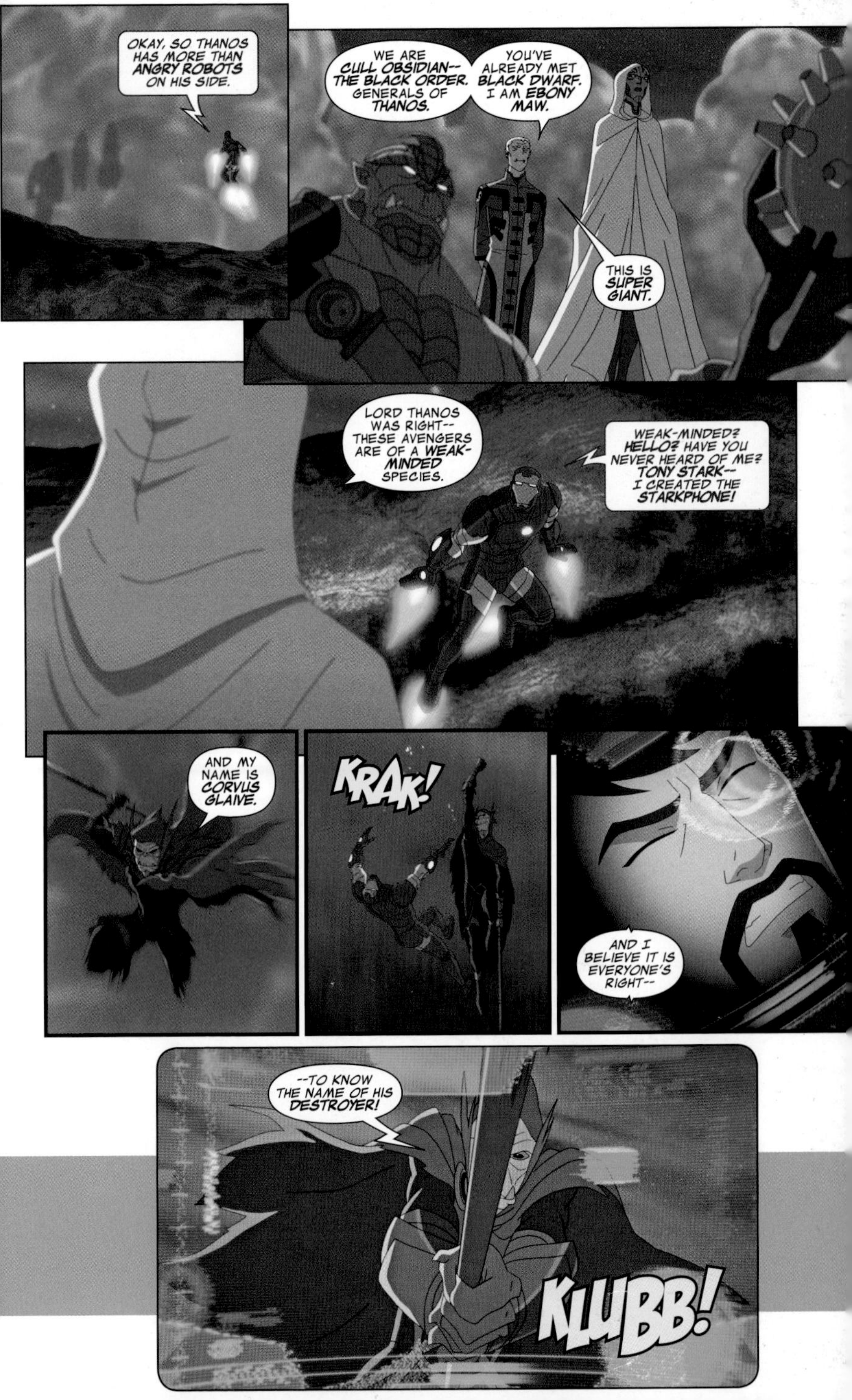

OKAY, SO THANOS HAS MORE THAN ANGRY ROBOTS ON HIS SIDE.
WE ARE CULL OBSIDIAN-- THE BLACK ORDER. GENERALS OF THANOS.
YOU'VE ALREADY MET BLACK DWARF. I AM EBONY MAW.
THIS IS SUPER GIANT.
LORD THANOS WAS RIGHT-- THESE AVENGERS ARE OF A WEAK-MINDED SPECIES.
WEAK-MINDED? HELLO? HAVE YOU NEVER HEARD OF ME? TONY STARK-- I CREATED THE STARKPHONE!
AND MY NAME IS CORVUS GLAIVE.
KRAK!
AND I BELIEVE IT IS EVERYONE'S RIGHT--
--TO KNOW THE NAME OF HIS DESTROYER!
KLUBB!

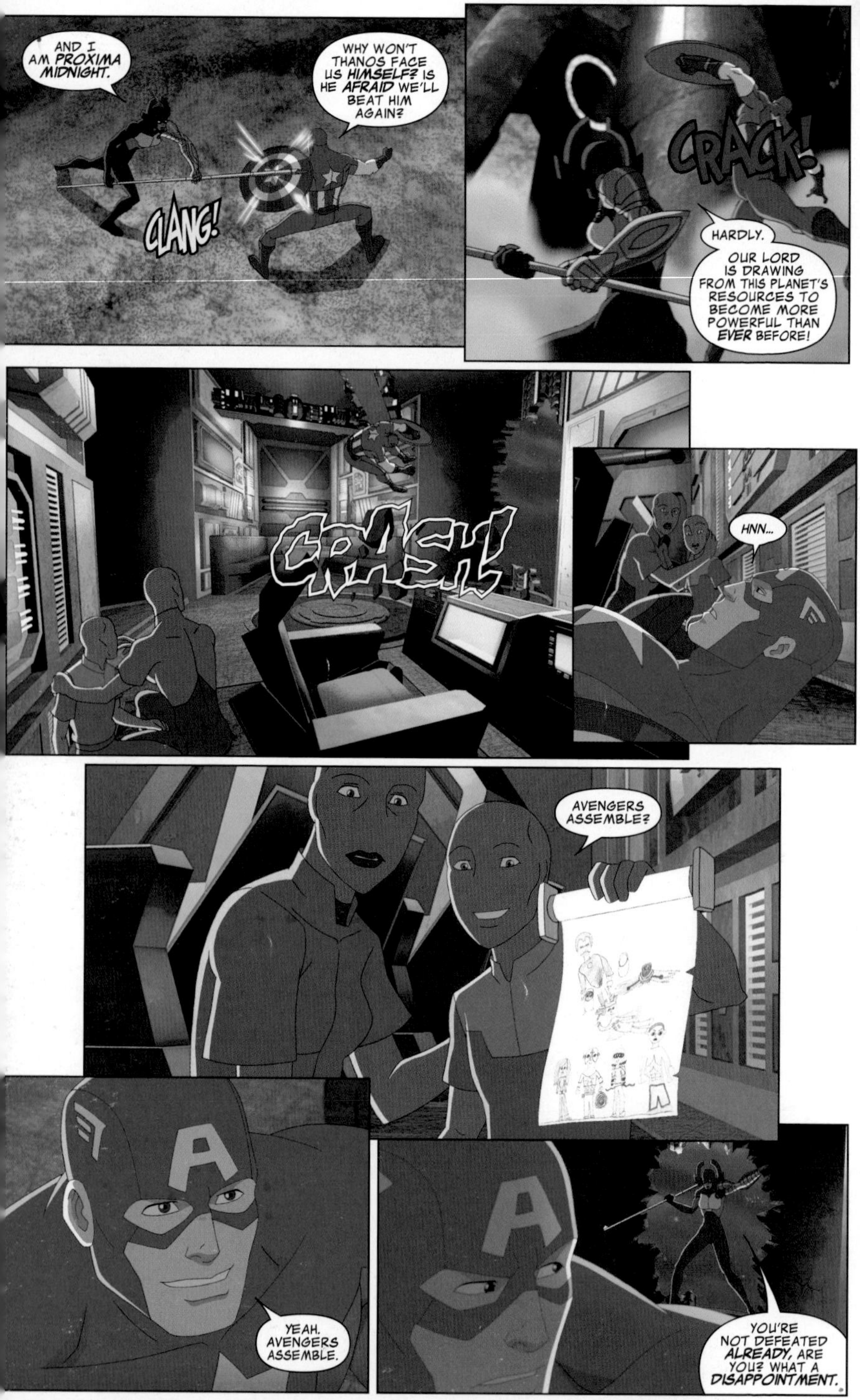

AND I AM PROXIMA MIDNIGHT.
WHY WON'T THANOS FACE US HIMSELF? IS HE AFRAID WE'LL BEAT HIM AGAIN?
CLANG!
CRACK!
HARDLY.
OUR LORD IS DRAWING FROM THIS PLANET'S RESOURCES TO BECOME MORE POWERFUL THAN EVER BEFORE!
CRASH!
HNN...
AVENGERS ASSEMBLE?
YEAH. AVENGERS ASSEMBLE.
YOU'RE NOT DEFEATED ALREADY, ARE YOU? WHAT A DISAPPOINTMENT.

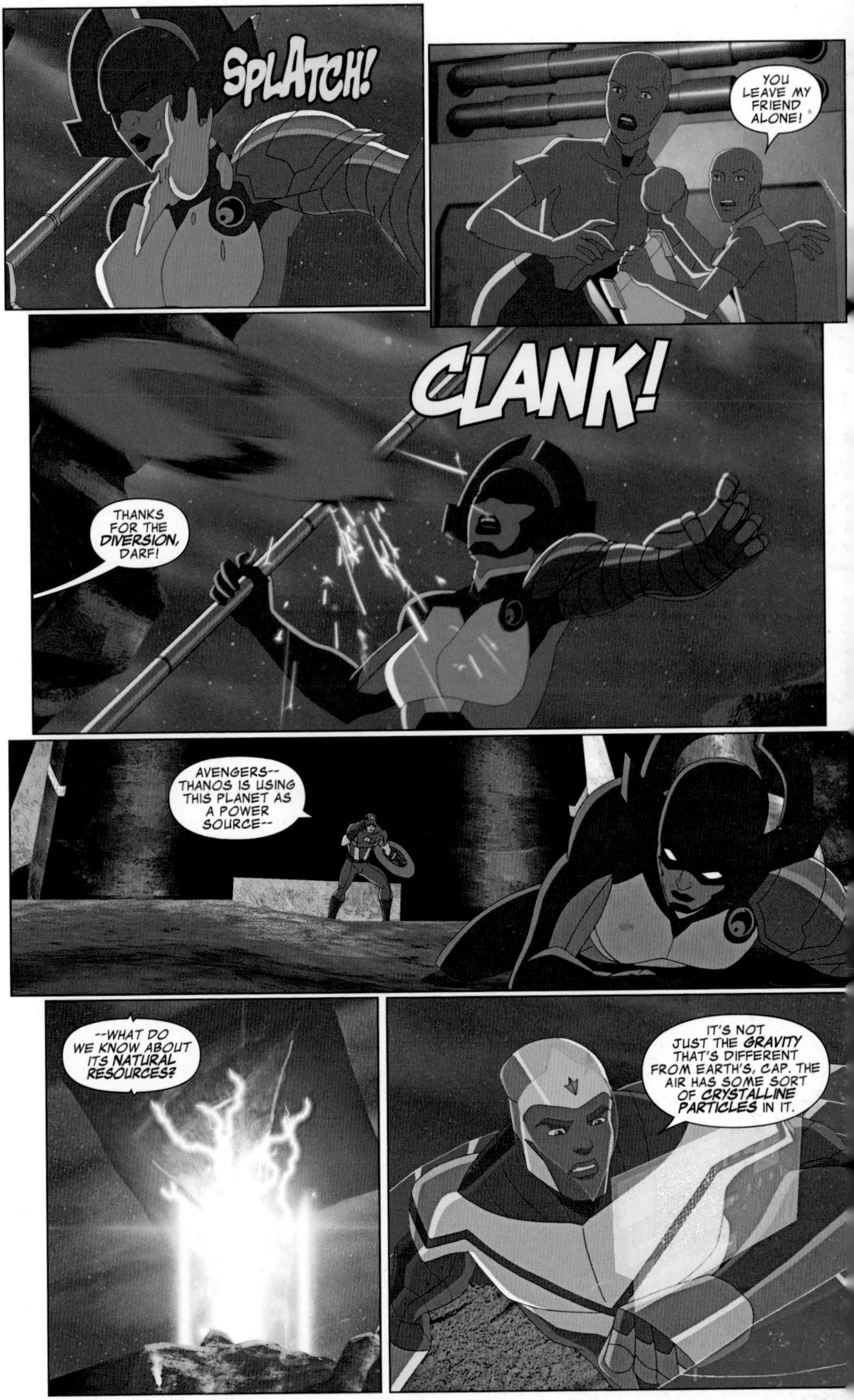
SPLATCH!
YOU LEAVE MY FRIEND ALONE!
CLANK!
THANKS FOR THE DIVERSION, DARF!
AVENGERS-- THANOS IS USING THIS PLANET AS A POWER SOURCE--
--WHAT DO WE KNOW ABOUT ITS NATURAL RESOURCES?
IT'S NOT JUST THE GRAVITY THAT'S DIFFERENT FROM EARTH'S, CAP. THE AIR HAS SOME SORT OF CRYSTALLINE PARTICLES IN IT.

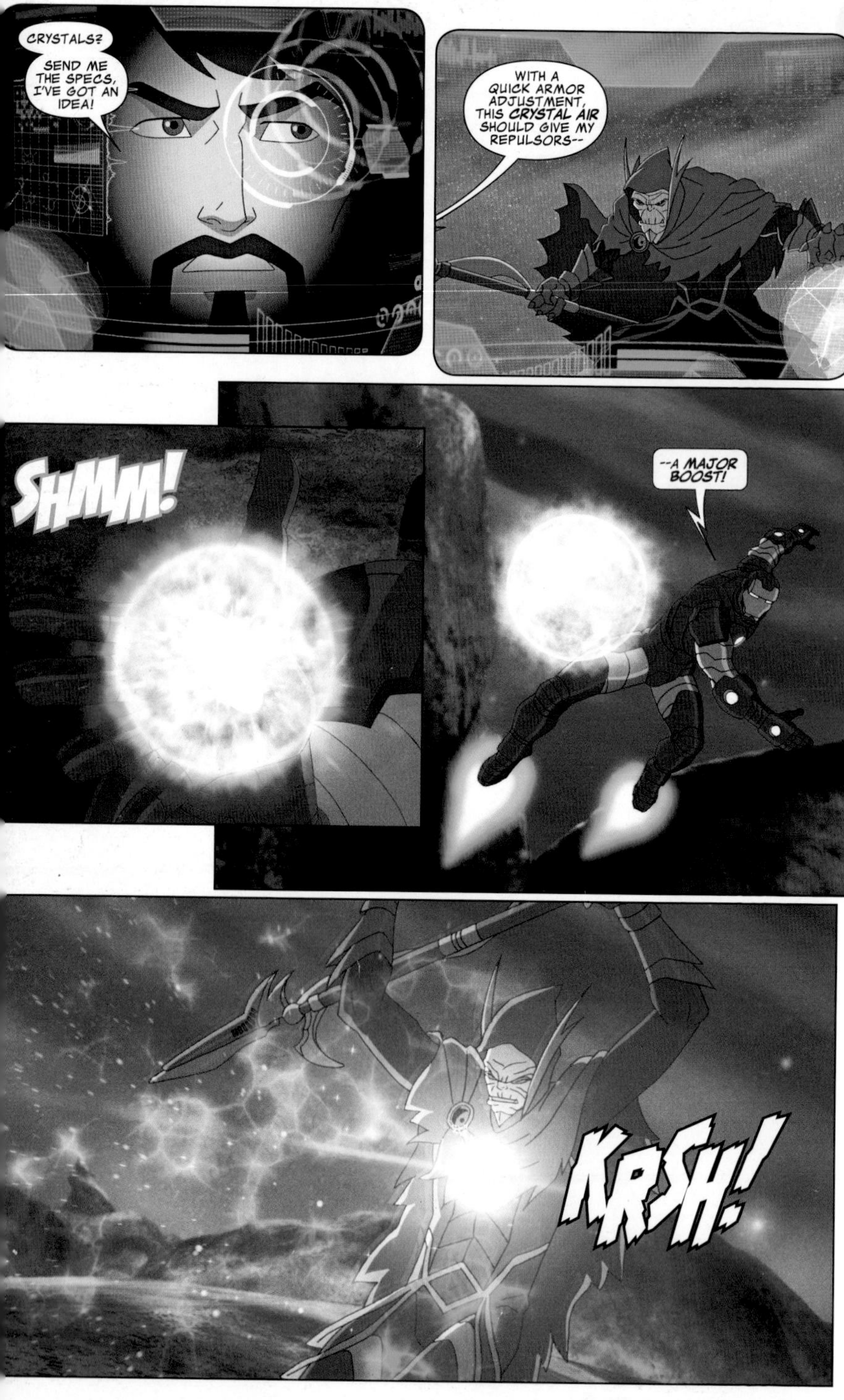
CRYSTALS?
SEND ME THE SPECS, I'VE GOT AN IDEA!
WITH A QUICK ARMOR ADJUSTMENT, THIS CRYSTAL AIR SHOULD GIVE MY REPULSORS--
SHMM!
--A MAJOR BOOST!
KRSH!

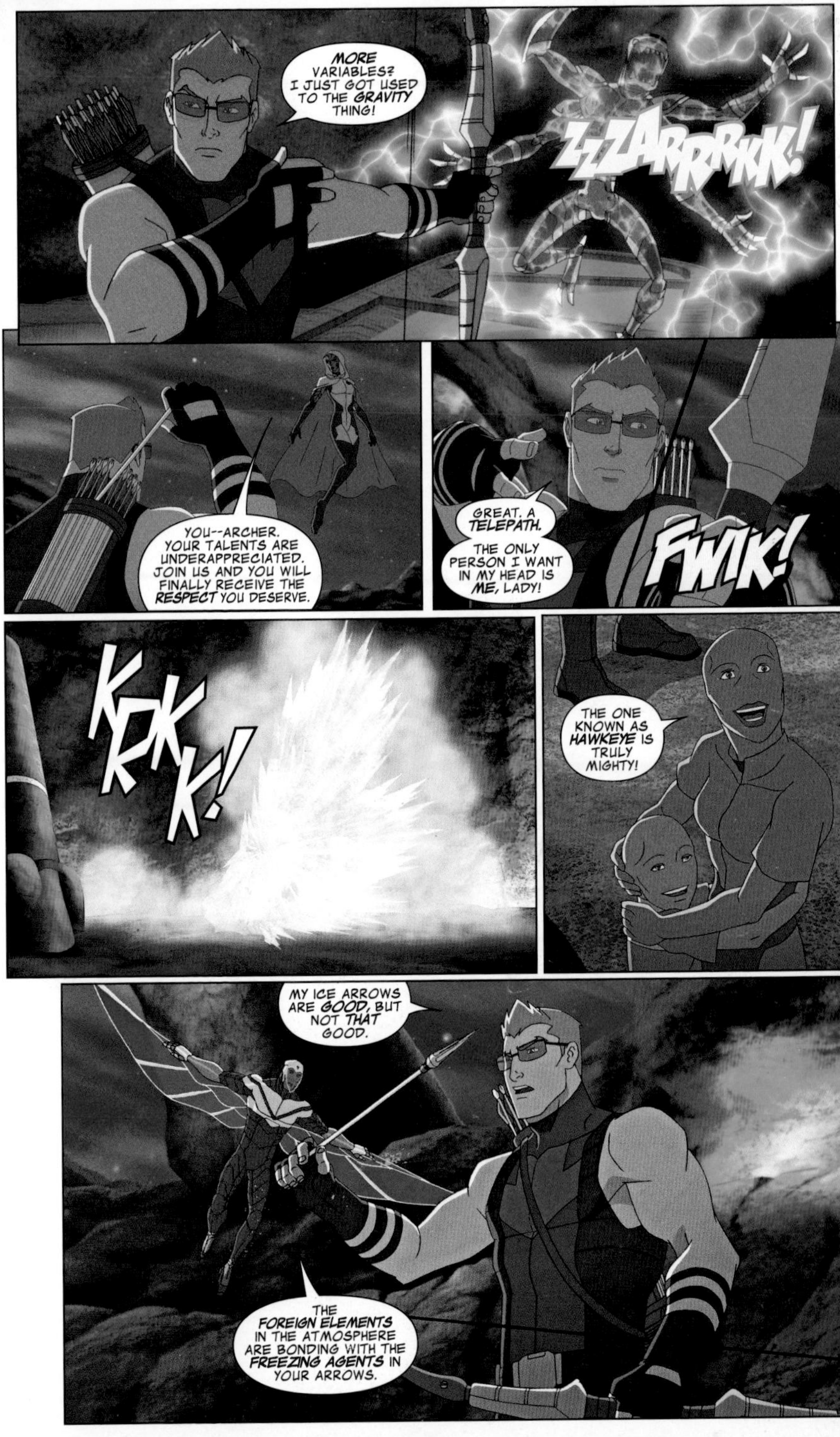

MORE VARIABLES? I JUST GOT USED TO THE GRAVITY THING!
ZZZARRRKK!
YOU--ARCHER. YOUR TALENTS ARE UNDERAPPRECIATED. JOIN US AND YOU WILL FINALLY RECEIVE THE RESPECT YOU DESERVE.
GREAT. A TELEPATH.
THE ONLY PERSON I WANT IN MY HEAD IS ME, LADY!
FWIK!
KRKRKK!
THE ONE KNOWN AS HAWKEYE IS TRULY MIGHTY!
MY ICE ARROWS ARE GOOD, BUT NOT THAT GOOD.
THE FOREIGN ELEMENTS IN THE ATMOSPHERE ARE BONDING WITH THE FREEZING AGENTS IN YOUR ARROWS.

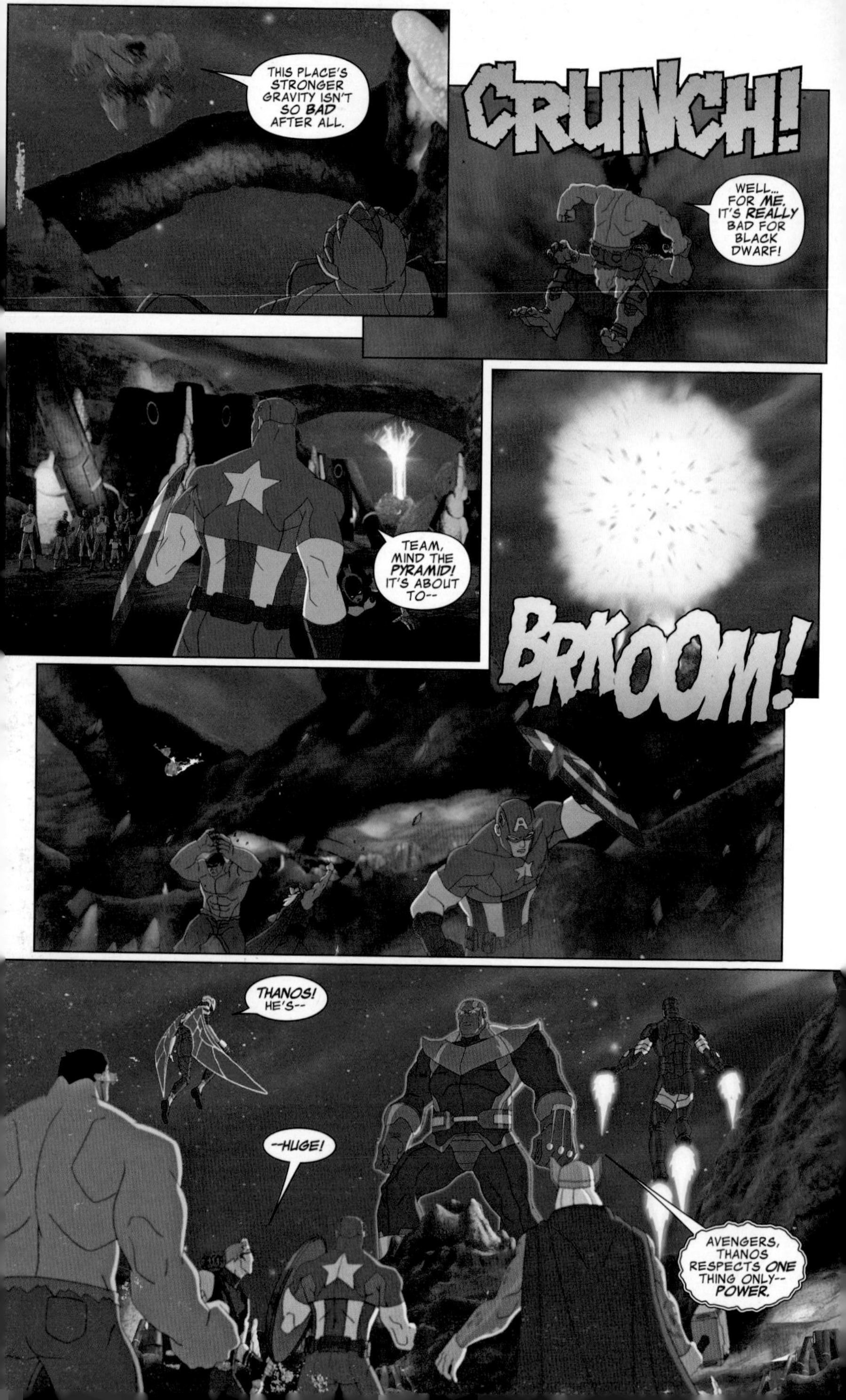
THIS PLACE'S STRONGER GRAVITY ISN'T SO BAD AFTER ALL.
CRUNCH!
WELL... FOR ME. IT'S REALLY BAD FOR BLACK DWARF!
TEAM, MIND THE PYRAMID! IT'S ABOUT TO--
BRKOOM!
THANOS! HE'S--
--HUGE!
AVENGERS, THANOS RESPECTS ONE THING ONLY-- POWER.

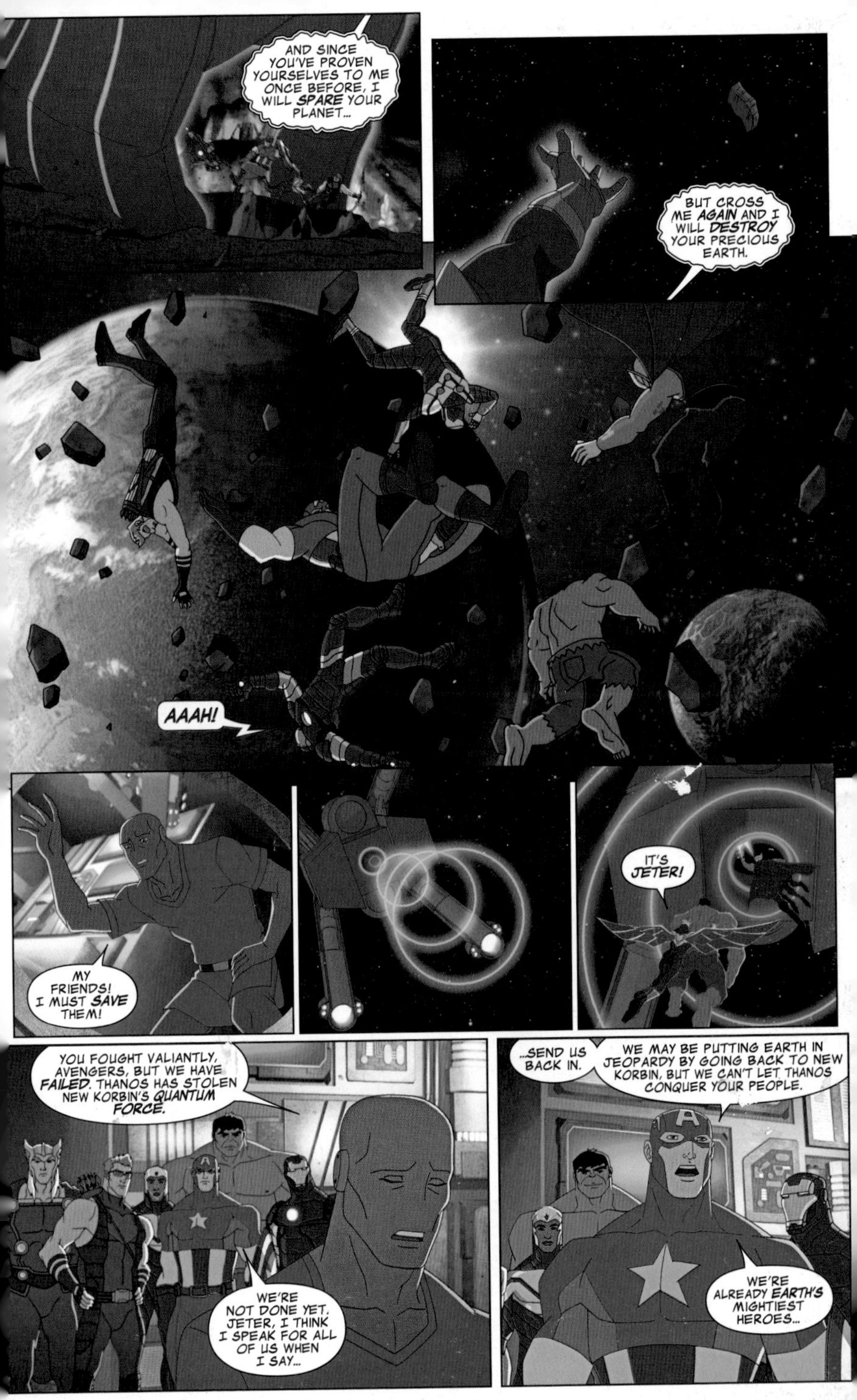
AND SINCE YOU'VE PROVEN YOURSELVES TO ME ONCE BEFORE, I WILL **SPARE** YOUR PLANET...
BUT CROSS ME **AGAIN** AND I WILL **DESTROY** YOUR PRECIOUS EARTH.
AAAH!
MY FRIENDS! I MUST **SAVE** THEM!
IT'S **JETER!**
YOU FOUGHT VALIANTLY, AVENGERS, BUT WE HAVE **FAILED**. THANOS HAS STOLEN NEW KORBIN'S **QUANTUM FORCE.**
WE'RE NOT DONE YET. JETER, I THINK I SPEAK FOR ALL OF US WHEN I SAY...
...SEND US BACK IN.
WE MAY BE PUTTING EARTH IN JEOPARDY BY GOING BACK TO NEW KORBIN, BUT WE CAN'T LET THANOS CONQUER YOUR PEOPLE.
WE'RE ALREADY **EARTH'S** MIGHTIEST HEROES...

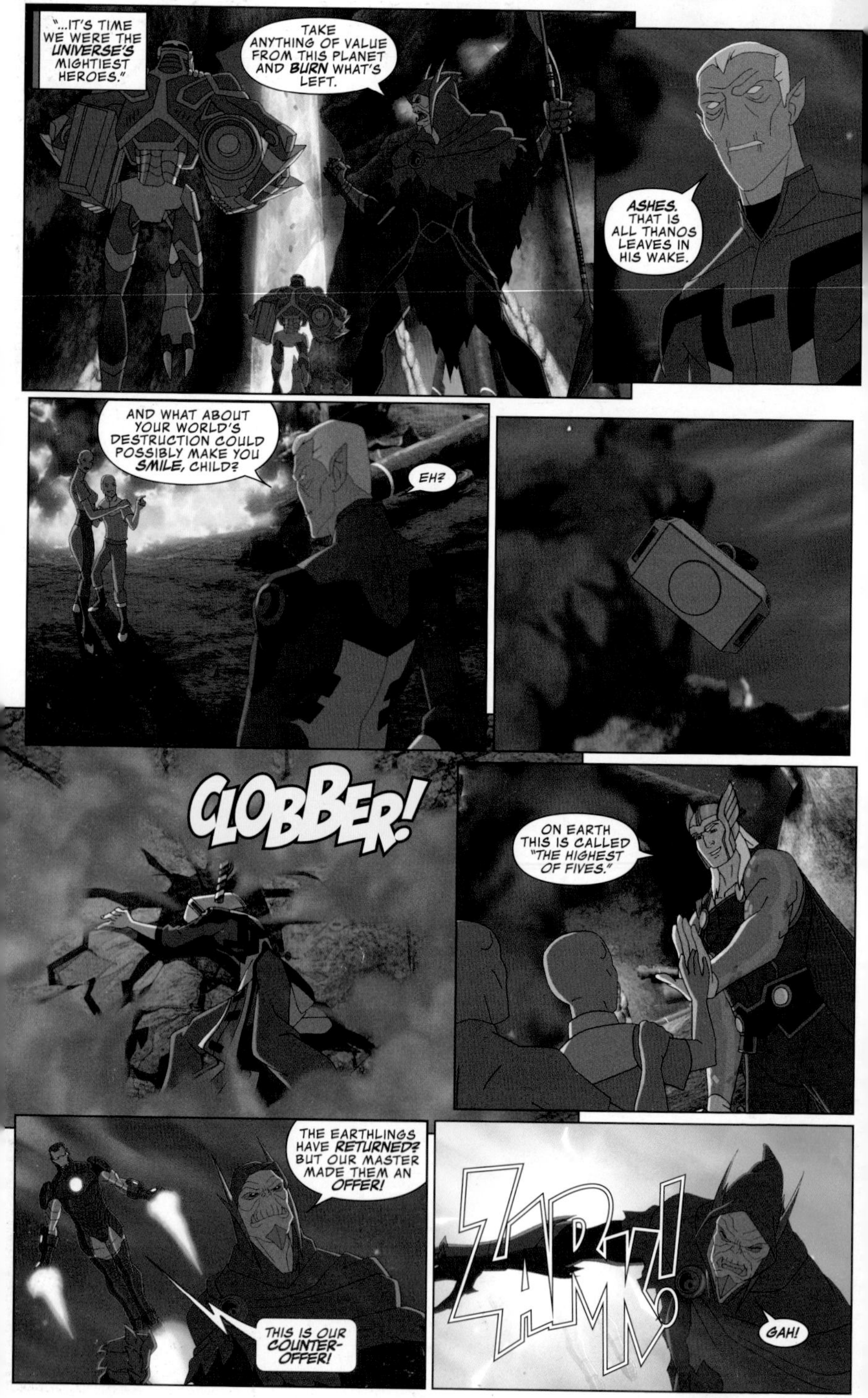
"...IT'S TIME WE WERE THE UNIVERSE'S MIGHTIEST HEROES."
TAKE ANYTHING OF VALUE FROM THIS PLANET AND BURN WHAT'S LEFT.
ASHES. THAT IS ALL THANOS LEAVES IN HIS WAKE.
AND WHAT ABOUT YOUR WORLD'S DESTRUCTION COULD POSSIBLY MAKE YOU SMILE, CHILD?
EH?
CLOBBER!
ON EARTH THIS IS CALLED "THE HIGHEST OF FIVES."
THE EARTHLINGS HAVE RETURNED? BUT OUR MASTER MADE THEM AN OFFER!
THIS IS OUR COUNTER-OFFER!
ZAP-THWAK!
GAH!

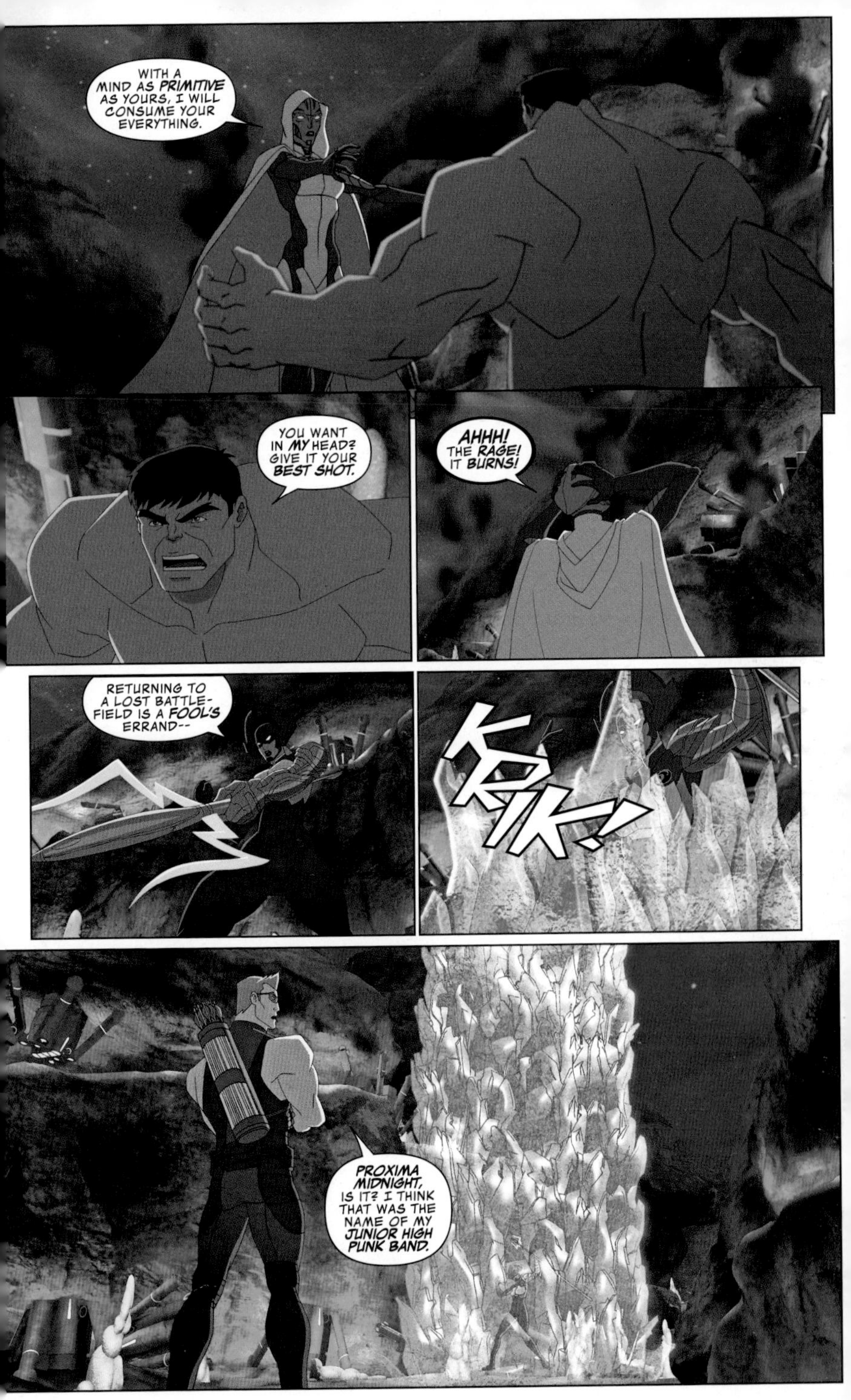
WITH A MIND AS PRIMITIVE AS YOURS, I WILL CONSUME YOUR EVERYTHING.
YOU WANT IN MY HEAD? GIVE IT YOUR BEST SHOT.
AHHH! THE RAGE! IT BURNS!
RETURNING TO A LOST BATTLE-FIELD IS A FOOL'S ERRAND--
KRIK!
PROXIMA MIDNIGHT, IS IT? I THINK THAT WAS THE NAME OF MY JUNIOR HIGH PUNK BAND.

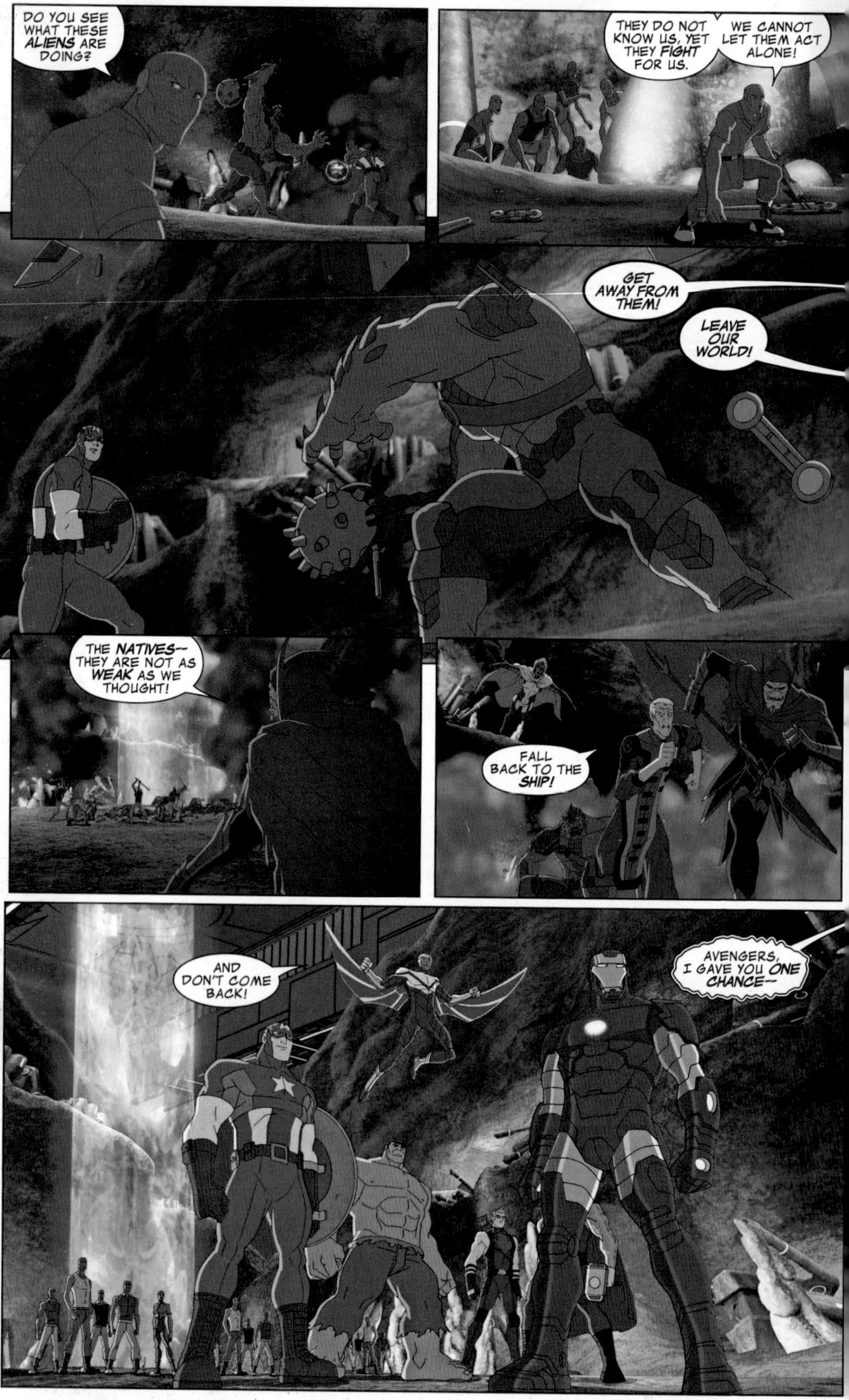
DO YOU SEE WHAT THESE ALIENS ARE DOING?
THEY DO NOT KNOW US, YET THEY FIGHT FOR US.
WE CANNOT LET THEM ACT ALONE!
GET AWAY FROM THEM!
LEAVE OUR WORLD!
THE NATIVES-- THEY ARE NOT AS WEAK AS WE THOUGHT!
FALL BACK TO THE SHIP!
AND DON'T COME BACK!
AVENGERS, I GAVE YOU ONE CHANCE--

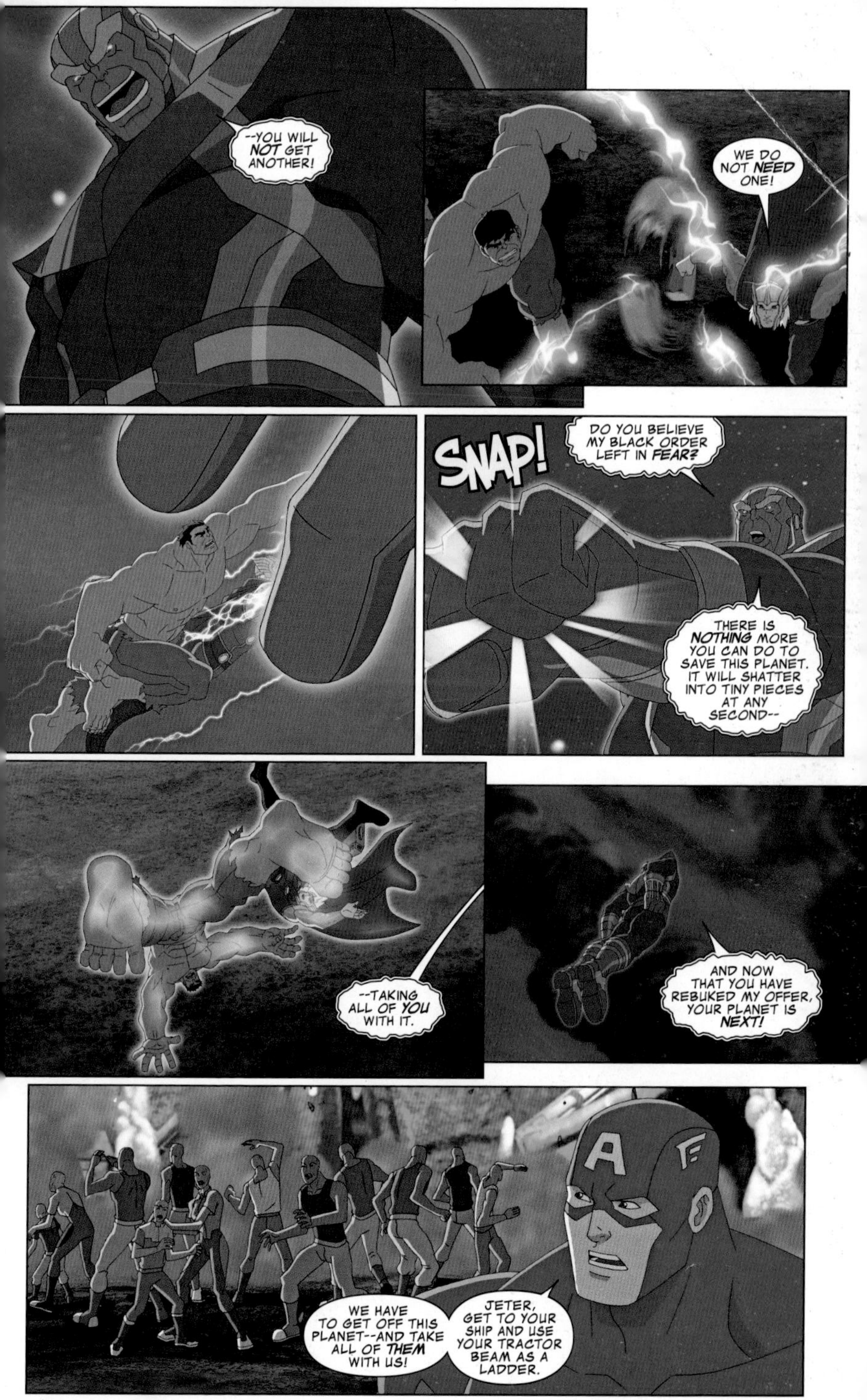
--YOU WILL NOT GET ANOTHER!
WE DO NOT NEED ONE!
SNAP!
DO YOU BELIEVE MY BLACK ORDER LEFT IN FEAR?
THERE IS NOTHING MORE YOU CAN DO TO SAVE THIS PLANET. IT WILL SHATTER INTO TINY PIECES AT ANY SECOND--
--TAKING ALL OF YOU WITH IT.
AND NOW THAT YOU HAVE REBUKED MY OFFER, YOUR PLANET IS NEXT!
JETER, GET TO YOUR SHIP AND USE YOUR TRACTOR BEAM AS A LADDER.
WE HAVE TO GET OFF THIS PLANET--AND TAKE ALL OF THEM WITH US!

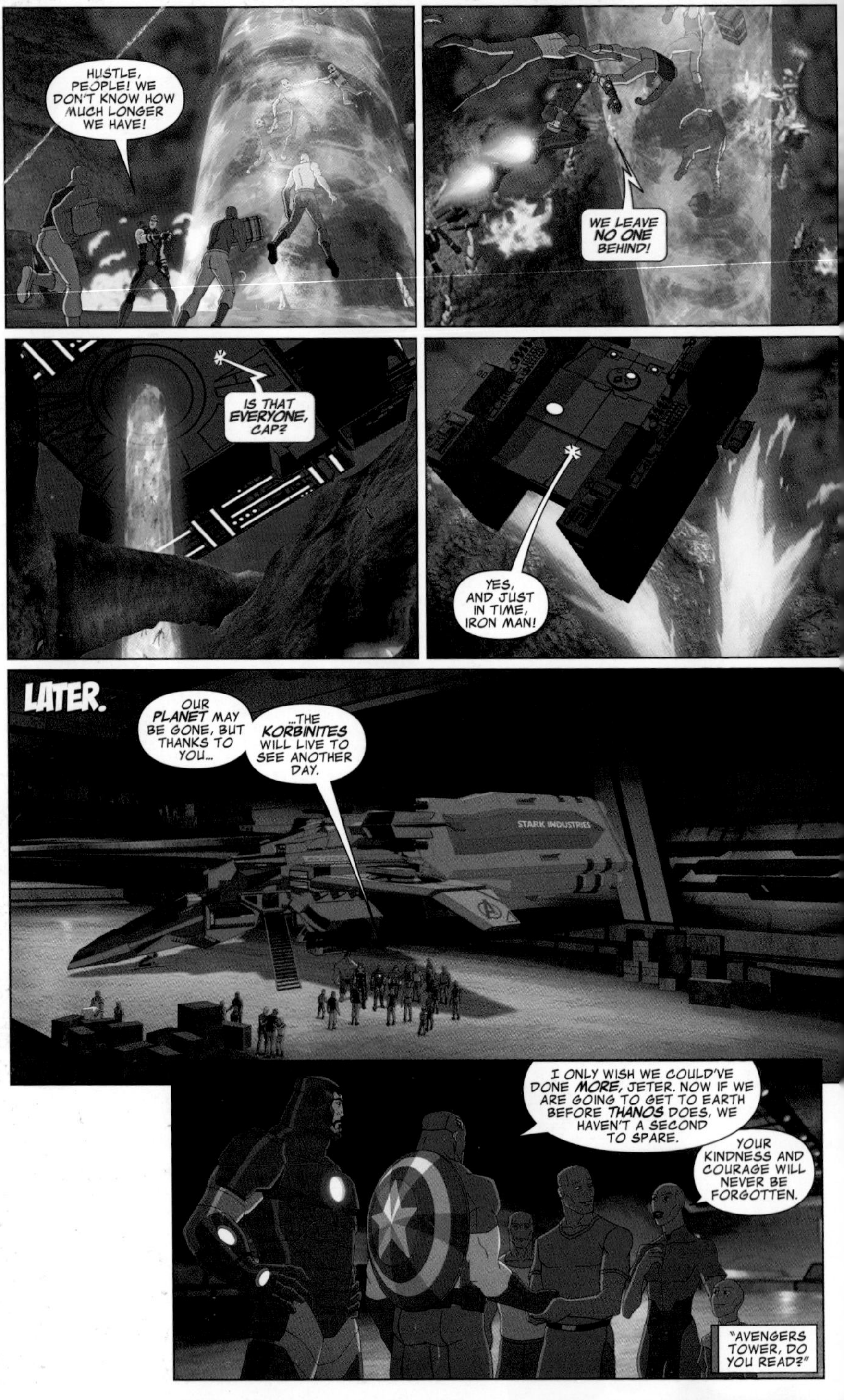
HUSTLE, PEOPLE! WE DON'T KNOW HOW MUCH LONGER WE HAVE!
WE LEAVE NO ONE BEHIND!
IS THAT EVERYONE, CAP?
YES, AND JUST IN TIME, IRON MAN!
LATER.
OUR PLANET MAY BE GONE, BUT THANKS TO YOU...
...THE KORBINITES WILL LIVE TO SEE ANOTHER DAY.
STARK INDUSTRIES
I ONLY WISH WE COULD'VE DONE MORE, JETER. NOW IF WE ARE GOING TO GET TO EARTH BEFORE THANOS DOES, WE HAVEN'T A SECOND TO SPARE.
YOUR KINDNESS AND COURAGE WILL NEVER BE FORGOTTEN.
"AVENGERS TOWER, DO YOU READ?"

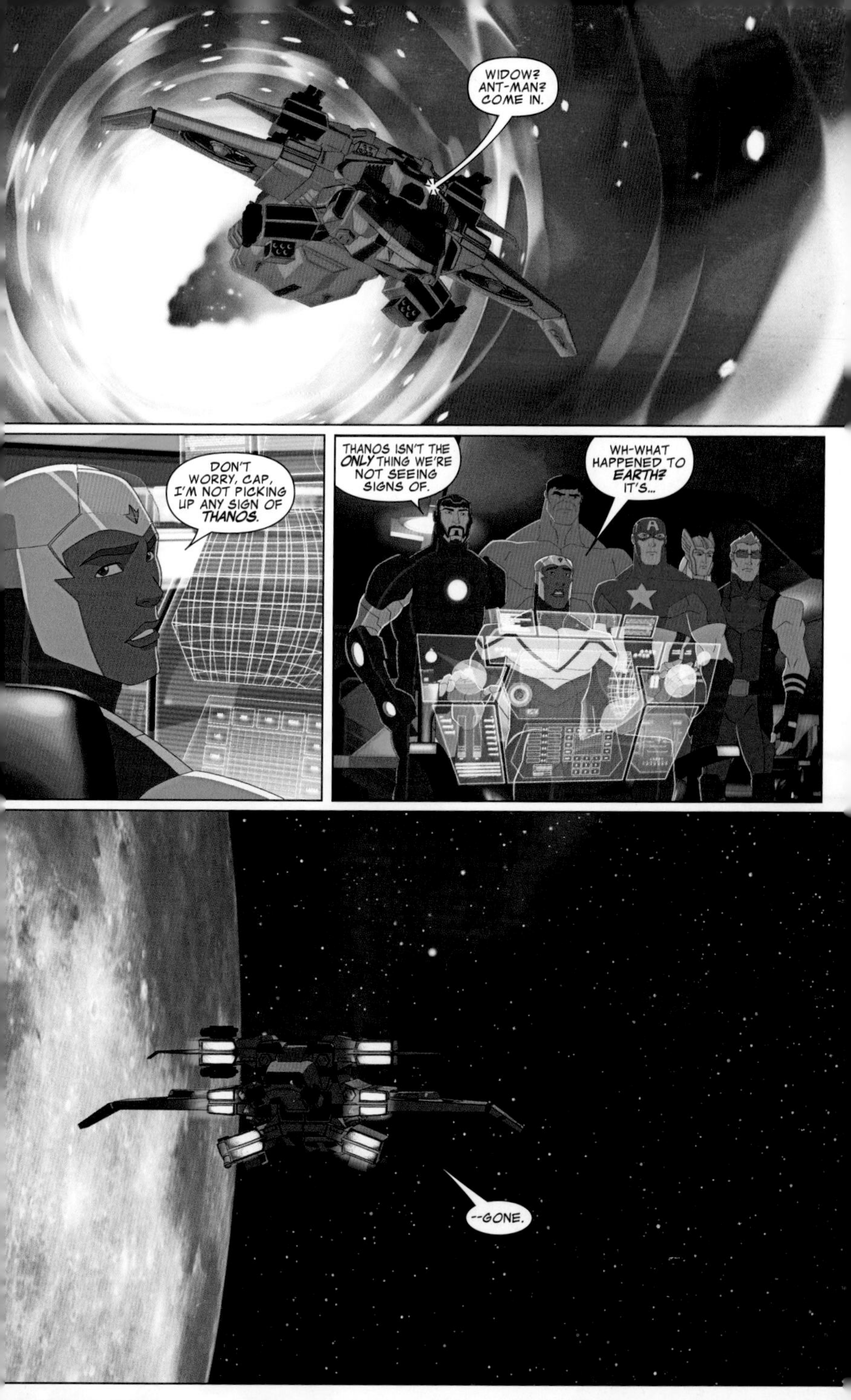

WIDOW? ANT-MAN? COME IN.
DON'T WORRY, CAP, I'M NOT PICKING UP ANY SIGN OF THANOS.
THANOS ISN'T THE ONLY THING WE'RE NOT SEEING SIGNS OF.
WH-WHAT HAPPENED TO EARTH? IT'S...
--GONE.

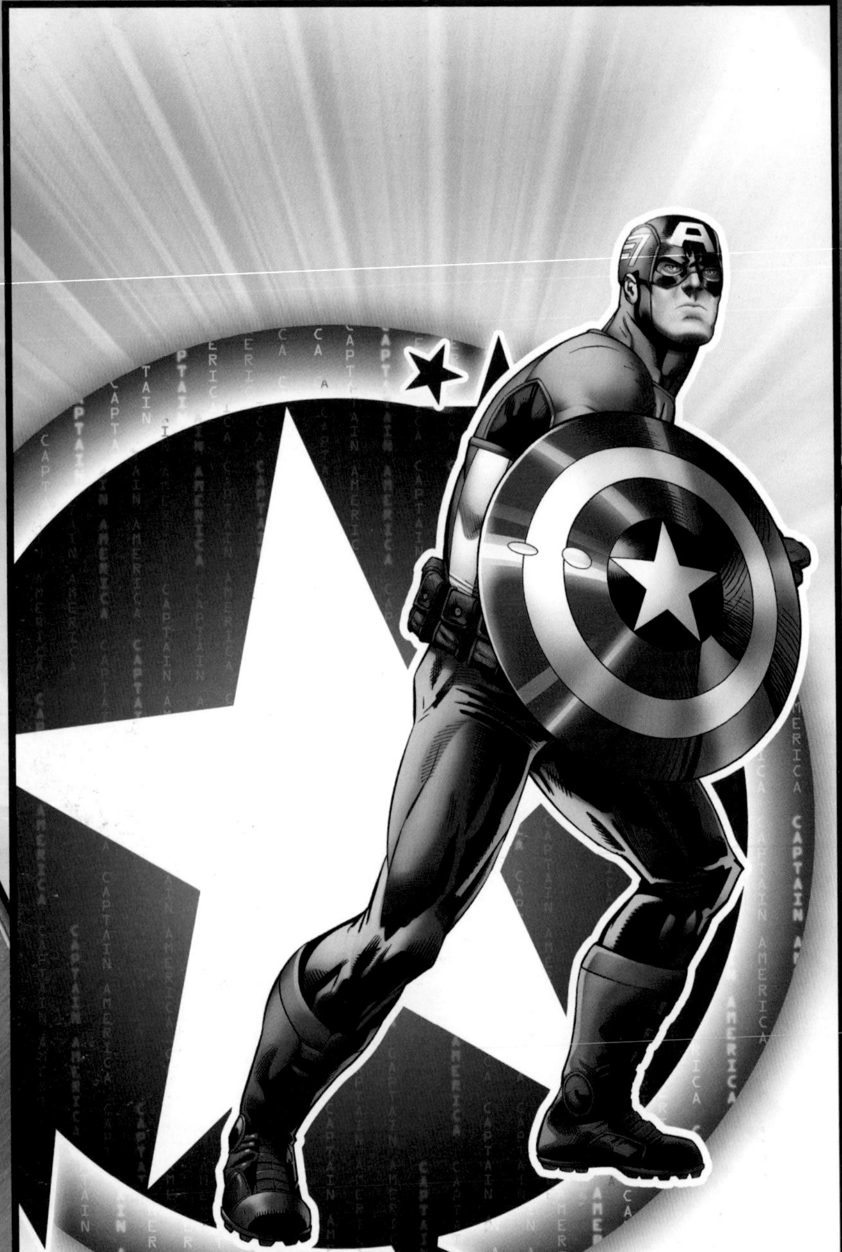
CAPTAIN AMERICA

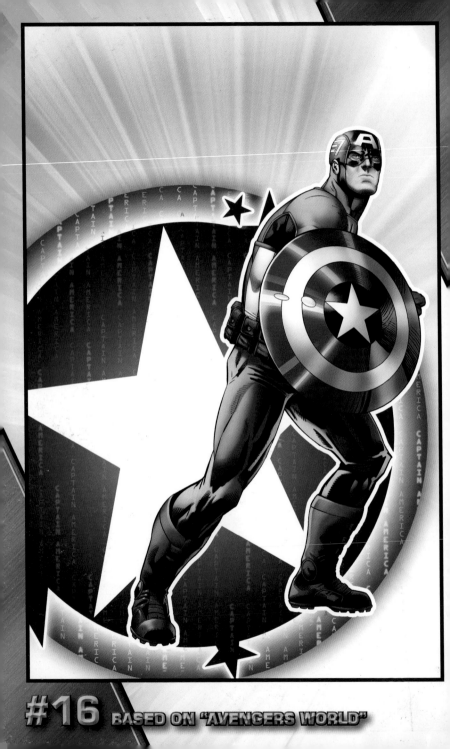

#16 BASED ON "AVENGERS WORLD"

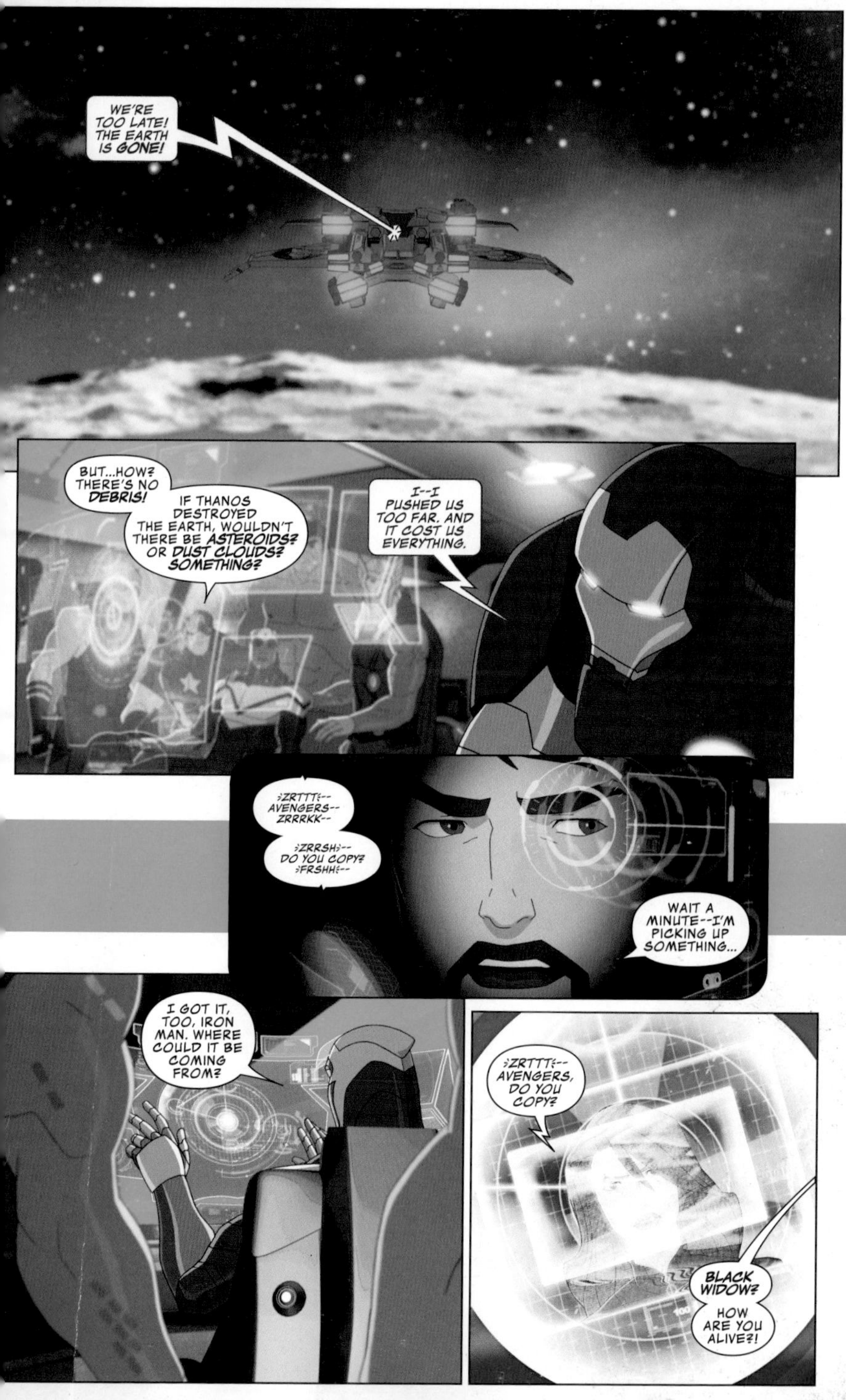
WE'RE TOO LATE! THE EARTH IS GONE!
BUT...HOW? THERE'S NO DEBRIS!
IF THANOS DESTROYED THE EARTH, WOULDN'T THERE BE ASTEROIDS? OR DUST CLOUDS? SOMETHING?
I--I PUSHED US TOO FAR. AND IT COST US EVERYTHING.
ZRTTT--AVENGERS--ZRRRKK--
ZRRSH--DO YOU COPY? FRSHH--
WAIT A MINUTE--I'M PICKING UP SOMETHING...
I GOT IT, TOO, IRON MAN. WHERE COULD IT BE COMING FROM?
ZRTTT--AVENGERS, DO YOU COPY?
BLACK WIDOW?
HOW ARE YOU ALIVE?!

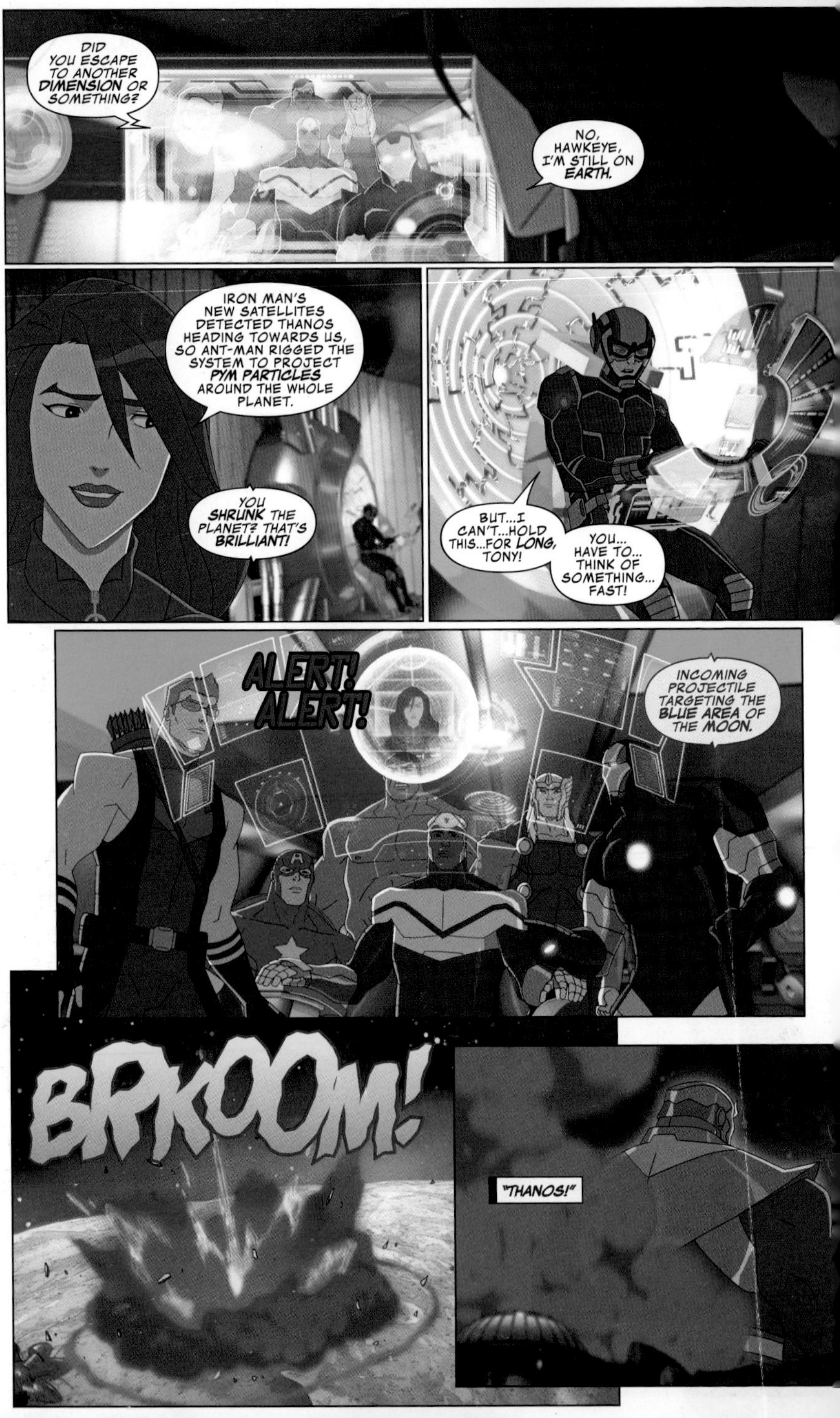

DID YOU ESCAPE TO ANOTHER DIMENSION OR SOMETHING?
NO, HAWKEYE, I'M STILL ON EARTH.
IRON MAN'S NEW SATELLITES DETECTED THANOS HEADING TOWARDS US, SO ANT-MAN RIGGED THE SYSTEM TO PROJECT PYM PARTICLES AROUND THE WHOLE PLANET.
YOU SHRUNK THE PLANET? THAT'S BRILLIANT!
BUT...I CAN'T...HOLD THIS...FOR LONG, TONY!
YOU... HAVE TO... THINK OF SOMETHING... FAST!
ALERT! ALERT!
INCOMING PROJECTILE TARGETING THE BLUE AREA OF THE MOON.
BRKOOM!
"THANOS!"

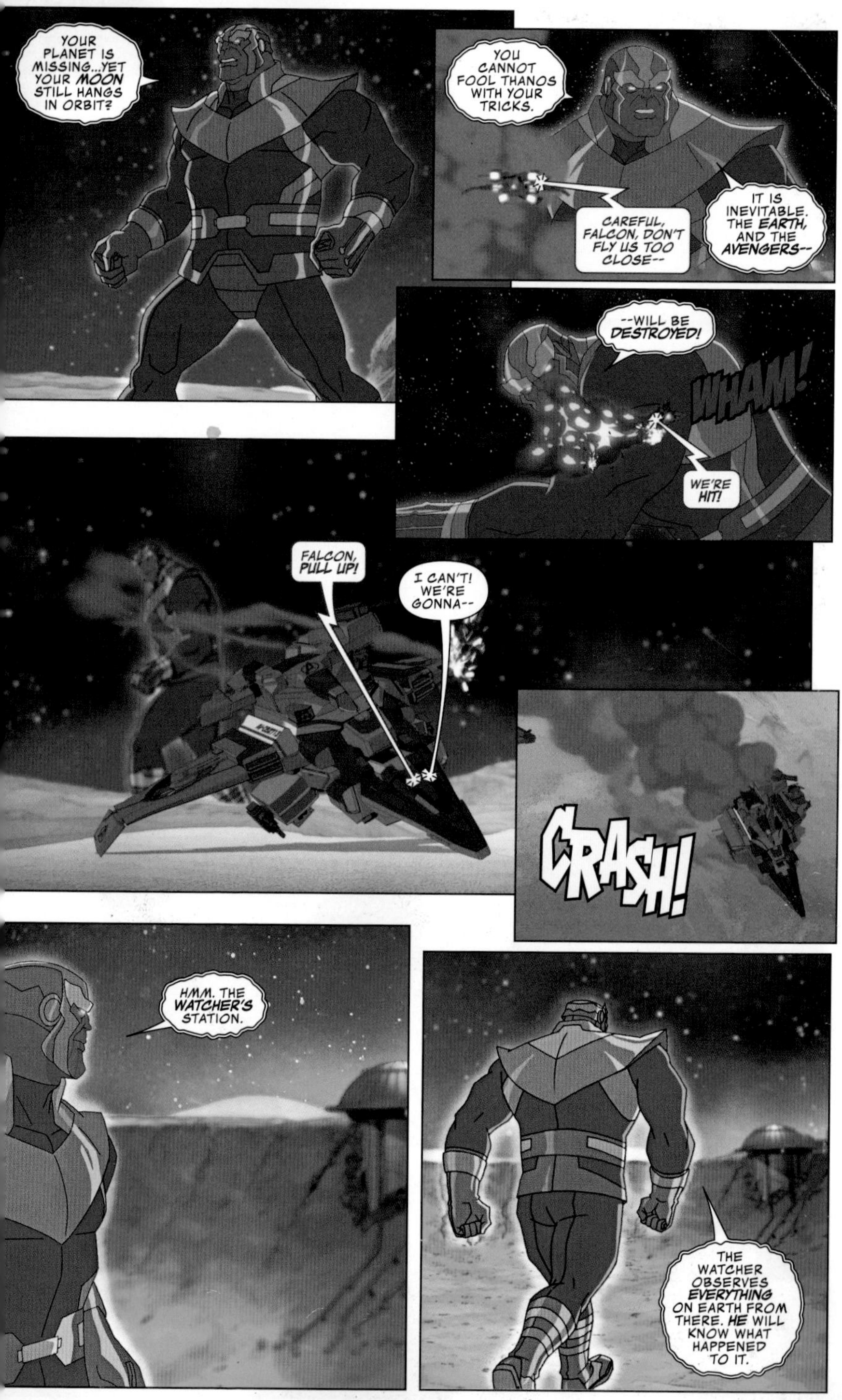
YOUR PLANET IS MISSING...YET YOUR MOON STILL HANGS IN ORBIT?
YOU CANNOT FOOL THANOS WITH YOUR TRICKS.
CAREFUL, FALCON, DON'T FLY US TOO CLOSE--
IT IS INEVITABLE. THE EARTH, AND THE AVENGERS--
--WILL BE DESTROYED!
WHAM!
WE'RE HIT!
FALCON, PULL UP!
I CAN'T! WE'RE GONNA--
CRASH!
HMM. THE WATCHER'S STATION.
THE WATCHER OBSERVES EVERYTHING ON EARTH FROM THERE. HE WILL KNOW WHAT HAPPENED TO IT.

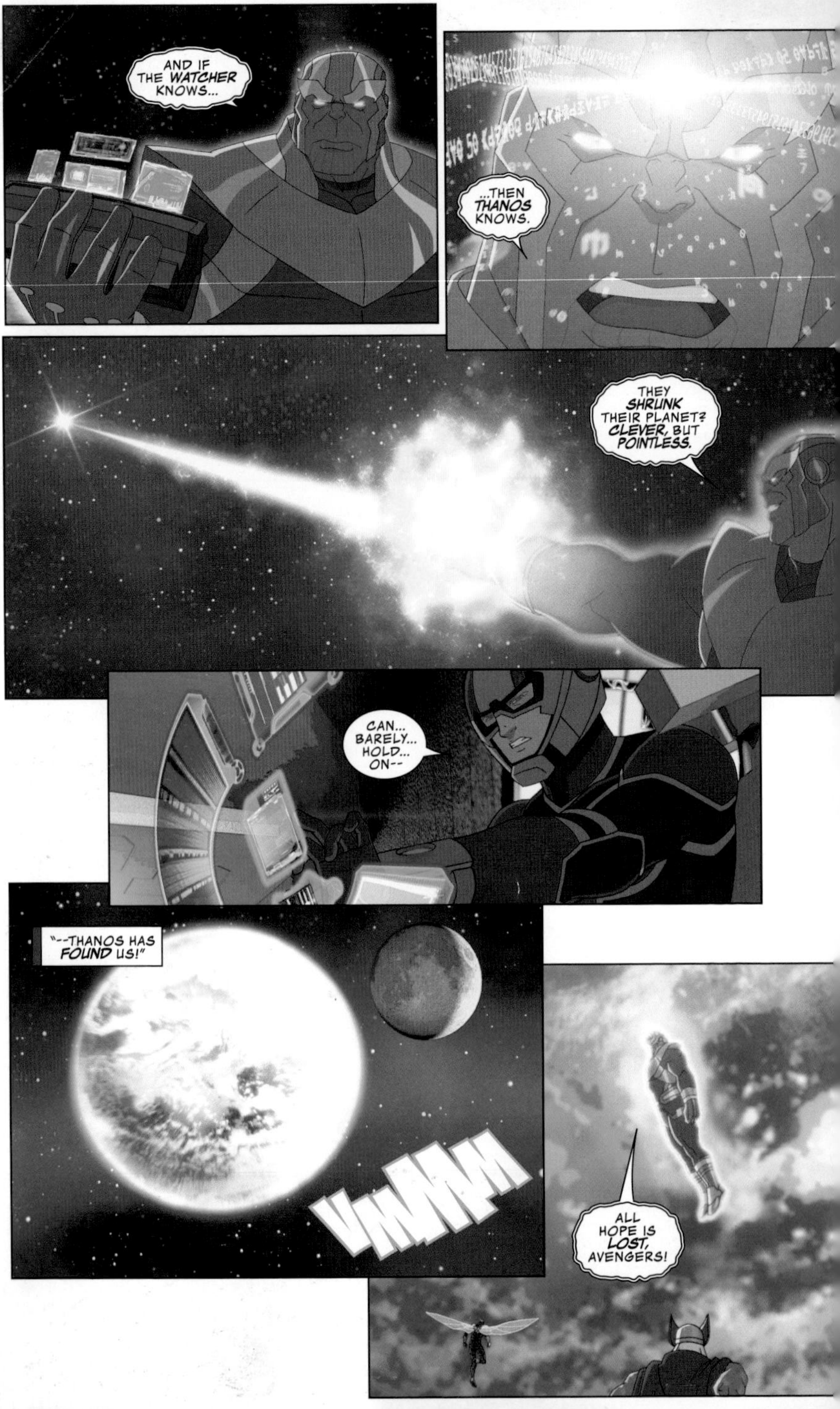

AND IF THE WATCHER KNOWS...
...THEN THANOS KNOWS.
THEY SHRUNK THEIR PLANET? CLEVER, BUT POINTLESS.
CAN... BARELY... HOLD... ON--
"--THANOS HAS FOUND US!"
VMMM
ALL HOPE IS LOST, AVENGERS!

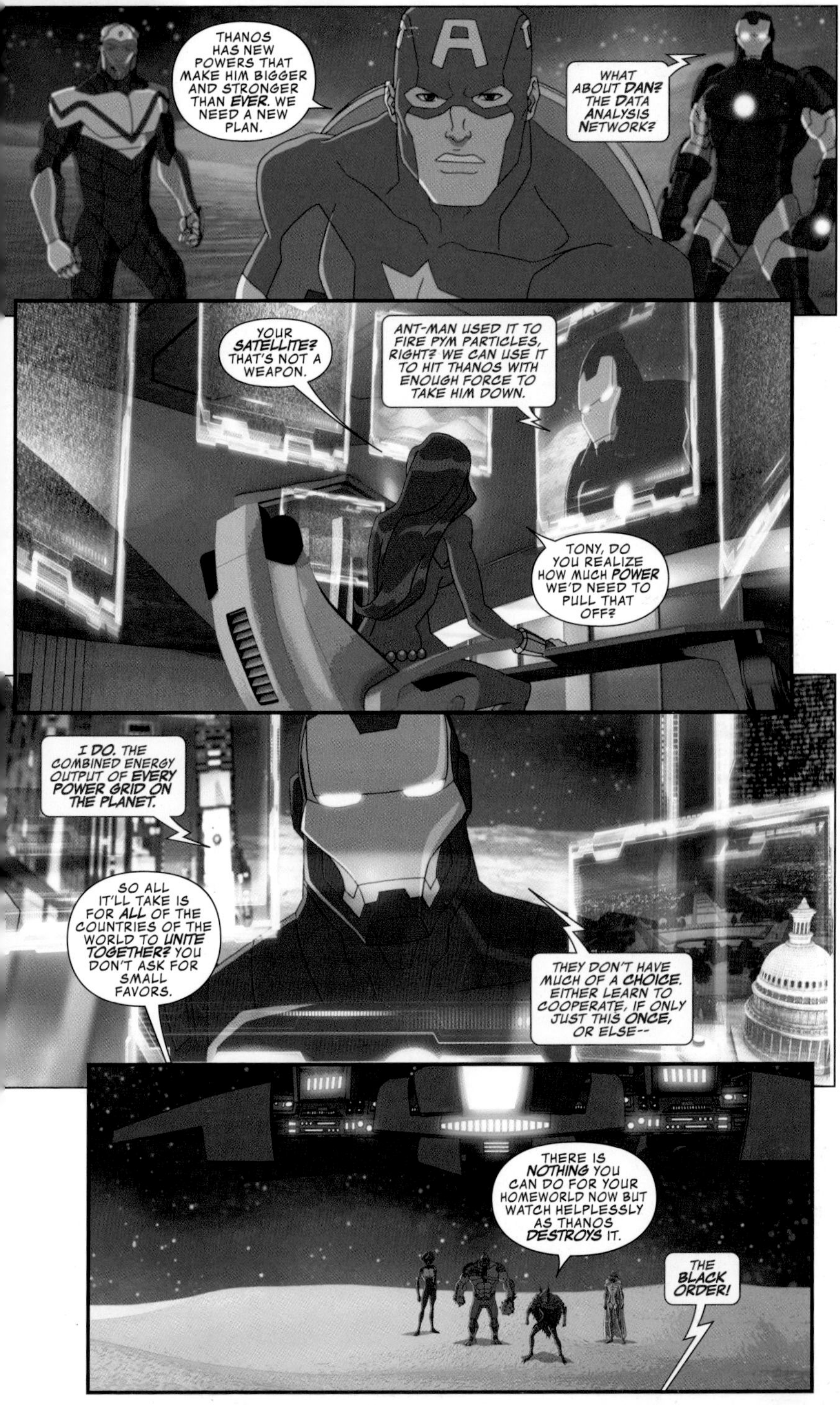
THANOS HAS NEW POWERS THAT MAKE HIM BIGGER AND STRONGER THAN EVER. WE NEED A NEW PLAN.
WHAT ABOUT DAN? THE DATA ANALYSIS NETWORK?
YOUR SATELLITE? THAT'S NOT A WEAPON.
ANT-MAN USED IT TO FIRE PYM PARTICLES, RIGHT? WE CAN USE IT TO HIT THANOS WITH ENOUGH FORCE TO TAKE HIM DOWN.
TONY, DO YOU REALIZE HOW MUCH POWER WE'D NEED TO PULL THAT OFF?
I DO. THE COMBINED ENERGY OUTPUT OF EVERY POWER GRID ON THE PLANET.
SO ALL IT'LL TAKE IS FOR ALL OF THE COUNTRIES OF THE WORLD TO UNITE TOGETHER? YOU DON'T ASK FOR SMALL FAVORS.
THEY DON'T HAVE MUCH OF A CHOICE. EITHER LEARN TO COOPERATE, IF ONLY JUST THIS ONCE, OR ELSE--
THERE IS NOTHING YOU CAN DO FOR YOUR HOMEWORLD NOW BUT WATCH HELPLESSLY AS THANOS DESTROYS IT.
THE BLACK ORDER!

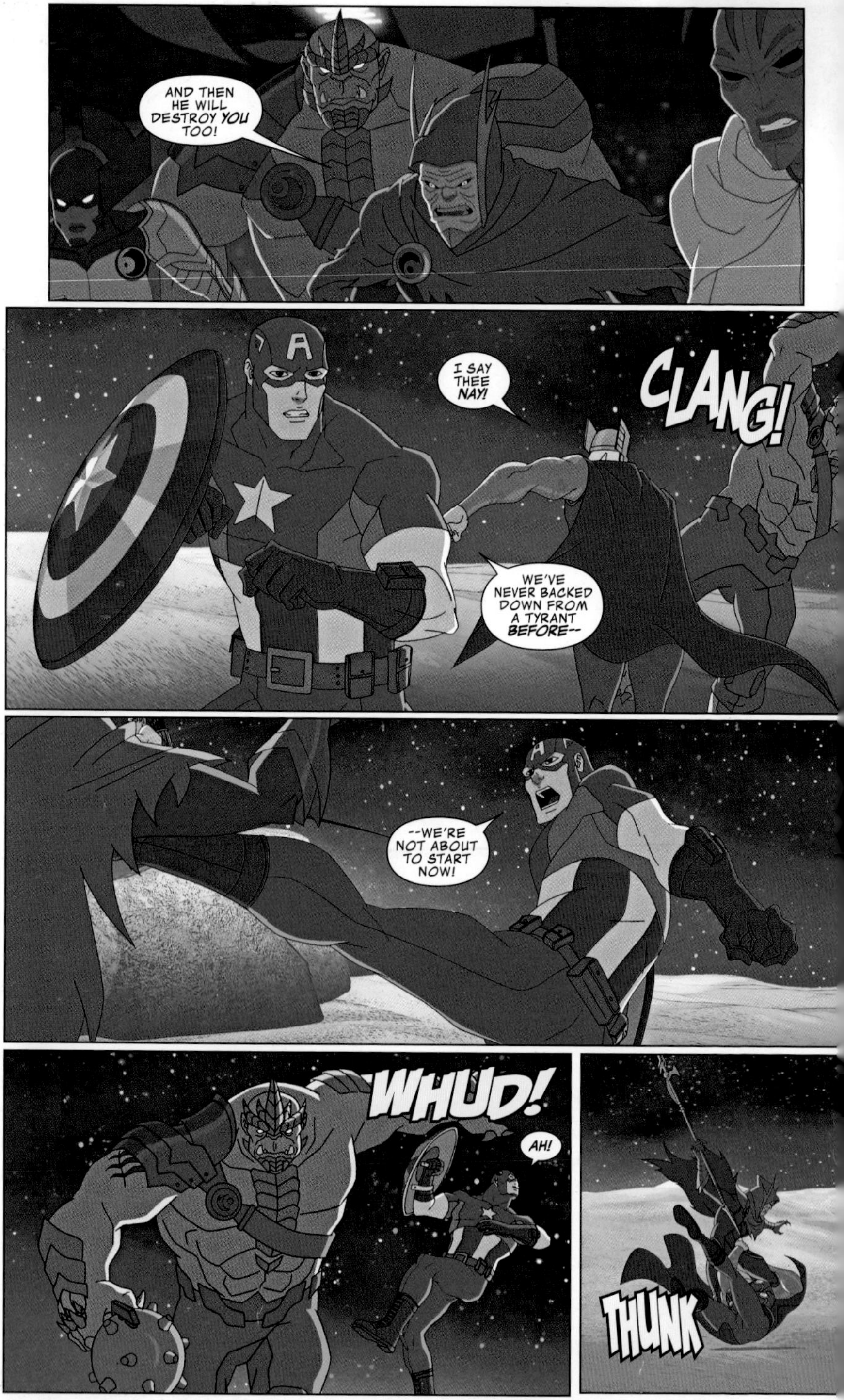
AND THEN HE WILL DESTROY YOU TOO!
I SAY THEE NAY!
CLANG!
WE'VE NEVER BACKED DOWN FROM A TYRANT BEFORE--
--WE'RE NOT ABOUT TO START NOW!
WHUD!
AH!
THUNK

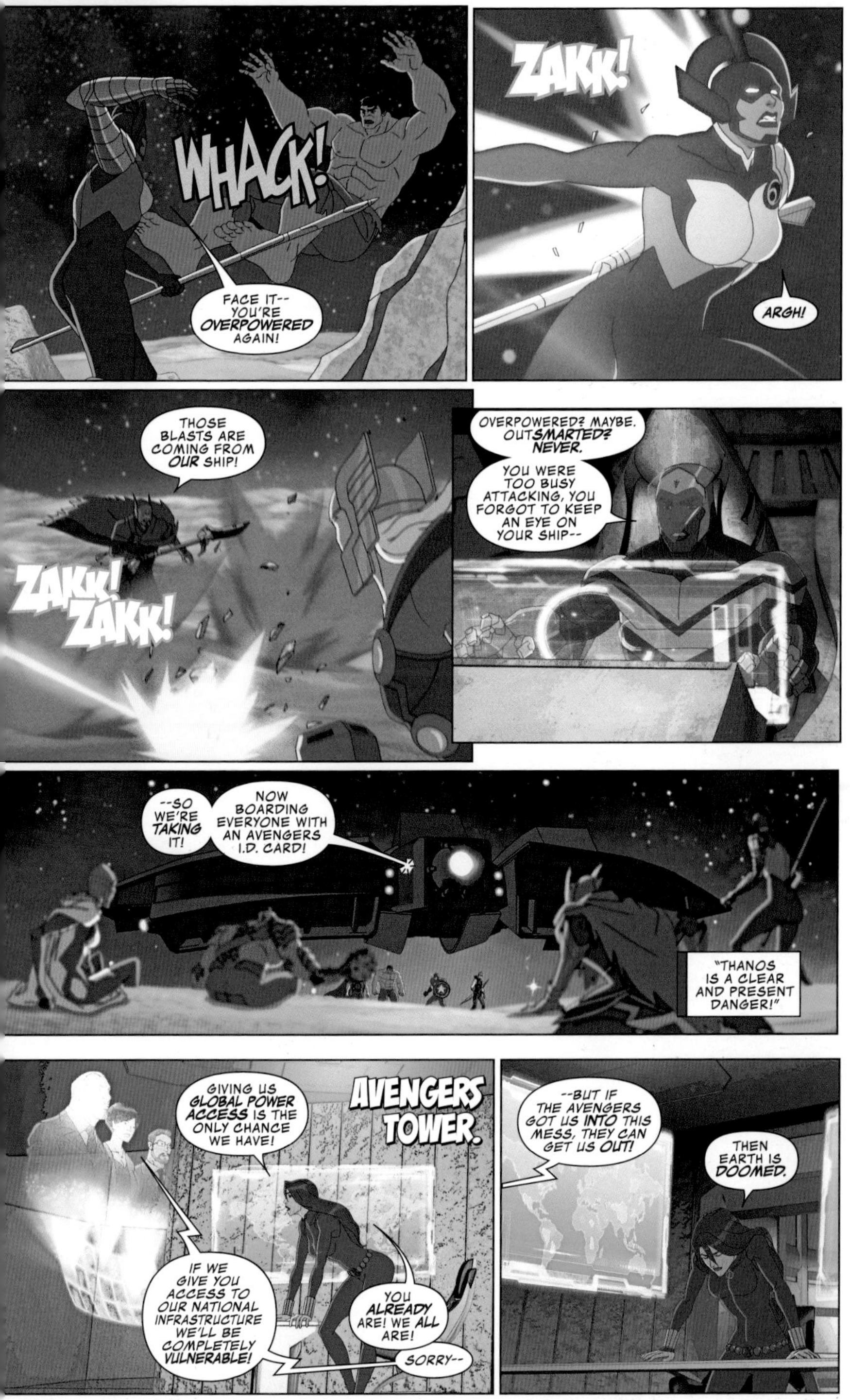
WHACK!
FACE IT-- YOU'RE OVERPOWERED AGAIN!
ZAKK!
ARGH!
THOSE BLASTS ARE COMING FROM OUR SHIP!
ZAKK! ZAKK!
OVERPOWERED? MAYBE. OUTSMARTED? NEVER.
YOU WERE TOO BUSY ATTACKING, YOU FORGOT TO KEEP AN EYE ON YOUR SHIP--
--SO WE'RE TAKING IT!
NOW BOARDING EVERYONE WITH AN AVENGERS I.D. CARD!
"THANOS IS A CLEAR AND PRESENT DANGER!"
AVENGERS TOWER.
GIVING US GLOBAL POWER ACCESS IS THE ONLY CHANCE WE HAVE!
IF WE GIVE YOU ACCESS TO OUR NATIONAL INFRASTRUCTURE WE'LL BE COMPLETELY VULNERABLE!
YOU ALREADY ARE! WE ALL ARE!
SORRY--
--BUT IF THE AVENGERS GOT US INTO THIS MESS, THEY CAN GET US OUT!
THEN EARTH IS DOOMED.

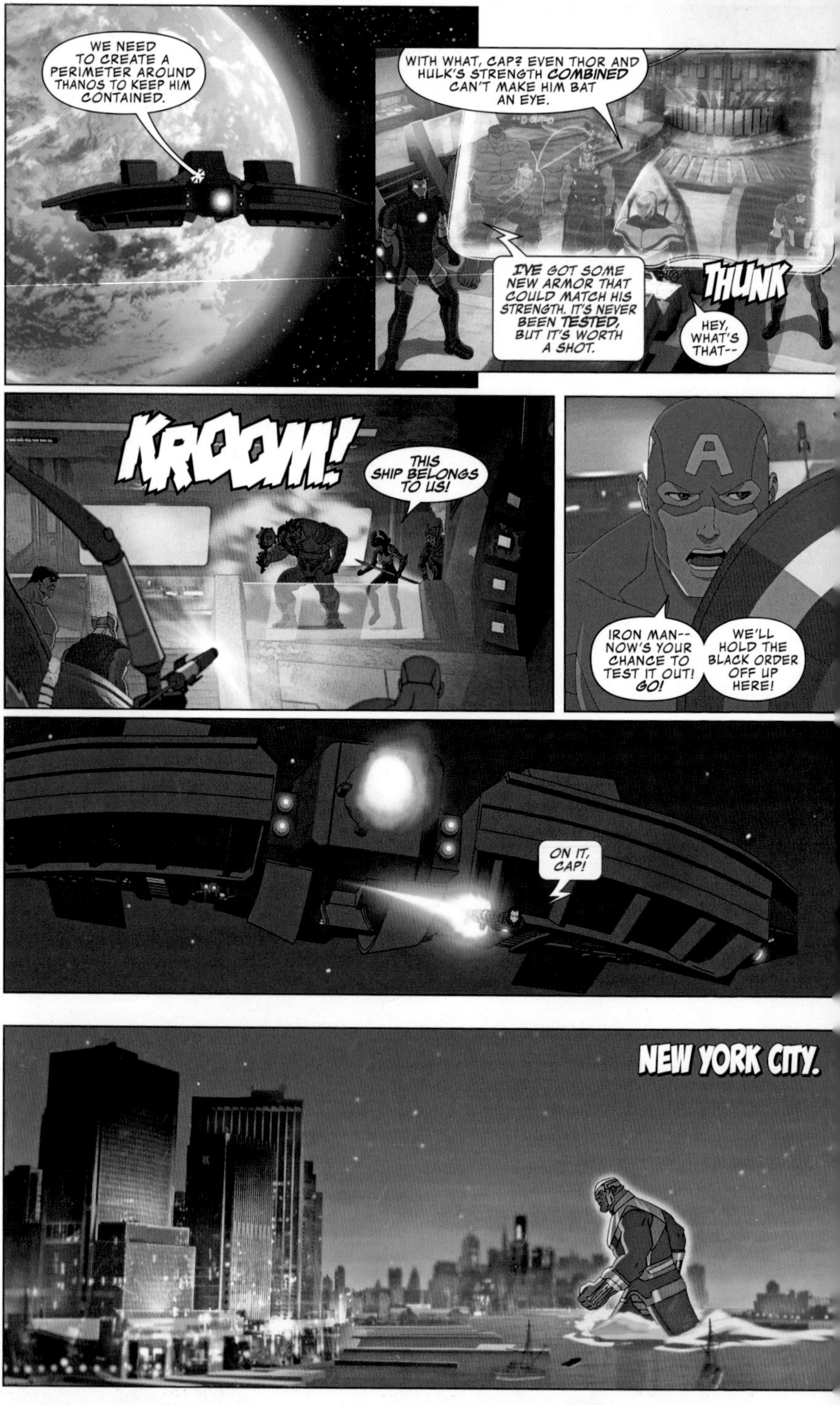

WE NEED TO CREATE A PERIMETER AROUND THANOS TO KEEP HIM CONTAINED.
WITH WHAT, CAP? EVEN THOR AND HULK'S STRENGTH COMBINED CAN'T MAKE HIM BAT AN EYE.
I'VE GOT SOME NEW ARMOR THAT COULD MATCH HIS STRENGTH. IT'S NEVER BEEN TESTED, BUT IT'S WORTH A SHOT.
THUNK
HEY, WHAT'S THAT--
KROOM!
THIS SHIP BELONGS TO US!
IRON MAN-- NOW'S YOUR CHANCE TO TEST IT OUT! GO!
WE'LL HOLD THE BLACK ORDER OFF UP HERE!
ON IT, CAP!
NEW YORK CITY.

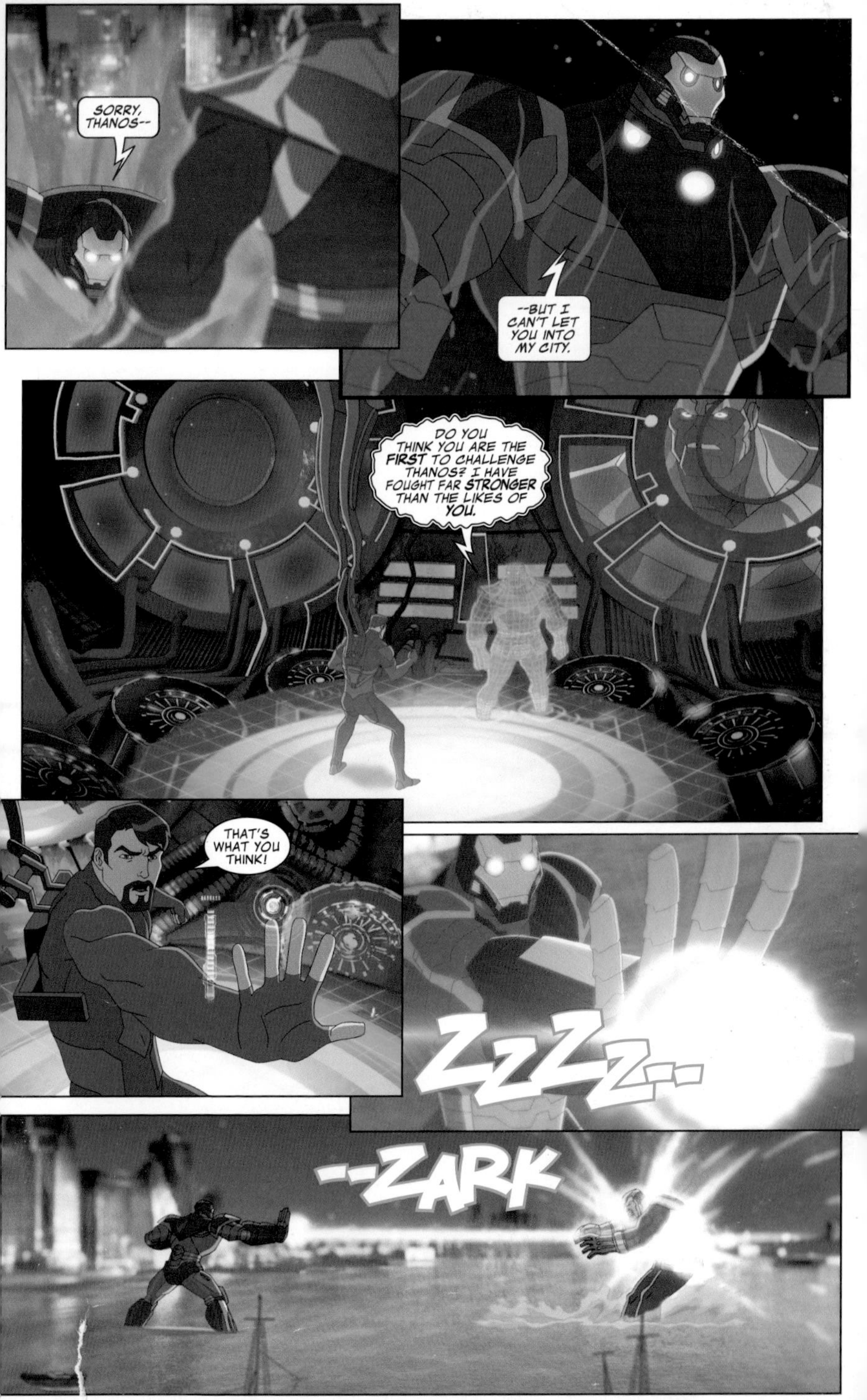
SORRY, THANOS--
--BUT I CAN'T LET YOU INTO MY CITY.
DO YOU THINK YOU ARE THE FIRST TO CHALLENGE THANOS? I HAVE FOUGHT FAR STRONGER THAN THE LIKES OF YOU.
THAT'S WHAT YOU THINK!
ZzZZ...
--ZARK

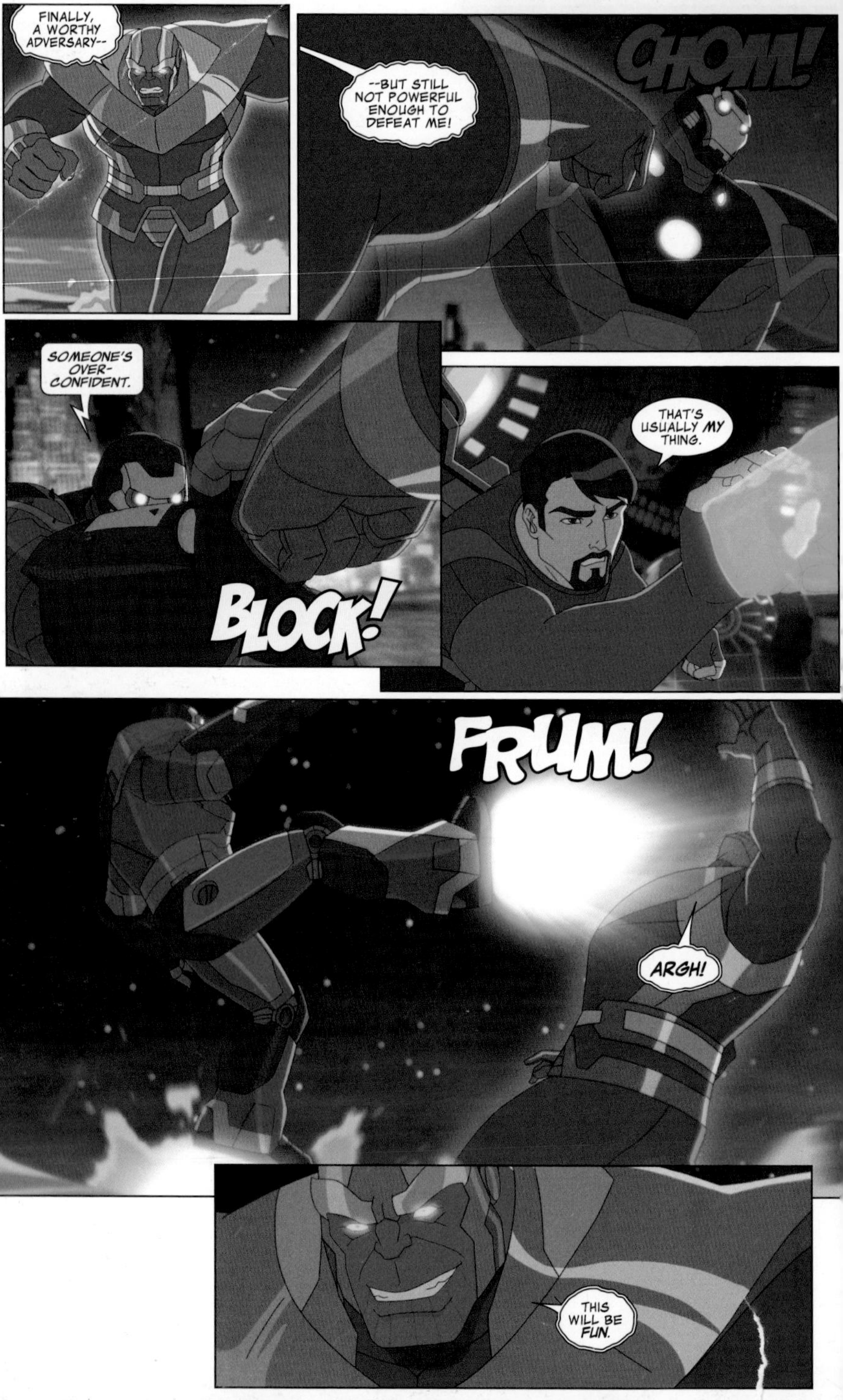
FINALLY, A WORTHY ADVERSARY--
CHOM!
--BUT STILL NOT POWERFUL ENOUGH TO DEFEAT ME!
SOMEONE'S OVER-CONFIDENT.
BLOCK!
THAT'S USUALLY MY THING.
FRUM!
ARGH!
THIS WILL BE FUN.

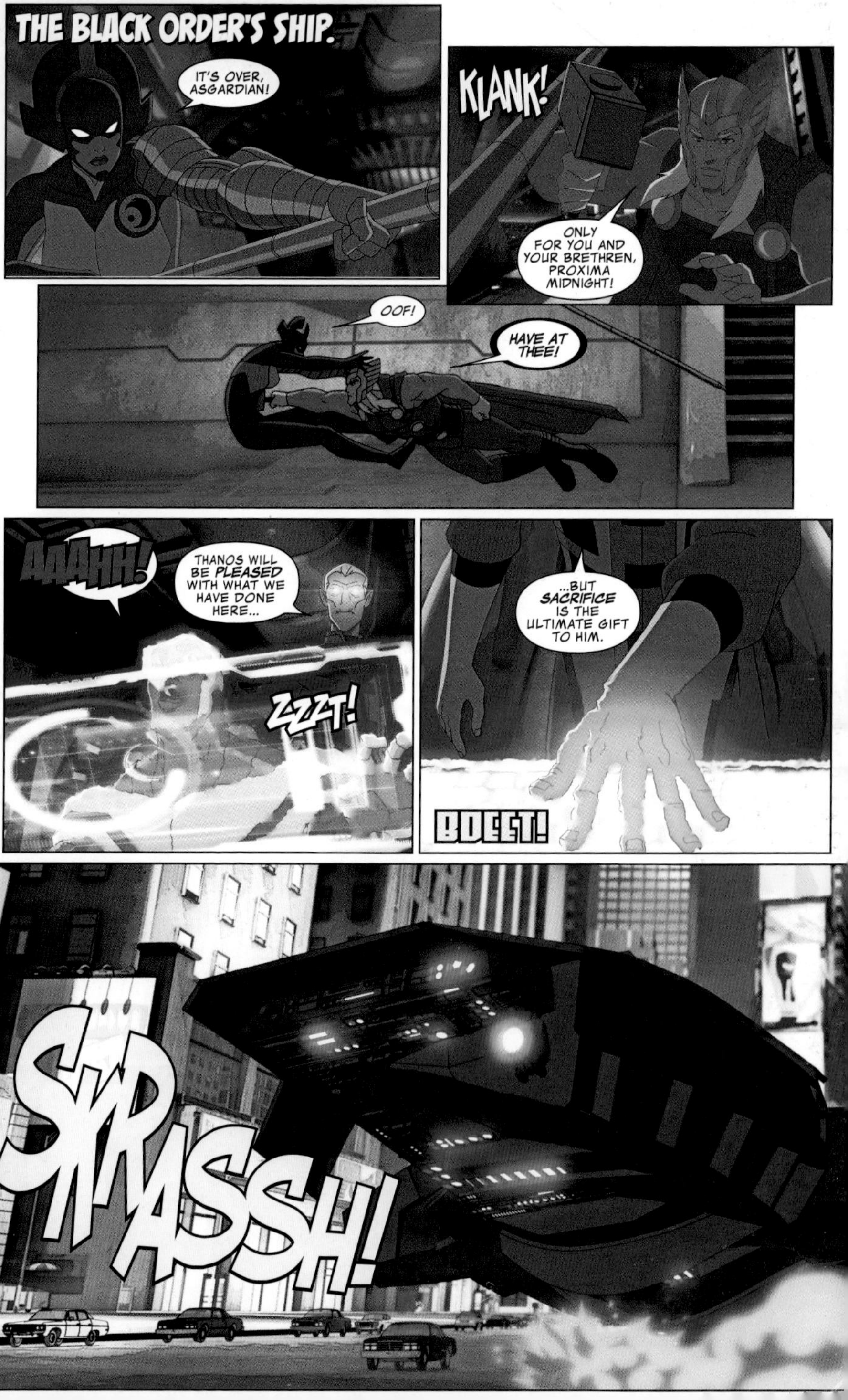

THE BLACK ORDER'S SHIP.
IT'S OVER, ASGARDIAN!
KLANK!
ONLY FOR YOU AND YOUR BRETHREN, PROXIMA MIDNIGHT!
OOF!
HAVE AT THEE!
AAAHH!
THANOS WILL BE PLEASED WITH WHAT WE HAVE DONE HERE...
ZZZT!
...BUT SACRIFICE IS THE ULTIMATE GIFT TO HIM.
BDEEET!
SKRASSH!

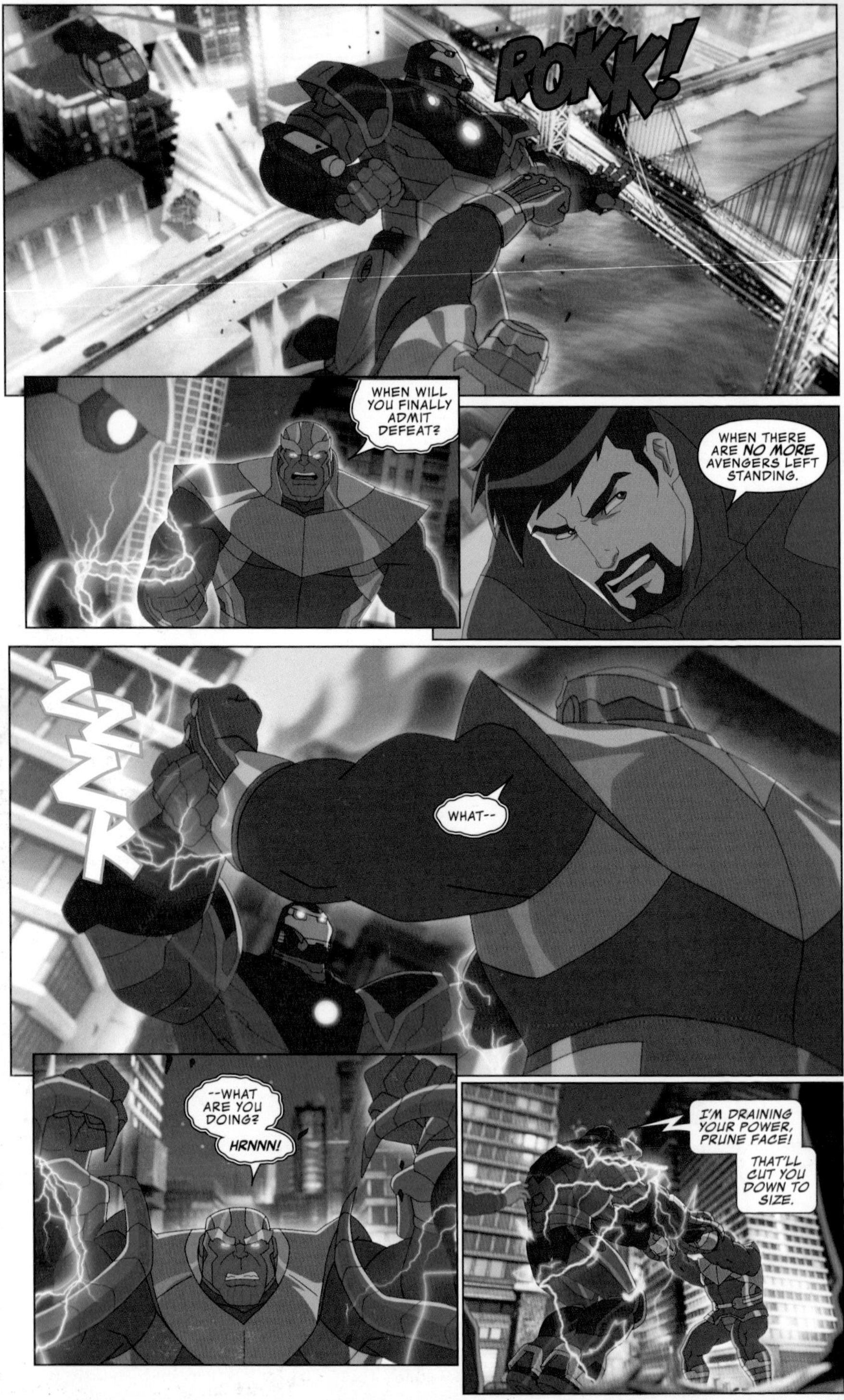
ROKK!
WHEN WILL YOU FINALLY ADMIT DEFEAT?
WHEN THERE ARE **NO MORE** AVENGERS LEFT STANDING.
ZZZK
WHAT--
--WHAT ARE YOU DOING?
HRNNN!
I'M DRAINING YOUR POWER, PRUNE FACE!
THAT'LL CUT YOU DOWN TO SIZE.

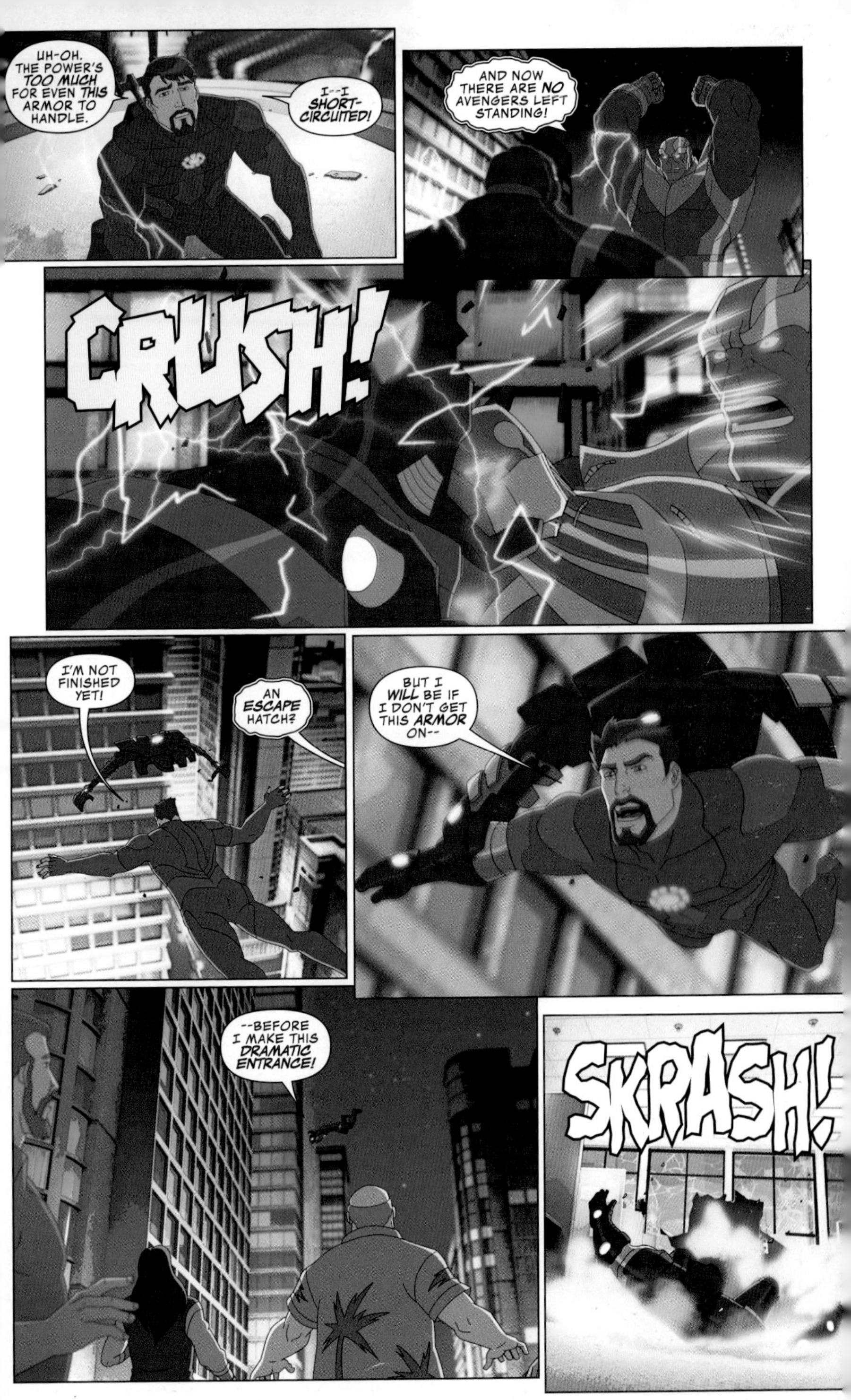
UH-OH. THE POWER'S TOO MUCH FOR EVEN THIS ARMOR TO HANDLE.
I--I SHORT-CIRCUITED!
AND NOW THERE ARE NO AVENGERS LEFT STANDING!
CRUSH!
I'M NOT FINISHED YET!
AN ESCAPE HATCH?
BUT I WILL BE IF I DON'T GET THIS ARMOR ON--
--BEFORE I MAKE THIS DRAMATIC ENTRANCE!
SKRASH!

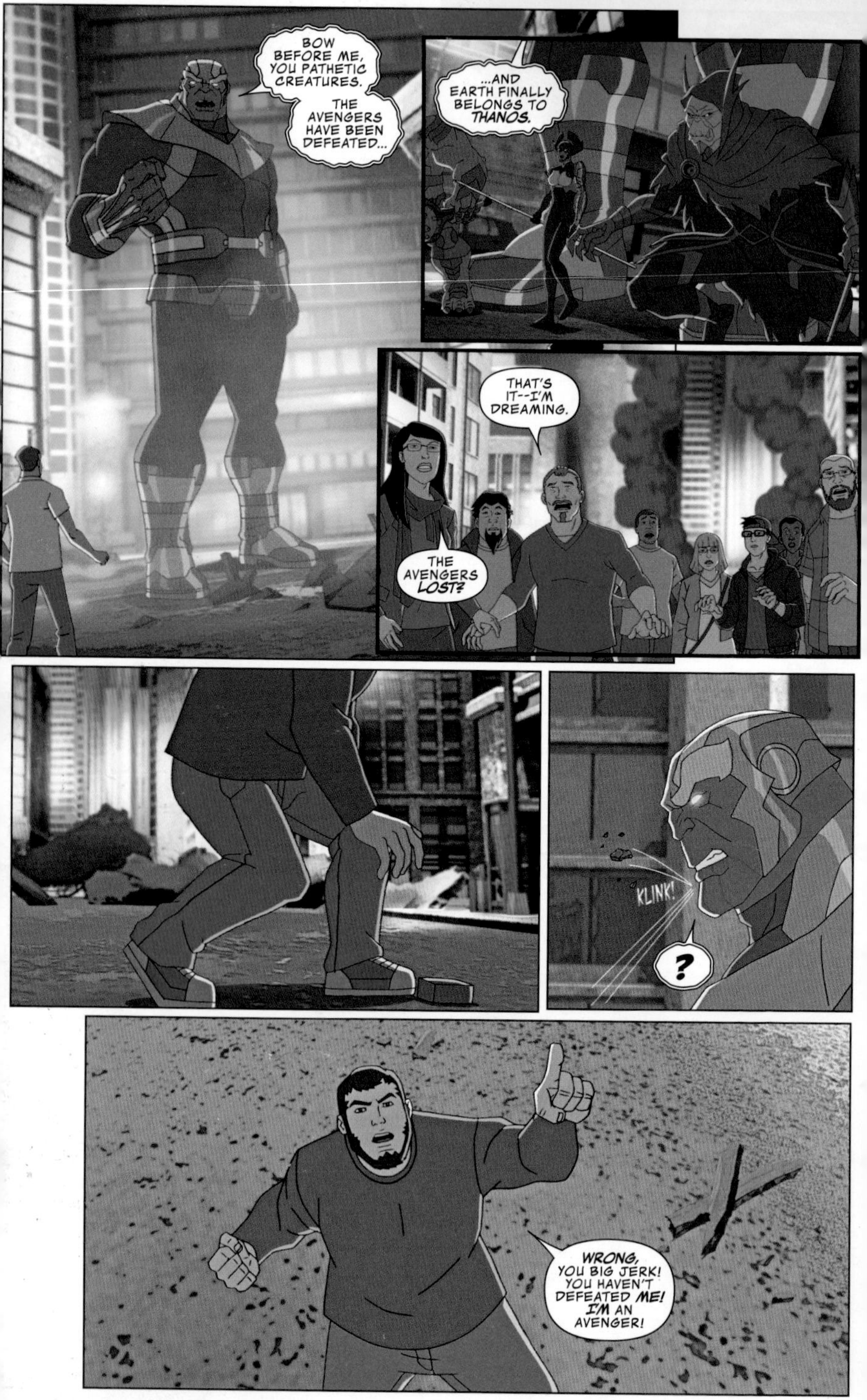
BOW BEFORE ME, YOU PATHETIC CREATURES.
THE AVENGERS HAVE BEEN DEFEATED...
...AND EARTH FINALLY BELONGS TO THANOS.
THAT'S IT--I'M DREAMING.
THE AVENGERS LOST?
KLINK!
?
WRONG, YOU BIG JERK! YOU HAVEN'T DEFEATED ME! I'M AN AVENGER!

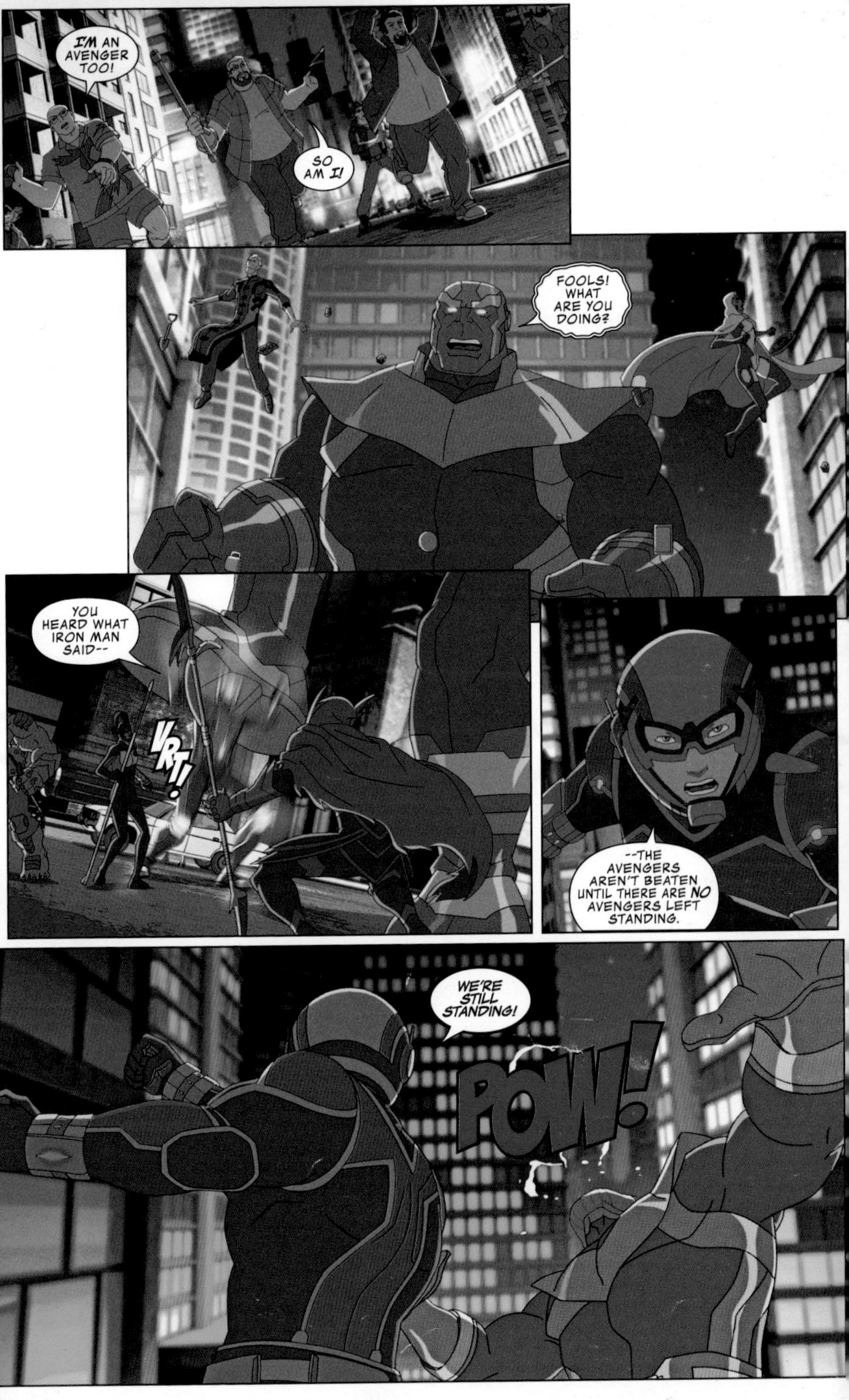
I'M AN AVENGER TOO!
SO AM I!
FOOLS! WHAT ARE YOU DOING?
YOU HEARD WHAT IRON MAN SAID--
VRT!
--THE AVENGERS AREN'T BEATEN UNTIL THERE ARE NO AVENGERS LEFT STANDING.
WE'RE STILL STANDING!
POW!

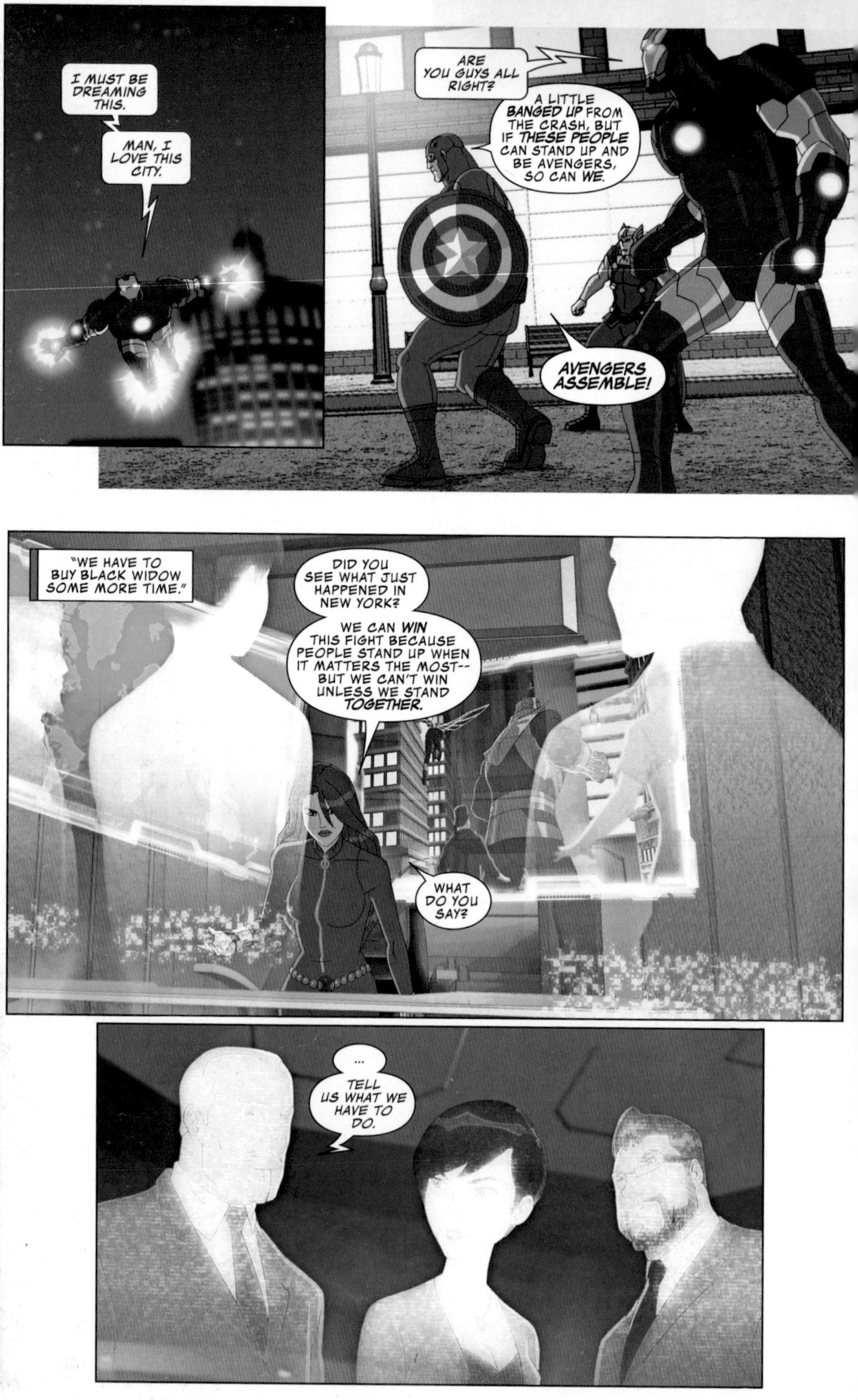
I MUST BE DREAMING THIS.
MAN, I LOVE THIS CITY.
ARE YOU GUYS ALL RIGHT?
A LITTLE BANGED UP FROM THE CRASH, BUT IF THESE PEOPLE CAN STAND UP AND BE AVENGERS, SO CAN WE.
AVENGERS ASSEMBLE!
"WE HAVE TO BUY BLACK WIDOW SOME MORE TIME."
DID YOU SEE WHAT JUST HAPPENED IN NEW YORK?
WE CAN WIN THIS FIGHT BECAUSE PEOPLE STAND UP WHEN IT MATTERS THE MOST--BUT WE CAN'T WIN UNLESS WE STAND TOGETHER.
WHAT DO YOU SAY?
...
TELL US WHAT WE HAVE TO DO.

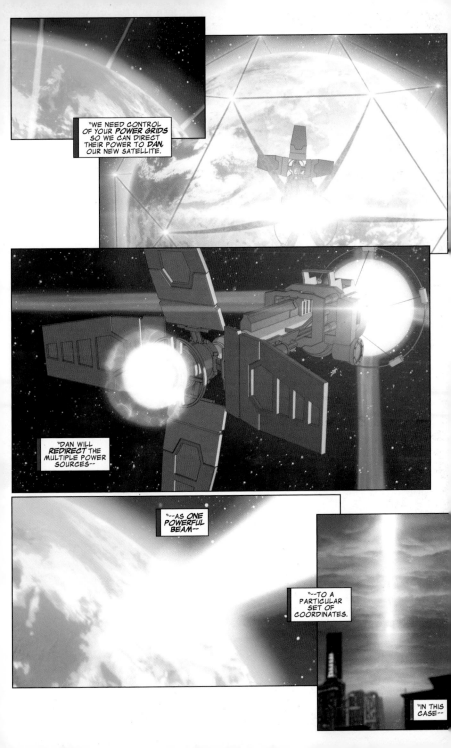

"WE NEED CONTROL OF YOUR *POWER GRIDS* SO WE CAN DIRECT THEIR POWER TO *DAN*, OUR NEW SATELLITE.

"DAN WILL *REDIRECT* THE MULTIPLE POWER SOURCES--

"--AS *ONE POWERFUL* BEAM--

"--TO A PARTICULAR SET OF COORDINATES.

"IN THIS CASE--

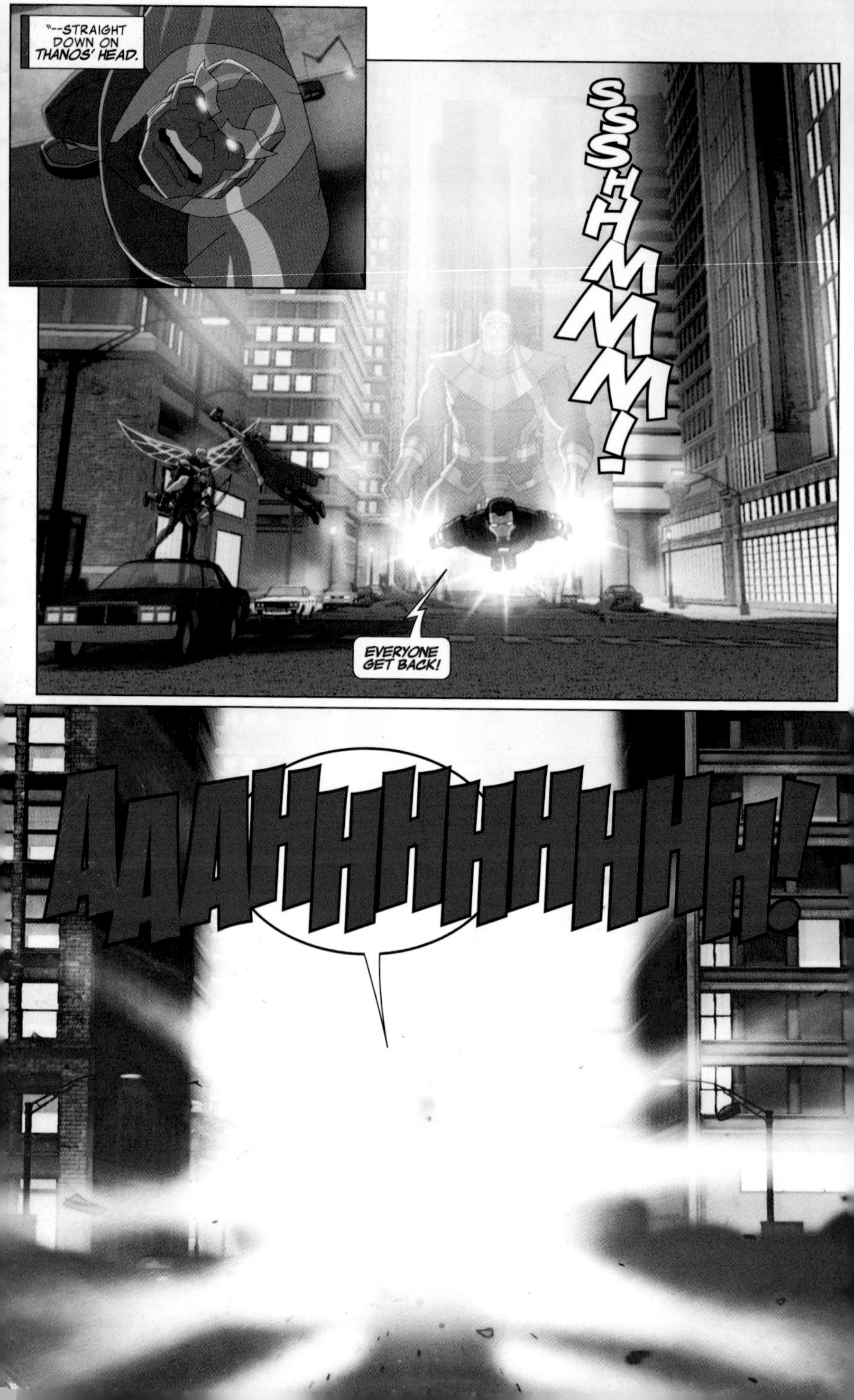
"--STRAIGHT DOWN ON THANOS' HEAD.
SSSHMMMM!
EVERYONE GET BACK!
AAAHHHHHHHHHH!

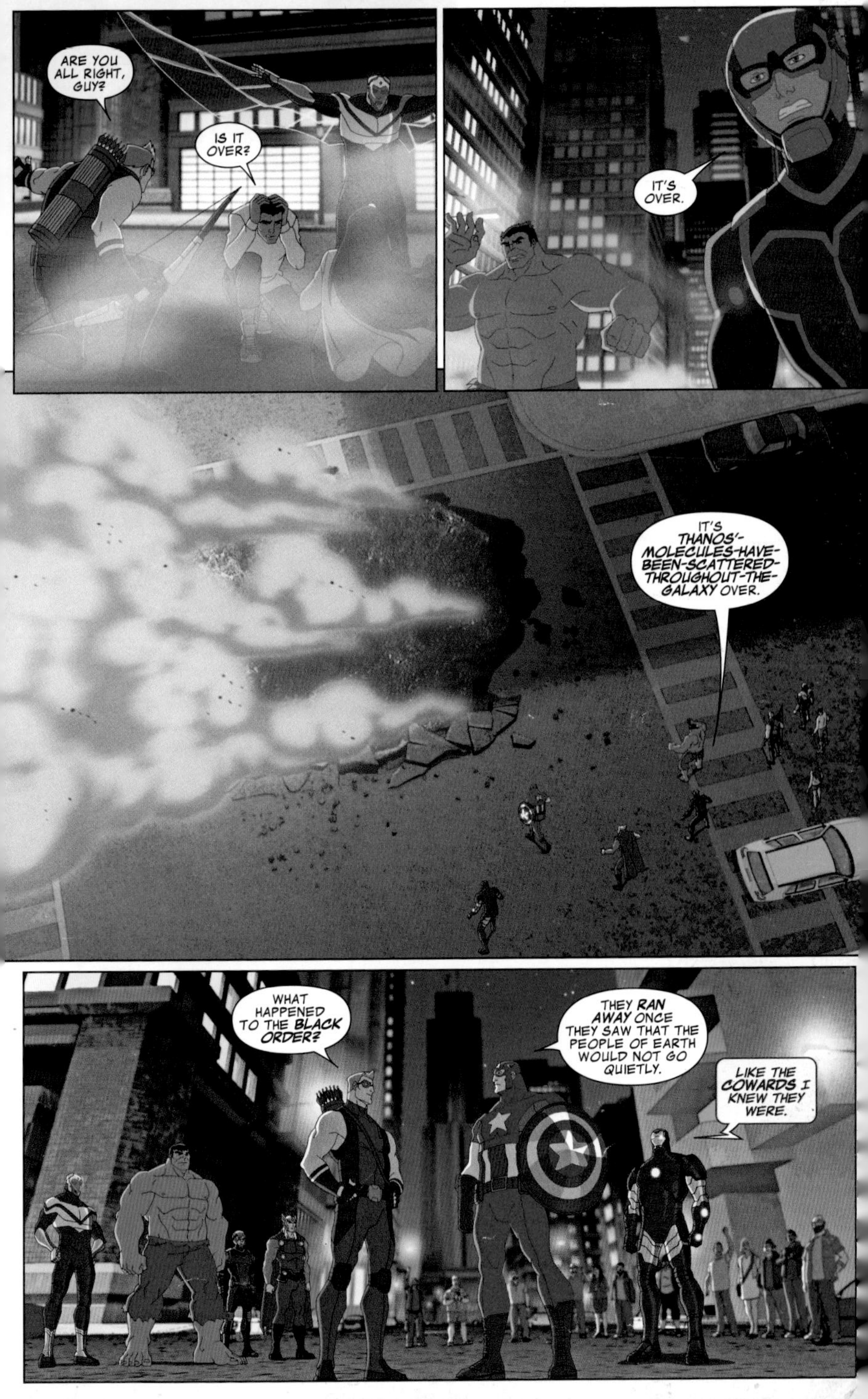
ARE YOU ALL RIGHT, GUY?
IS IT OVER?
IT'S OVER.
IT'S THANOS'-MOLECULES-HAVE-BEEN-SCATTERED-THROUGHOUT-THE-GALAXY OVER.
WHAT HAPPENED TO THE BLACK ORDER?
THEY RAN AWAY ONCE THEY SAW THAT THE PEOPLE OF EARTH WOULD NOT GO QUIETLY.
LIKE THE COWARDS I KNEW THEY WERE.

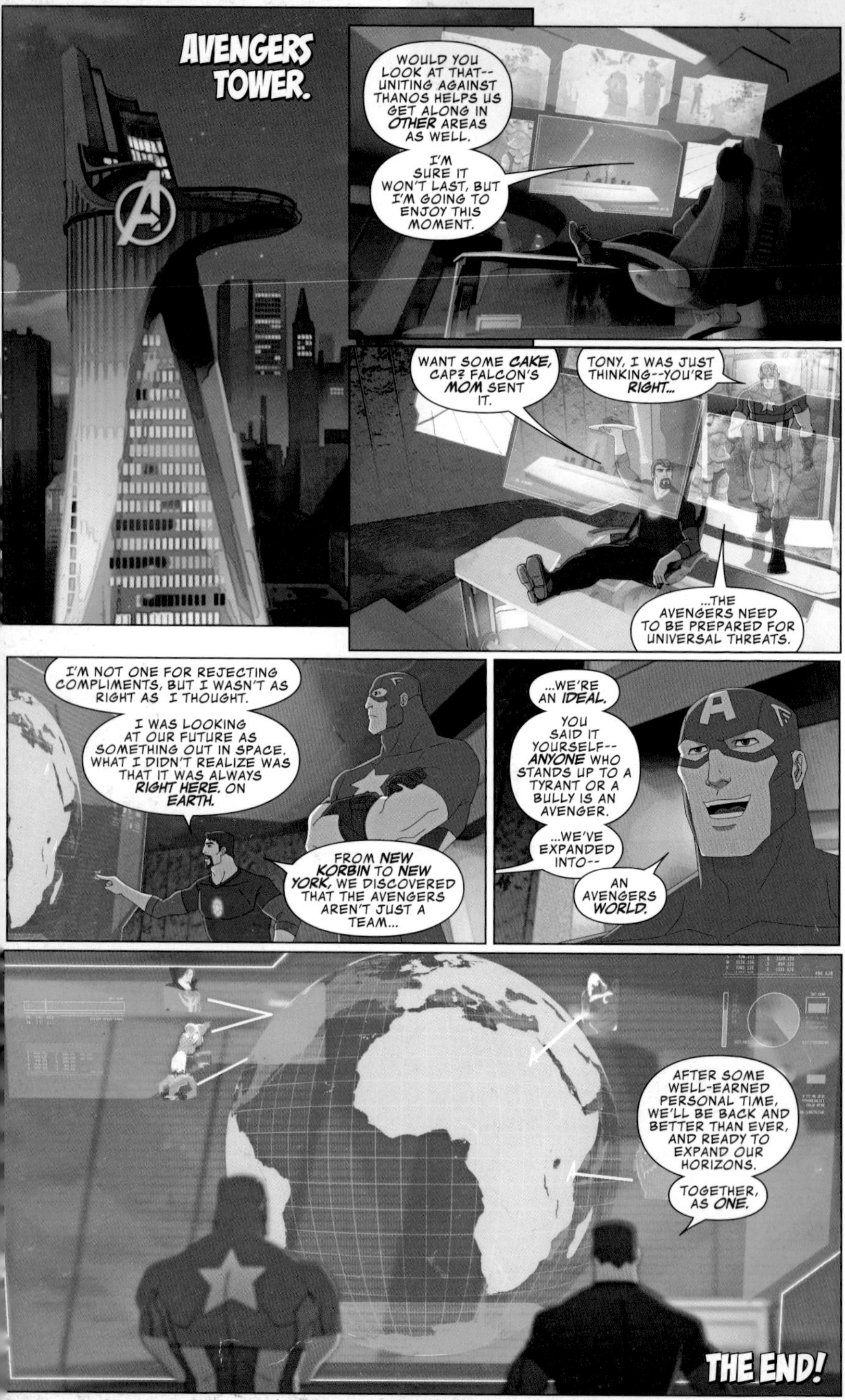
AVENGERS TOWER.
WOULD YOU LOOK AT THAT--UNITING AGAINST THANOS HELPS US GET ALONG IN OTHER AREAS AS WELL.
I'M SURE IT WON'T LAST, BUT I'M GOING TO ENJOY THIS MOMENT.
WANT SOME CAKE, CAP? FALCON'S MOM SENT IT.
TONY, I WAS JUST THINKING--YOU'RE RIGHT...
...THE AVENGERS NEED TO BE PREPARED FOR UNIVERSAL THREATS.
I'M NOT ONE FOR REJECTING COMPLIMENTS, BUT I WASN'T AS RIGHT AS I THOUGHT.
I WAS LOOKING AT OUR FUTURE AS SOMETHING OUT IN SPACE. WHAT I DIDN'T REALIZE WAS THAT IT WAS ALWAYS RIGHT HERE. ON EARTH.
FROM NEW KORBIN TO NEW YORK, WE DISCOVERED THAT THE AVENGERS AREN'T JUST A TEAM...
...WE'RE AN IDEAL.
YOU SAID IT YOURSELF--ANYONE WHO STANDS UP TO A TYRANT OR A BULLY IS AN AVENGER.
...WE'VE EXPANDED INTO--
AN AVENGERS WORLD.
AFTER SOME WELL-EARNED PERSONAL TIME, WE'LL BE BACK AND BETTER THAN EVER, AND READY TO EXPAND OUR HORIZONS.
TOGETHER, AS ONE.
THE END!

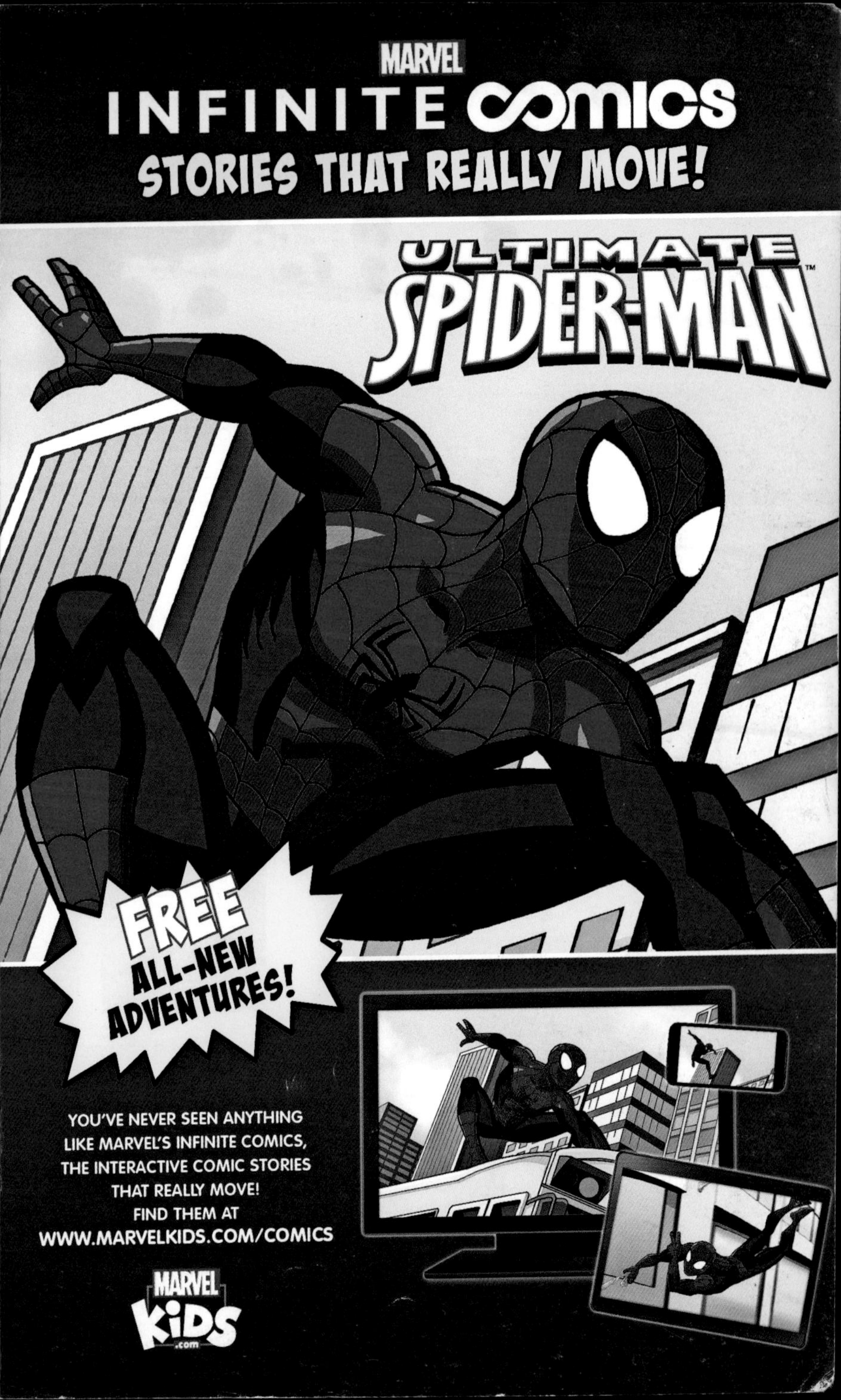
MARVEL
INFINITE COMICS
STORIES THAT REALLY MOVE!
ULTIMATE SPIDER-MAN
FREE ALL-NEW ADVENTURES!
YOU'VE NEVER SEEN ANYTHING LIKE MARVEL'S INFINITE COMICS, THE INTERACTIVE COMIC STORIES THAT REALLY MOVE! FIND THEM AT WWW.MARVELKIDS.COM/COMICS
MARVEL KiDS .com

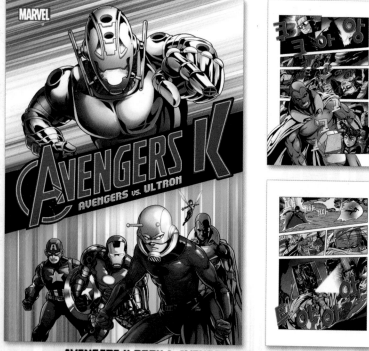

MARVEL

AVENGERS ASSEMBLE

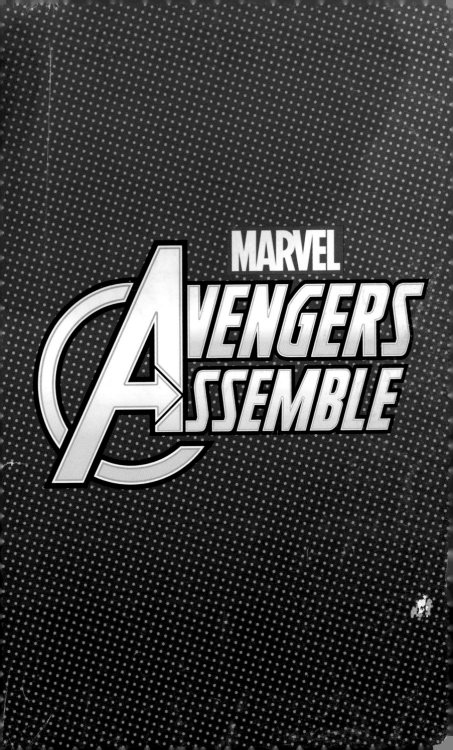

MARVEL

AVENGERS ASSEMBLE

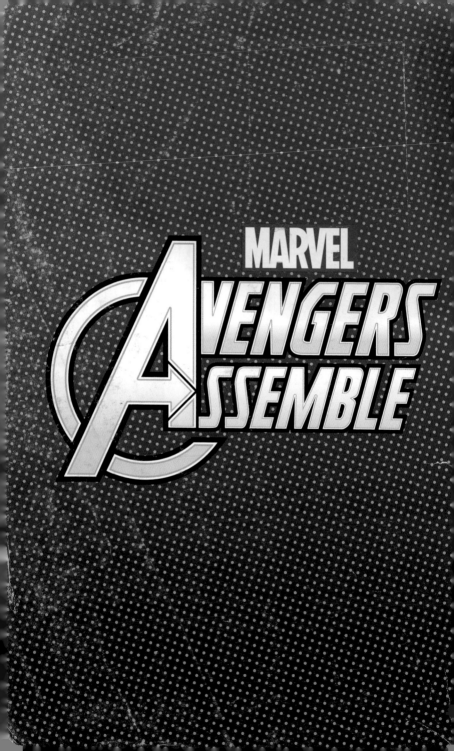